THE
LAST
SCALP

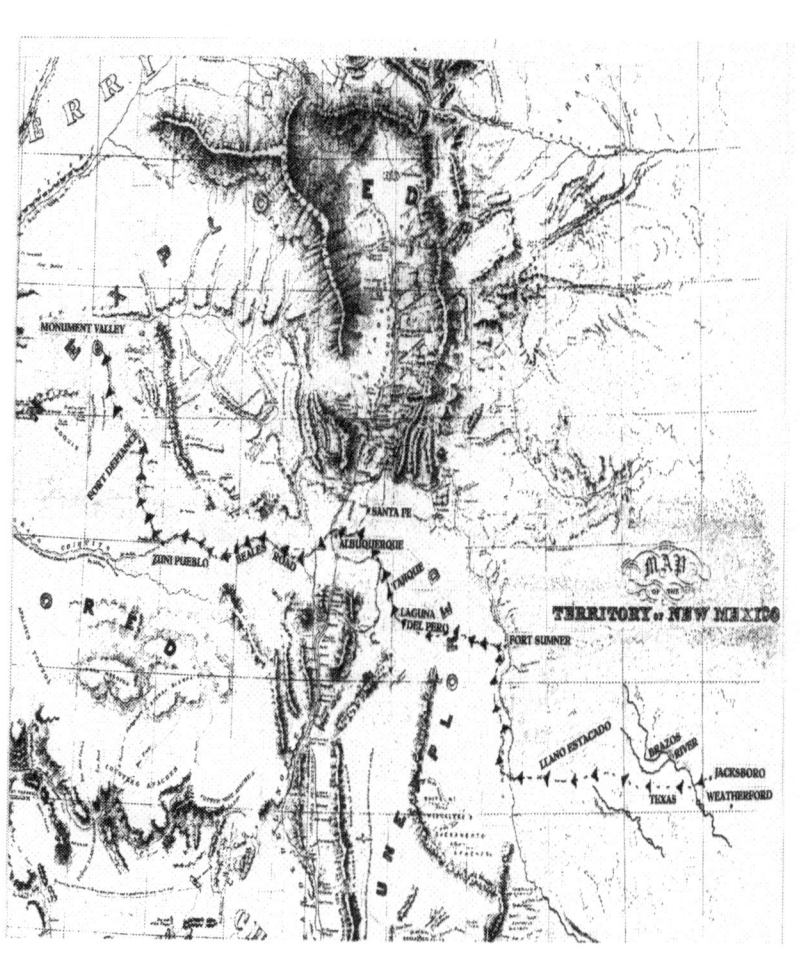

MONUMENT VALLEY

ZUNI PUEBLO

SANTA FE

ALBUQUERQUE

LAGUNA
DEL PERO

FORT SUMNER

MAP
OF THE
TERRITORY OF NEW MEXICO

LLANO ESTACADO

BRAZOS RIVER

JACKSBORO

TEXAS

WEATHERFORD

THE LAST SCALP

Paul Cox

Llumina Press

ISBN: 978-1-62550-470-8

CHAPTER ONE

The wagon road had all but disappeared under the summer grass and its ruts were lined with inch-thick saplings. Overhead, leaves rocked quietly in a warm breeze. Patches of sunlight flickered through and danced across a broad-brimmed hat and shoulder-length black hair.

Sitting motionless on a roan gelding, a man in a faded calico shirt and knee-high moccasins watched and listened. Under his right leg in a leather boot was a Henry repeating rifle. On his hips, with butts forward, were two Navy pistols, and tucked snugly into a shoulder holster was a Whitney hideout gun. In his hands was a 10-gauge shotgun.

Just ahead of the rider was a clearing. It was there, before the barrels of the shotgun had been sawed short, that his mother had used the weapon on a raiding Apache. The blast of buckshot was deflected by the Indian's buffalo shield and failed to kill him, but he left a trail of blood. Then, without the bright red drops, Sam Bucklin could never have followed them...but that was four years ago.

Now, his dark eyes studied the blades of grass, the small stones and even the dust on the plants. He saw where a rabbit had fed the night before and the tracks of a centipede. There was old deer sign and the partial print of a gray wolf, but nowhere did he see evidence of Indians.

The roan's ears were at ease. Turning slowly in the saddle, he scanned a stand of brush then glanced behind him at a second horse at the end of a lead rope.

Saddled, but with no rider, a buckskin stood three-legged in the heat enjoying the short rest. On the far side of its saddle was a Sharps buffalo rifle and balancing it on the other was a Long Tom shotgun. Alongside it was tied a round shield of thick animal hide and a bow and quiver of arrows.

Facing the clearing again, the rider eased forward to the edge of a spring then stared at the muddy tracks along its banks. He had first heard of Jacksboro in a Yankee prison camp up in Illinois. There was fertile land for the taking, and it was a country nearly forgotten by the war. It was on the Texas frontier and there were some Indians, but to a man of Arkansas's "Bloody Seventh," a band of savages was nothing to fear. And his father had grown up in Arkansas when it was on the frontier. Caddo Indians stalked the woods then and they had always gotten along by treating them right. It all sounded good to him in prison, but when Reconstruction took hold it sounded even better. It would be a chance for a fresh start in a new land and, with his encouragement, the men of the family were ready to go. After a long night's talk the women trusted to their judgment and the decision was made.

The family learned of Oak Springs when they arrived in Jacksboro, which lay a mere three miles to the south. They had gone as far west as civilization would allow and this was a good piece of dirt. It was late in the year and time to make a crop so they agreed on the springs, and for a short time it became the Bucklin settlement. But a few months later it was remembered only as the site of the Oak Springs Massacre.

Sam Bucklin looked up from the tracks with eyes hard as flint. After checking his back trail he dismounted and pulled the cork from his canteen then squatted to hold it under the cool water. Bubbles popped on the surface of the pool as insects buzzed from a large oak tree that stood in the middle of the meadow. Under it was a pile of fire-blackened logs. A few steps away, the weathered tops of four wooden grave markers rose just above a tangled growth of weeds.

He was away hunting when the attack came. Without warning they were on them. First his brother, then his father. His wife was next and then his mother fell to be scalped and left for dead. They took his sister and his child with them. But a few hours later he found his infant daughter.

Bloody, naked, and cold, she hung by her jaw from a tree, a sharpened branch protruding out her small mouth. Dried tears streaked her tiny face. He was still holding her when the Texas Rangers found him.

After taking a drink from the canteen Bucklin opened his saddlebags and pulled out a small linen pouch closed tight by a knotted draw string. Crossing to the charred logs he uncovered a rusted hammer and a square spike. With his knife he split the bag open and drew out a crusted mass of coarse black hair. Pressing the scalp to the tree he drove the nail through the dried skin and buried the shaft deep into the trunk.

Taking a step back he glared at the matted hair as it hung on the gray bark. In seconds red ants began crawling into the blackness, attracted first by the dried blood, then by the nits. In a few days the hairs would be picked clean and the rain would wash them straight again. Then, like the fourteen scalps next to it, it too would dangle in the wind over the graves.

"It's done, Sara," he said emptily as he turned to the faded markers and took off his hat. "I been away a long time, but the last of them is hanging on the tree there."

'That gray-haired one Ma said took our baby, I never did see. He weren't with them from the very first day, but I always kept looking for a big buck with that look and that kind of hair, but he never come back to the band in all the years I trailed them. All along I figured it was him Ma had hit with the buckshot and he died right off. Likely the wolves took him, Sara, 'cause there just ain't no more of them left."

Pausing for a moment, the man stared down at the graves of his family, then continued, "I done all I can for us, I can't do no more good."

"Ma died last winter, Pa. She's buried back home at Hope. Aunt Joy figured it was on account of how Ruthy turned out. But they're all here, Pa. I nailed their hides, every last one. I smote them hip and thigh, until they paid to the last farthing."

"Jeb, I saw some deer sign coming in. Likely be good hunting come fall."

"Baby Elizabeth... Baby... Daddy loves you!"

Dropping the hammer to the ground, Sam Bucklin fell to his knees and wept.

Two dozen steel shoes pounded heavily over the road to Jacksboro, pulling a lunging stagecoach and a half-acre of dust into the town square. Amid the rattle of trace chains and churning hooves, the driver belched out a command and leaned back on the reins bringing the stage to a bouncing halt in front of a stone courthouse.

"End of the line," announced the driver. "Hotel and facilities across the street."

The battered stage door swung open and stepping out first, in a black broadcloth suit, was a small blond-haired man in his early twenties. After him came an older man in a well-tailored, pin-striped suit and derby hat. Then a third man, similarly dressed but considerably younger, emerged only to turn and extend his arm. Taking it firmly with a white-gloved hand was a wedge-faced woman in an uncomfortable-looking but fashionable velvet dress. Glancing at the two-story courthouse and then the stores and hotel across from it, the young woman forced a smile.

"What a quaint little village," she said. "Just as I had pictured a town on the frontier."

The older man brushed a layer of dust from his lapels. "Yes indeed, Margret. Quite a bit more than I expected from what we've heard. Very impressive, wouldn't you say, Rockwell?"

The third man raised an eyebrow. "I expected a fortress with barricades," he answered. Tugging on the bottom of his silk vest he added, "Everything here seems quite secure and obviously unmolested."

Passing by the small group with a woman's traveling trunk on his shoulder, the burly stage driver snorted. "Pumpkin rollers," he muttered, then spat a long stream of brown tobacco into the dusty street. "Couldn't drive nails into a snow bank!"

"If you would all like to register at the hotel, Mr. Coyler," offered the blond-haired man, "you may make yourselves comfortable while I see if Mr. Wallace is in town."

"Thank you, Mr. Lanham," replied the gray-headed Coyler. "It has been an exhausting journey. How soon can we expect Mr. Bucklin?"

"Soon. Maybe tomorrow. I'll know more after talking to Mr. Wallace."

"Very well, Mr. Lanham. Margret, Rockwell, I believe the hotel awaits."

After the three easterners were out of sight, Thomas Lanham heaved a sigh of relief. Had they heard the driver's insults? Had they understood what he said? But then it didn't really matter. They were in Texas now. They would hear worse said about them. Much worse.

Walking up the courthouse steps and through the double doors, Lanham stuck his head in the first room to his right. "Bigfoot in town?"

A rawboned man with a sheriffs badge glanced up, "Thomas Lanham! How ya been?"

"Seen better days, Nathan."

"Bigfoot and a couple of his Rangers come in yesterd'y. Most likely he's down to Joyner's eatin' his dinner about now."

"Did he have Sam Bucklin with him?"

Standing, suddenly excited, the sheriff asked, "Sam? Sam comin' in?'

"Maybe. I need to talk to Bigfoot about that to see if and when he is. I got some bigshot easterners that want to meet him."

"Yankees?'

"Worse," replied Lanham. "They're from the Board of Indian Commissioners."

"Hellfire, Thomas. You best stay clear of them."

Lanham shook his head. "It's not my idea of a hoedown.

It's the governor's business."

"What's that carpetbaggin' Davis got to do with you?"

"I guess you haven't heard yet," sighed Lanham. "I was elected district attorney for Weatherford. Davis is already politicking with my job."

"Yankees, carpetbaggers, and now Injun lovers. Damn! We shoulda won that war Thomas, we surely shoulda."

Thomas Lanham nodded his head. "Too late for that," he said then turned and hurried out of the courthouse.

Just past the center of town Lanham looked down a side street. Several horses stood at hitch rails in front of a long low-roofed log building that served as the unofficial head-quarters of the Texas Rangers when they weren't chasing Indians.

Glancing back at the hotel Lanham swore under his breath. With a knot forming in his stomach he started for Joyner's. He hoped Sam Bucklin wouldn't be there. But who was he to say what was best for Sam. Maybe it would work out. Maybe, just maybe, there would be no trouble.

In the middle of the crowded room, five men in stained and faded red shirts sat on both sides of a plank table. All were lean with a hardness about the eyes that only the Rangers seemed to possess. Each wore a Colt and a Bowie-style knife.

Entering Joyner's Saloon in his broadcloth suit, Thomas Lanham felt awkward and out of place even though he knew most of the men who would be there.

Pausing just inside the doorway, he squinted into the dim light, waiting for his eyes to adjust.

"Over here, Thomas," called a large man with thinning white hair. "Light and set." To the bartender he added, "Another plate of beef 'n beans, Moses, and another cup."

Crossing the hard-packed dirt floor, Lanham nodded to the Rangers and shook hands with the biggest of them. "Glad you made it, Bigfoot," he said, stepping over the crude bench and sitting with the others.

"Have any luck finding Sam?"

Bigfoot Wallace glanced down the table. "Sweeney crossed his trail a week ago. He give him the word we wanted to see him here in town."

Lanham looked anxiously at Sweeney. "How'd it go?"

Sweeney smiled through his full beard and chuckled. "It almost never got started," he began, as the bartender shoved a metal plate and cup in front of Lanham, then set a black kettle of red beans in the center of the table.

"I got word from up around Palo Duro he was headed back this way so I was lookin' fer that double set of tracks he leaves. If'n I hadn't a know'd it was him I saw, I'd sure 'nough shot him for certain."

Taking his turn at the pot, Sweeney spooned his plate full of beans. "It'd been a couple a years since I seen 'im last. He looked like a damn Comanche."

Bigfoot smiled. "He's got some of the look all right. His grandma was a Caddo."

Setting down a platter of charred steaks, Moses interrupted. "Who's part Caddo?'

"Sam Bucklin," answered Wallace, forking a steak into his beans.

Moses scratched the greasy shirt that stretched tight over his drooping belly. "Well, more power to him. Maybe that's why he's kept his hair so long."

"Long?" agreed Sweeney, "I should smile. It's down past his shoulders and he must shave every day. From a ways off he could be took fer Injun, which is what I near done."

Lanham seemed concerned. "How did he act, Sweeney? Did he seem like himself?"

Swallowing a mouthful of beans, Sweeney washed it down with a big gulp of coffee, then wiped his lips with the back of his hand. "Chew that a little finer, Thomas."

"You all heard of Old Isaac Lynn over in Mason County?"

Several of the men nodded, but Sweeney drew a blank.

Bigfoot shook his head solemnly. "I talked to an army officer at Fort Richardson last month. Isaac's been following after their patrols hoping to get more scalps.

Since the Apaches murdered his daughter he's been a bubble off plumb. Gettin' worse all the time."

Sweeney took another drink from his cup, then set it down thoughtfully.

"No," he said, "Bucklin ain't crazy. Not by a long shot I'd say. He moves slower'n any man I ever saw. A crazy man ain't that cautious. And he reads sign better'n any white man I know."

"What did he say when you told him we wanted to see him?"

"Not much, 'cept he'd come. Seems all it took was the callin' of your name and Bigfoot's. I could see he set store by you two."

Bigfoot Wallace nodded gravely as he carved on his steak. "Thomas knowed him from the war. I met up with him 'bout four years back when me and six other Rangers was trailin' a small raidin' party that come up from Fredricksburg. We seen the smoke from Oak Springs, but was too late."

Forking a chunk of meat into his mouth, he chewed while he talked. "From the sign, we could tell they'd joined another band and we took out after the fresh trail. We found Sam a sittin' under a tree holdin' his dead baby. We tried to get him to go back, but it weren't no use so we sent one of the boys back with the body and lit out.

"Old Mr. Bucklin had some tarantula juice at the settlement and them Apaches had found it and took it with 'em, so we figured to wait till dark and let 'em git liquored up some.

"We had some field glasses with us and Sam got holt of 'em. He kept workin' closer and closer to their camp until we thought he'd sure 'nough git hisself caught. Kep' lookin' through them damned glasses all the while."

Obviously puzzled, Sweeney worked at a piece of meat stuck between his two front teeth. "What fer?"

"Hell, we didn't know it at the time, but he was lookin' fer his kid sister."

Sweeney's eyes flared with hatred. "Was she there? Did them red devils have her?"

Wallace grunted, his face stiffening, "She was out of sight behind some bushes so Sam couldn't see. He didn't know what them bucks was doin' there goin' back and forth whoopin' and carryin' on. Just before dark he snaked his way back up to us.

"Told us what he'd been lookin' fer and then what he'd seen. We all knew they was 'passin' her on the prairie', but we didn't tell 'im. Couldn't tell what he might do and git us kilt.

"We jumped 'em at dark and got his poor sister and kilt three before they scattered. There was fiftteen bucks in that band and Sam got a good, long look at ever' one of 'em. When

the shootin' was done he took his knife to two of the dead Injuns and scalped 'em. Well, more like skint 'em. On the last
one, I showed 'im how it was done proper."

Sweeney swore under his breath. "That's how it started.
The scalp tree?"

"Yep," answered Wallace, "last I saw that oak they's
eleven hides on it."

"Fourteen last fall," offered another Ranger.

"That's why we've got to get him out of this country,"
protested Lanham. "He's known by every redskin from the
Pecos to the Canadian. Sooner or later they'll get him like
they did Brit Jonson."

"That was a good nigger," admired Wallace, "and brave
as hell."

All at the table agreed grimly as Lanham went on. "And
Brit was caught just outside of town here and shot full of
arrows. Right outside of town!"

"I don't know," shrugged Wallace. "We need ever'
good man we can muster. Hate to lose a man that knows
Injuns like he does. He ought not to be out there by hisself,
but if he joined up with the Rangers, it'd be differn't."

"You already tried that, Bigfoot. He didn't bite."

"Naw, not then. But could be he's had his fill of revenge
killin'. By now he might be ready to give up huntin' just
that one band and light out with us after the rest of 'em."

Lanham reached for the beans and filled his plate. Eyeing Wallace thoughtfully, he said, "Those commissioners
came all the way down here from Fort Sill and they're expecting to hire Sam Bucklin. If they don't get him, they'll
get someone else with similar qualifications. They pay
double what a Ranger takes in.

"You need all the Rangers you can get and everybody
in West Texas knows you're the only effective fighting
force we have against the Apaches and Comanche-
Kiowas. But Sam fights best alone. He's got his own

ways of doing things and his style doesn't include a partner. He's a lone wolf and you all know it. And that's just what those people asked for. Governor Davis asked for a recommendation and I gave them Sam's name."

"You never did say what the job was exactly."

"I still don't know all the details, but like I said it's Indian work. He'll be assigned to a reservation as a kind of detective."

"Reservation," blurted Wallace. "I thought Grant give all that work to them Quakers. That there Society of Friends, that's about as useful as tits on a boar hog."

"This is different, Bigfoot. It's the Navajos they want him for."

Leaning back in his chair, Wallace folded his arms. Sucking his teeth, his eyes narrowed in thought. "Them Navajos now, I heard tell they was some differn't kind of Injun. A shade more human than these gut-eatin' Apaches and Comanches."

"He'll be on the north end of the reservation. Not many Apaches raid that far up. Mostly Utes and Paiutes cause all the trouble."

Wallace took a mouthful of coffee, then gulped it down with a croak from his throat. "Wouldn't be a bad idea at that," he admitted. Rubbing the back of his sun-wrinkled neck, Wallace paused, his eyes wandering. "He's been grievin' a mighty long time. Do 'im some good to leave Oak Springs behind. Lord knows he done right by 'em now."

"Good," smiled Lanham, reaching for the steaks. "Then I can count on you?'

"We owe 'im, Thomas, the both of us surely do."

"One more thing, Bigfoot, and this goes for everybody: the less said about that scalp tree the better off Sam will be."

"Why not?' objected Sweeney. "If'n they're lookin' fer a Injun fighter, they had oughta know Sam's one of the best in Texas. When it comes to fightin' and scrappin', he's hard as hammered hell."

Lanham dropped his eyes and shook his head. "Everybody on the frontier knows the Apache, the Comanche, and the Kiowa braves live just to murder, rape, and steal. But distance, my friends... distance breeds ignorance and enchantment.

"When Texans catch sight of a renegade warrior, we do our damnedest to shoot him, but these easterners think of them as mistreated government pets. They lay the fault of Indian depredations at the feet of the white man and feel great sympathy for what they call... the Noble Savage."

Dumbfounded by Lanham's words, the Rangers were stunned into a long silence.

"Them folks," said Bigfoot finally, "had better be told to keep their ideas to theirselves. Was a man over 'n Macon County that said somethin' like that and a total stranger come up and shot 'im dead on the street."

"Good 'nough fer 'im," retorted Sweeney. "And them three'll be as welcome around here as a rattler in dog town."

"If we're lucky," agreed Lanham, "they'll be gone by tomorrow."

CHAPTER TWO

Stopping his horses in an elm thicket, Sam Bucklin pulled his saddle strings and unrolled a buckskin jacket. There was no evening breeze and the mosquitoes were already swarming when he pulled it on and buttoned up the front.

A half-mile across an open field, the framed windows of Jacksboro were beginning to fill with pale yellow lights. It had been months since he had eaten at a table, had a hot bath, or slept between clean sheets. But he was alive because he took no unnecessary chances. For a few more minutes he waited in the trees, patiently brushing the mosquitoes from his face and hands.

When it was still light enough to see, but too dark for an Indian to use a rifle, Bucklin spurred his horses into a canter and crossed the field. Just before entering town, he slowed to a walk.

Riding down a deserted main street, he passed the darkened courthouse, then rode on toward the livery at the end of the street. Inside the barn a young boy sat on a stump under a hanging kerosene lantern. As Bucklin approached, he looked up suddenly, startled.

"You like ta s'queered the life outa me, mister," he said, catching his breath. "Thought ya was a Injun'. You shouldn't be a comin' in so late."

Bucklin half-smiled at the boy, no more than nine years old. "What do you mean?"

"Ma says they's Injuns about and when it gets dark they come out and prowl around. If they ever ketch me out after dark they'll skin me alive."

"You best listen to your ma, son," said Bucklin, riding more into the flame's soft light. "You in charge here?"

"Yes, sir," answered the boy. Noticing the armored horses, his eyes widened. "Ever'body else is at supper. I done et."

Swinging to the ground, Bucklin unbuttoned his jacket and handed the split reins to the boy, then went to the trailing horse and untied the latigo strap. "What's your name, son?"

"Jeramiah."

"You spend the night in here, Jeramiah?"

"No, sir. Only supper time. Mr. Copeland comes back then and he stays until mornin'. Otherwise the Injuns'll steal the horses."

Lifting the saddle and its gear off the gelding, Bucklin dropped it onto a saddle tree, then hung the blanket over a heavily cribbed stall divider. After doing the same for the lead horse, he glanced at the wide-eyed youngster.

"That a real Injun shield, mister?"

"It is."

Walking closer to the saddles, Jeramiah gazed at the rifles and shotgun, then caught sight of the twin pistol butts under the buckskin jacket. "I ain't never seen so many guns on one person before unless maybe it was that Sam Bucklin."

"You know Sam Bucklin, do you?"

"Sure. Ever'body in these parts knows he's a Injun fighter. He's kilt a hundred Injuns all by hisself, maybe more. Nobody knows on account of he don't talk about it to nobody and Ma says folks know it ain't fittin' to ask. Ma says it's a private matter.

"But I seen 'im once. Ma says I did. I weren't very big then and can't hardly 'member. He brung us back some of the horses the Apaches stole away when they kilt my Pa. I was only five then."

Bucklin took a harder look at the youth, then stared in wonder.

"How is your ma, son?"

"Who, Ma? Oh, she's tolerable 'cept when she whoops me. She got married agin last year to a storekeeper in town."

Bucklin nodded sincerely. "That's good, Jeramiah, that's a fine thing."

Stepping into the darkness, he paused and listened, then said quietly, "I'll be at Joyner's for the night. Ya'll keep an eye on my gear fer me?"

"Yes, sir," replied Jeramiah, walking to the edge of the lighted barn. Calling after the stranger, he asked, "What's your name, mister?" But there was no reply, there was no sound at all.

Tobacco smoke filled Joyner's Saloon and the air smelled of stale sweat and horses. At the bar, a crowd of well seasoned, tough-looking men stood shoulder to shoulder, tossing down drinks while a few still sat at the cluttered tables eating. A steady clatter of tin plates filtered through the laughter and garbled conversations as Bucklin made his way to the far end of the bar and into the kitchen.

"Got any supper left, Moses?"

The barkeeper grunted, then looked up from a dirty tub of dishwater.

"Sam Bucklin," he blurted as he extended his dripping hand and shook hands.

"It's been a coon's age, boy. How ya been?"

"Good. And you?"

"Can't complain much. Ain't as many folks as they used to be 'round here 'cause of the Injuns, but tonight I got me a load of Yankee teamsters just in from Fort Griffin."

"They clean ya out of food?"

"Not by a long shot, Sam. You have a seat out there and I'll bring you some beef 'n beans. Got some biscuits left, too, and plenty of coffee."

Bucklin started for the tables, then paused. "Moses, you still got that shed room out back? I'm up to sleepin' in a bed tonight, and havin' a bath, too."

Moses grinned. "Got it all, Sam, and glad to have you stay. I'll start up some hot water and have the tub full by the time you're done eatin'." Avoiding the clamorous teamsters, Bucklin made his way to a dimly lit corner and took a seat in one of the few chairs in the saloon. Tossing his hat on the small table, he leaned back and restfully closed his eyes.

He hadn't had biscuits since last spring and had run out of coffee a month ago. For the last week, he had eaten jerked venison and berries, when he could find them, but tonight he would eat well.

There would be no risk to consider in building a cookfire, no worry of the wind carrying the smell of smoke or food, no danger that he might be discovered and killed. And then he would sleep, if he could, the entire night through.

A booming voice from the bar broke rudely into his thoughts, then sounded again. "We want more rye, barkeep. Are ya deaf?"

"Hang onto your horses," returned Moses, crossing to the darkened corner with a pot of steaming coffee and a metal cup. "Be right with ya, boys."

Setting the cup on Bucklin's table he filled it. "Thought you might like some while you're waitin' Sam. Be 'bout ten minutes yet."

Bucklin took a sip and nodded gratefully, "It's been a while at that."

As Moses turned and left, a hulking teamster with red hair and thick, brown beard pulled away from the bar and stared into the corner. "I don't like to be kept waitin'," he roared, then took a step away from the other men who had suddenly grown silent. More massive and several inches taller than those behind him, the teamster swaggered a few more feet, then stopped. Holding up his grimy wool britches was a wide leather belt. On it hung a Bowie-style knife.

"What you got back there?" he demanded as he shifted his knife forward. "Looks to me like one of them damn blanket Injuns."

Standing uneasily in the middle of the room, Moses replied, "He ain't no Injun, mister, believe you me. No, sir. Now, come on and let's get at that whiskey."

"Come on, McCarty," came a fainthearted-voice from the bar, "he ain't done nothing to you."

"I say he's Injun," snarled McCarty as he started for the corner.

Moses quickly stepped in the big man's path. "I tell you he ain't Injun. Why he's..."

A sweeping backhand from McCarty slammed the pot into Moses' chest, knocking him to the floor as scalding coffee gushed over his neck and face.

Screaming and swearing, Moses scrambled to his feet, then tripped and fell again before making it to the kitchen.

Switching the coffee to his left hand, Bucklin took another drink, relishing the taste as McCarty came closer. Easing his right hand under the table, he took a bone-handled skinning knife from the top of his moccasin.

McCarty stopped at the edge of the table and grinned wickedly, but before he could blink, the butt end of the skinning knife crashed into his temple, snapping the meaty head back and away. His eyes rolled as he stumbled backward and fell.

Still holding his cup, Bucklin slid the knife back into its sheath and wiped some spilt coffee from his jacket. He took another sip...as much as the flavor, he had missed the smell and warmth.

McCarty's eyes began to focus. No one moved at the bar, but Moses had found a wet rag and now held it to his neck and over one eye. "Mister, you ought to have better manners," remarked Bucklin calmly.

Glaring viciously at Bucklin, McCarty rubbed the side of his head and came slowly to his feet. "I'll kill you for that," he gritted, then more violently shouted, "you're a dead man!"

Without taking his eyes off the teamster, Bucklin carefully set his cup down.

"Mighty sorry to hear your intentions, mister," he said, scooting his chair back and standing. Then in one deliberate but fluid movement, both pistols came out of a crossdraw and blasted fire, smoke, and lead into both sides of McCarty's heart.

The barrel chest jerked from the impact of the slugs, then, like heated wax, McCarty slowly crumpled to the floor. Both legs stiffened in a wild spasm, shoving the lifeless heap full length onto its face. As the fingers twitched, the last breath of Red McCarty hissed past his lips and disappeared into the bloody dirt.

Shifting his eyes to the teamsters at the bar, Bucklin kept his guns steady. "Moses, if you still keep that 8-gauge around, I'd appreciate to borrow it."

Reaching under the back of the bar, Moses drug out a long double-barreled shotgun, broke it and dropped in two huge shells.

"Bring it around the side and put 'er down on my table," said Bucklin evenly. "I come in here fer supper and coffee, not fightin' and killin'."

Hurrying along the edge of the room, Moses carefully laid the shotgun down, then stepped off against the wall. Bucklin holstered his left pistol, picked up the 8-gauge, then holstered his right and cocked both hammers of the shotgun.

"Now, anybody else that's goin' to kill me better wait till I'm done eatin'."

From the darkness outside the front door came an anxious, but commanding voice, "This is Sheriff Nathan Johnson. Sam, Moses, I'm comin' in."

"Come ahead on," answered Bucklin. "You're just in time fer supper."

Pistol in hand, Sheriff Johnson walked cautiously into the saloon and paused. "Don't nobody move too quick or I'll start shootin'. Sam, you can ease up on that artillery. Bigfoot and Sweeney's comin' around back."

Carefully resetting the hammers, Bucklin laid the shotgun on the table. Then relaxed into his chair. Palming his cup, he watched the two Rangers emerge from the kitchen and position themselves behind the teamsters. The coffee was strong. A whisp of steam swirled up from its blackness and it tasted good.

Johnson went to the dead man and knelt down on one knee. Looking him over closely, he asked, "What happened, Moses? Who is he?"

"He's a teamster, like these others. They called him McCarty."

"That's right," said a tall man with deep set eyes and distinct northern accent. "Red McCarty, and that halfbreed coward never gave him a chance."

"Who are you?"

"The name's Miller. I'm in charge of this outfit. We're government-contracted drivers. Red never had an even chance."

Rolling the thickset body over, Johnson examined the twin bullet holes. "Chance to do what?"

Miller balked. Glancing at the other men and then at the people gathering outside, he said, "Well... Red had been drinking some and..."

"He said he was gonna kill Sam," interrupted Moses. "Said it twice real loud so ever'body could hear his brag." Then to those gathering at the front door, he repeated clearly, "The man said he was gonna kill Sam Bucklin."

A low rumble of excitement rippled through the growing crowd and down the street as the name of Bucklin echoed back and forth.

Johnson's eyes narrowed. "That right, Miller?"

"Maybe. Sure. He said a few things, but he no more than finished his last word and he was shot dead." Listening to the threatening tone of the spectators outside, the teamsters' outrage weakened with uncertainty. As the sheriff came to his feet, the crowd grew quiet.

"Wherever you men came from," began Johnson sternly, "you better know you ain't there no more. Out here a man's taken at his word. You go braggin' you're gonna kill a man, he ain't likely to wait fer no ambuscade. Besides that, this here McCarty has a knife and it sure weren't fer whittlin'."

Miller snarled and pointed at Bucklin, "You mean you're not going to arrest that man?"

"A man's got aright to defend hisself. There ain't no such thing as an idle threat on a man's life." Before they could object, Johnson cocked his pistol. "And that goes fer any of his friends. If I see any of ya'll hangin' around town tonight I'll arrest you for attempted murder. But that ain't nothin' compared to what the Texas Rangers'll do to you if they ketch you on the prowl. I want ya'll gone by tomorra. Now git."

For a moment no one moved. Miller struggled for something to say, but finally started his men for the door. Before going out, he turned.

"Governor Davis is going to hear about this, Sheriff. And he knows how to deal with Texas Rebels and murderers."

As Miller rejoined his men, Thomas Lanham charged through the kitchen into the saloon, then slid to an abrupt halt and dropped into a half-crouch. Holding a pocket pistol and gasping for air, his eyes darted around the empty room. With his chest heaving and drops of sweat streaking his forehead, Lanham's attention focused on the sprawled corpse.

"It's all right, Thomas," said Bigfoot. "Sam's over there in the corner and the trouble just left."

Straightening slowly, Lanham watched the last of the teamsters file past the front window, then cautiously opened his coat and replaced his pistol. Squinting in the dim light and walking across the floor, he asked, "That you, Sam?'

"Afraid so, Thomas."

"What the hell happened?"

"Have you et yet, Thomas?" returned Bucklin easily.

"Eaten?"

"I'm about to have supper."

Glancing at the body a few feet from the table, Lanham looked back at Bucklin with concerned anxiety. "I ate at the hotel."

Bucklin nodded. "Have a seat," he offered politely, then to the others, he added, "Ya'll are welcome if you have a mind, but Moses has got to get supper ready."

Bringing a small bench with them, Bigfoot and Sheriff Johnson casually stepped over the body and sat down next to Lanham as Moses went back to his cooking and Sweeney strolled out into the darkened street.

"Sorry to cause trouble for ya'll my first night in town."

"Weren't nothin' you could do," said Johnson, then quickly explained to Lanham.

"Self-defense," agreed Lanham. "The court would rule it the same. It would've been a tougher decision if he weren't armed, but even then, I'm certain no one in Jacksboro would see it any different."

"Now, there's where there might be trouble," grumbled Bigfoot. "That Miller, that one said he run the whole she-bang, talked like he was gonna bring the governor in on us. He weren't no southerner. Called us Rebels."

Lanham was surprised. "He said he was going to Governor Davis?"

"It's what he said," confirmed Johnson. "You think it'll make any difference?"

Thomas Lanham thought hard for a moment, then said worriedly, "If he presses charges and takes the case to some east Texas county, he could fill the jury with Reconstructionists and Carpetbaggers. Sam could be in for it.

"If Miller has connections in Reconstruction politics, who knows? We're ex-Confederates. We don't have the same rights as Yankees and there's so many worms in this new government almost anything can happen."

"Don't matter, does it, Thomas?' asked Bigfoot. "You got a job offer fer Sam, don't ya?"

"Oh…right," affirmed Lanham as he glanced at Bucklin with a reserved smile. "That's what we wanted to talk to you about, Sam. Bigfoot and I…we both agree that you're the man for the job."

Nursing his coffee, Bucklin asked blandly, "What am I good fer that you think is so important?'

"I'll put it to you straight, Sam. There's a problem on the Navajo reservation up in the New Mexico Territory. They want a man that can work alone and that knows Indians, especially Apaches. You'd be working for the Board of Indian Commissioners that's been appointed by Grant himself. These people are supposed to watch over the Indian appropriations and make sure they're dealt out fair and square."

Bucklin was silent, but surprisingly made no objections, so Lanham continued.

"The trouble is on the north end of the reservation where the Utes and some allied Apaches are raiding the

Navajos. Gunrunners are selling arms to both Utes and Navajos and the Mormons are suffering depredations from both sides. Running in the same territory is a bunch of renegades headed by one of the Apaches, called Cabeza Blanca. They go after anyone, white or red.

"Before the military is called in, the commissioners want to defuse the situation as quietly as possible."

"You know about Brit Johnson, Sam?' asked Bigfoot. "That the Apaches got 'im?"

"I heard."

"Me and Thomas figured it's time you think about gettin' off this frontier anyway. You're knowed too well, just like old Brit, and that makes you a prime target, but on further west, it won't be so bad."

"This is my home, Bigfoot. Where my family's buried. My wife...and my baby are here."

"Sure they are, Sam," encouraged Lanham, "but you can always come back. The land will still be yours, I'll make sure of that. I'll fix it so no one else can homestead on it."

Bucklin twirled his cup on the table, staring blankly into it as the others watched expectantly. Finally he asked, "What do they want done?'

Relieved, Thomas Lanham leaned back in his chair. "I don't know the particulars, but three of the commissioners are in town and want to talk with you. I took the liberty of recommending you to them several months ago."

"What are they doin' way out here?'

Lanham shrugged. "They said they wanted firsthand knowledge of the Indian situation on the Texas frontier. They've worked their way up from San Antonio."

"Be best for them," added Johnson, "if you see 'em real soon before there's trouble."

Bucklin glanced up. "You mean 'cause of McCarty?'"

Waving a disregarding hand at the cooling body, the sheriff sneered, "Naw. Not that. It's on account of the way they been talkin' over at the hotel. They sure as hell are Injun lovers and damned Yankees to boot. The way folks feel, it'd be good to git 'em out of Texas as soon as we can. Otherwise they're gonna get hurt."

"If they're like that, why do you want me?" asked Bucklin warily.

"All they know," answered Lanham, "is that you know Indians as good as any man in Texas and you know more than most about the Apache. I didn't tell them how it is you came by your knowledge."

"Maybe they ought to know," said Bucklin. "Might make a difference."

Lanham hedged. "No, Sam. They're from Washington, too far removed to understand."

Bigfoot nodded in agreement, but the sheriff scratched curiously at the stubble on his chin then asked, "How do they figure he come to know Apaches less'n he hunted 'em?"

"Who knows, Nathan," sighed Lanham. "They certainly have no idea what life is like for a settler on the frontier. Perhaps instead of farmers and ranchers they believe most of us are Daniel Boones or Davey Crockets. But I do know they're sympathetic toward Indians in general and they don't know an Apache from an Arapaho."

Responding slowly, Bucklin raised an eyebrow. "How could it be they don't know about the Apaches and the Comanches. You said they was Indian commissioners, government folks. People have been writin' Washington for years tellin' of the murderin' and stealin' and all the while beggin' for help."

Scowling suspiciously, Lanham thought for a moment. "It tempts one to vile speculations indeed. The way Congress stalled on the Medicine Lodge treaties a few years back, then stalled on giving out their meager appropriations, it almost seems as if they want trouble with the Indians. They immerse themselves in the reconstruction politics of the State, but ignore the depredations of its ex-Confederate citizens."

"While we got 'em down here," said Bigfoot, "maybe we ought to give 'em a education, show 'em all the burned-out chimneys and graves and such."

"That's a fact," agreed Johnson. "Nobody ever come to see fer theirselves before. We ought to be able to make it real clear what's happenin'."

"They'll not likely listen to a district attorney," said Lanham, "but the three of you might do some good. What do you say, Sam?"

Bucklin sat up in his chair and glanced patiently at the kitchen. "If it'll help folks, but fist I'm gonna eat and clean up."

Again rubbing his beard, the sheriff grinned and said, "I could use a little sprucin' up myself. Where and when do we meet, Thomas?"

Pulling out his pocketwatch, Lanham flipped open the case. "It's seven-thirty. Let's be at the hotel in an hour. I'll set it up with the commissioners, but remember we just talk about the Indian depredations. They don't need to know about any other particulars or this powwow could backfire."

CHAPTER THREE

Gritting against the tearing pain, Sam Bucklin pressed his palm over the purple-red scar on his thigh and shoved his hand back and forth. Only two months old, the wound was raw to the touch and still a mass of twisted flesh. The Comanche arrowhead was torn out quickly and there had been little infection, but it would take months of work to break the skin free from the knotted muscle below.

It had been the same for the two white scars on his left side where a bullet passed between his ribs and the single round one in his shoulder where he still carried a lead ball next to the bone.

The water in the battered copper tub was turning lukewarm when Moses walked into the back room. "Want any more water, Sam?"

"No. I'm clean as I'm gonna get, Moses."

Tossing a rolled bundle on a nearby bench, Moses smiled. "I brung you a clean shirt. Thought you might be needin' one since you been out so long."

"Thanks, Moses. Mine needs a good washing before it's fit for company."

"Bigfoot's waitin' in the saloon, Sam," said Moses as he left the room.

"Says you got about ten more minutes."

Stepping out of the tub, Bucklin dried off and pulled the heavy cotton shirt over his head and tucked it into his buckskin trousers. After tying his moccasins, he adjusted the hideout pistol and its holster, then covered it with his jacket. Grabbing his belt with the Colts, he went through the kitchen and into the saloon.

Handing the pistols to Moses, he said, "Keep an eye on these for me."

Glancing at the Ranger leaning against the bar, he buttoned the front of his jacket. "You ready, Bigfoot?"

"Sure 'nough," answered Wallace, crushing a cigarette under his boot and casually eyeing the bulge of the shoulder pistol. "Thought it best to walk you down. Some of them mule skinners might not listen so good."

Stepping out of the stale saloon and into the shadows, both men paused. A horse nickered from the stable while crickets rattled musically in the drifting night air. Across town a dog barked continuously until a sudden yelp put an end to it.

When their eyes had adjusted to the darkness, the two men started cautiously for the hotel saying nothing until stopping at the corner of Main Street.

Bigfoot Wallace strained his eyes in the poor light, trying to see how Bucklin would react to what he had to say. "I was surprised at first when you seemed interested in this job offer," he said. "Didn't figure you would be. It took me a while, but I caught on finally."

Bucklin raised his head and looked into a cloudless sky. "The air smells sweet this time of year. Folks will be plowing and planting."

"You finished, didn't you, Sam? You done it?'

Bucklin inhaled deeply, then sighed, "I never found the gray-haired one. Maybe it's best to believe that Ma shot him after all."

"She put lead into 'im, all right," agreed Wallace. "You figure it was enough to kill 'im?"

"Must have. I never laid eyes on him. Not even...not even on that first day."

"Well, you done us all a favor, Sam. At least there's one band won't butcher no more folks. Lord knows they done more'n their share."

Avoiding the noisy boardwalk, Bucklin and Wallace again started for the hotel, keeping to the edge of the street until they came to a lone figure leaning against a hitching rail.

"Nathan?" questioned Bigfoot. "That you that smells like lilac water?"

"I ain't never met no rich folks before," replied the sheriff. "Least not this rich, and besides, one of 'em is a lady."

"What makes you think they're so rich?" asked Bigfoot.

"Thomas says these commissioners got so much money they give it away fer no reason. Called 'em philanderers or some such thing. I can't imagine the likes. And that old one, Coyler, paints pictures and makes money at it, too. High falootin' I tell ya."

"Don't count for much out here," said Bucklin. "They die like ever'body else. Only they likely don't figure it that way."

"We found a man like that once," added Wallace. "The Kiowas had stripped 'im like they do and he was scalped and gutted, but his money was layin' all around 'im like leaves that had fell out of a tree."

Through the hotel window, the three men saw Thomas Lanham sitting at a table with Commissioner Coyler. A bottle of brandy and several glasses stood ready and waiting.

"That's the one that makes pictures," whispered Johnson. "Them other two went down the street a while ago."

"Looks friendly enough," commented Bigfoot as he laid his hand on the brass doorknob. "Let's see what kind of pilgrim he is."

Lanham stood at the sight of the men and waved them over. As they neared, Coyler smiled genially and came to his feet.

"I want you all to meet Vincent Coyler of the Indian Commission," announced Lanham formally. As the men shook hands, he continued, "Mr. Coyler, this is W.A. Wallace, Texas Ranger for nearly thirty years. And this is Sheriff Johnson of Jacksboro and, as you have no doubt surmised, this is Mr. Sam Bucklin."

"Have a seat, gentlemen," offered Coyler, his eyes lingering appraisingly on Bucklin. "Mr. and Mrs. Flitcher will be here directly."

Taking the bottle of brandy, he filled two glasses and handed them to Wallace and Johnson. As he reached for the third, Bucklin stopped him. "Thanks. But I lost my taste for it a few years back. Just as soon keep it that way."

Surprised, but impressed, Coyler replaced the cork. "Our time is short, gentlemen, so I shall come straight to the point. We have come to Texas for two reasons. One, of course, is to hire Mr. Bucklin, but the other is to ascertain the *true* extent of the Indian depredations along the western frontier in the fifth district.

"Mr. Lanham has informed me you are all experts in your fields and might be able to shed some light on the subject. Perhaps we could begin by discussing your local experiences."

"May I suggest, Mr. Coyler," said Lanham, "that considering the importance of what these men have to say that it might be best if we wait for Mr. and Mrs. Flitcher. We could talk over the New Mexico situation first."

Coyler smiled agreeably. "Certainly, Mr. Lanham. You are correct of course. Sometimes my fascination with the frontier proves embarrassing."

Lanham took a sip of brandy trying to relieve the uneasiness in his stomach. "I told Mr. Bucklin just a bit of your proposal, Mr. Coyler, but he was interested in more of the details."

Coyler's cordial expression grew more serious, his brow furrowing with concern. "Mr. Bucklin, the Indians we are trying to protect are called the Navajo or Dine. They are a splendid example of our success in civilizing the red man. Before the forces under Kit Carson defeated them eight years ago, they were quite warlike, and even though they farmed and raised sheep, they continually raided the Mexicans to the south and the whites to the north.

"The military took them three hundred miles from their homeland to Fort Defiance and there attempted to relocate them. Unfortunately the weather and pestilence destroyed what crops they managed to plant, and they were constantly raided by neighboring Apaches for what little appropriations they received. The entire affair was a miserable failure and after two years the entire tribe, six thousand of them, were escorted back to their land.

"The promised sheep are just now beginning to arrive and some meager appropriations are finally being disbursed, but considering the terrible conditions, the people as a whole are behaving admirably. Most have stayed on the reservation as was agreed."

"You mean the raids are still goin' on," said Bigfoot. "Settlers is still bein' kilt and the Injuns doin' the murderin' escape back to the reservation with their scalps and booty. We got the same problem with Fort Sill, and the last thing them redskins need is protection."

Coyler flinched at the blunt remarks, his thoughts momentarily scattering.

"Fort Sill, you say? We're scheduled to be in Fort Defiance soon, but perhaps we could visit there as well. But I have been in contact with the agent at Fort Sill. He has mentioned nothing in his letters of Indians leaving the reservation."

Bigfoot Wallace fought back a sneer, but said sternly, "You got eight thousand Injuns up there and one Quaker who hardly never leaves his house, to look 'em over. And he says none of his Injuns has left, none of his Injuns is doin' the killin' and stealin'. Hell, I've trailed 'em back there many a time myself. Seen it with my own eyes."

Gathering his composure, Coyler's lips thinned with a faint, patronizing smile. "I do recall discussing these claims with General Sherman shortly before we left Washington, Mr. Wallace. Let me assure you that he is looking into any complaints that might be registered with his office. In fact he is planning a trip to Texas next spring to view firsthand the condition of the frontier in this regard.

"But let me say also that the Navajo are sincere in their desire to end the hostilities and settle down to farming and raising their sheep. The raiding they are doing only continues out of fear and frustration, which is why we need Mr. Bucklin's aid."

"I never heard of no Injun farmin' stock," interrupted Johnson. "And I been all over this country. Before the war, I fought Sioux and Cheyenne up north and then the Kiowa, Comanche, and the damned Apaches. None of 'em would be caught dead behind a plow."

"That's precisely why the Navajo are so critical," said Coyler excitedly. "They will be an example to all red men, showing them the success of taking the white man's road. But as I mentioned, there is unrest in the area. Several trading posts have set up business along the San Juan River on the north end of the reservation and some are trading whiskey to the Indians, Utes as well as Navajo.

"Also reported is a man known only as Harry who deals exclusively with the Indians and renegades in trading contraband for firearms. He has never been identified.

"Most importantly, however, is the presence of a band of hostiles headed by one the Apaches call Cabeza Blanca. The renegades, a most terrible lot, are composed of Utes, Paiutes, Apaches, and Comanches, but they raid the friendly Utes and Navajos as well as the Mexicans and whites."

"Excuse me, Mr. Coyler," said Bucklin patiently, "I don't see how all of this fits together with what I can do. Sounds more like a job for the army."

"That is just what we hope to avoid, Mr. Bucklin, but you are not alone in your thinking. The Mormons have suffered severely from the unfriendly Utes for several years and now the return of the Navajo depredations has them demanding another military campaign to restore order. But it is vital that this situation never again fall into the hands of the War Department. It must remain in control of Indian Affairs. If the soldiers were brought in it would be a terrible setback, and the little trust the Navajos have in us would be destroyed.

"No, Mr. Bucklin, this is a job for one man or perhaps a few individuals. Our goal is to remove the influence of this Cabeza Blanca, for he is at the heart of the crisis perpetuating the turmoil."

"Why's that?" asked Bucklin.

"Cabeza Blanca is so efficient in his atrocities that the Navajo can find no place to hide from him. He finds them even in their most secret hiding places that Carson himself missed. The Navajo have lost much of their crop and livestock as well as having many of their men killed and women captured.

"Out of fear, the Navajo desire guns and ammunition and are able to get them through this Harry I mentioned. However, to trade for the guns, they must provide contraband and thus they raid the Mormon settlements and take what they need. The more Cabeza Blanca raids the Navajo, the more they raid the whites. As you can see, it is a circle that must be broken before the entire area is engulfed in another war."

"That circle as you call it," said Bigfoot, "has been goin' on for as long as I can remember, even before there ever was a Cabeza Blanca."

"Perhaps, Mr. Wallace," returned Coyler mildly. "But during the Carson Campaign it ceased and afterward was quiet for some months. Those in the area believed the defeat of the Indians had a profound and lasting effect, but then the raids began again, just as the renegade band of Cabeza Blanca appeared."

"I thought you said the Navajo were moved to Fort Defiance," said Lanham. "How did the raids start back up so soon?"

"As many as two thousand Navajo never reported to the new reservation and actually were never found by Carson's forces. They were too remote and well hidden in the many canyons that cut through the country. But oddly enough, they continued to visit their relatives at Fort Defiance and then return home.

"At first they bragged about their bravery and independence, but then they began to trickle in with tales of destruction. These were the Ricos, the holdouts, the richest, most powerful of the Navajo, and they were being defeated one by one by a new enemy. One they could not defend against, Cabeza Blanca. And these raids have continued now for four years."

Bucklin's eyes began to narrow slowly. "This Cabeza Blanca then, you're sayin' he showed up just four years ago? Before that they never heard of 'im?"

"That is correct, Mr. Bucklin. And presently he stands in the path of peace and progress for an entire tribe."

"Any other particulars you know about him?"

Coyler glanced at the hotel door as it swung open. "Only that he is the most ruthless individual and by all accounts is an Apache. He is larger than most of his band and the Navajo that have seen him and survived say he walks with a distinct limp."

Only Bigfoot Wallace had noticed Bucklin's mild interest turn into suspicion and now he watched as the young man's face darkened with smoldering rage.

Before Coyler said anything more, he slid his chair from the table and stood formally. Proudly extending his hand toward a couple entering the lobby he said, "Gentlemen, I would like you to meet two more commissioners, my daughter and her husband, Mr. and Mrs. Rockwell Flitcher."

Wallace and Johnson awkwardly stood up as their chairs tipped and scraped over the wooden floor. Bucklin hesitated, then disinterestedly glanced over his shoulder and slowly joined the others. He did not listen to the remainder of the introductions nor did he notice that no one shook hands. And he was totally unaware of the scowl on Rockwell Flitcher's face and the aroused fascination in the woman's eyes.

Flitcher's nostrils flared above a neatly trimmed mustache. "We've just returned from a chance meeting with a government-employed wagonmaster named Miller. Before that, we had already made several inquiries concerning this…Mr. Bucklin…of the townspeople."

Bewildered by Flitcher's rudeness, Coyler shrugged, "And?"

Pausing to form a sophisticated sneer, Flitcher said, "It seems our Mr. Lanham is either an extremely poor judge of character, or is indeed nothing more than a ruffian himself. His recommendation that we hire Mr. Bucklin for our purposes has turned out to be a grotesque blunder."

"Whatever do you mean?" choked Coyler.

Flitcher turned to Sheriff Johnson and pointed his finger at Bucklin. "I demand you arrest that man, sir. He is a murderer."

Sam Bucklin broke away from his thoughts, his eyes focusing on Flitcher for the first time. Quickly evaluating the easterner, he dismissed the worth of the man, but searched carefully for any weapon he might be carrying. Then, looking briefly at the homely woman next to him, he said politely, "Good evening, ma'am. Nice to make your acquaintance."

Coyler was shocked into silence. Before he could recover, Bucklin tipped his hat to the woman and started for the door.

"Sheriff, arrest him, I say, "commanded Flitcher as Bucklin walked past him ignoring his accusing finger. "Arrest him for the murder of Red McCarty and untold numbers of innocent Indians."

His intimidation melted away by the ludicrous spectacle. Sheriff Johnson laughed, "You arrest him, Mr. Commissioner. I ain't of your partic'lar persuasion."

"If he reaches for that door," boasted Flitcher, "I shall do just that."

Without breaking his stride, Bucklin spoke clearly, unemotionally, "You go for that belly gun hid in your coat and I'll kill you, Mr. Flitcher."

As Bucklin pulled the door open, Margaret Flitcher threw her arms around her husband and screamed, "No, Rockwell, no."

Bucklin turned smoothly. A cloud of blue-white smoke exploded from his right hand shattering the brandy bottle into pieces and showering the table with liquor.

Then, with his brown eyes holding on Flitcher, he smiled flatly. "You take good care of your man while he's in Texas, ma'am. Otherwise he'll get hisself kilt."

Halfheartedly struggling against his wife's embrace, Flitcher feigned an effort to follow. After the door had closed and with the color drained from his face, he quivered, "He's a madman. A madman I tell you. He tried to kill me. Me!"

Margaret Flitcher was on the verge of tears, but was too frightened to let them fall. "Barbarians," she gasped. "Barbarians and illiterate hooligans."

Consoling his wife, Flitcher said, "The sooner we're away from here the better. Shall we be leaving in the morning, Vincent?'

Wallace smoothed his mustache and fought off a grin. "Sam wasn't tryin' to kill you, Mr. Flitcher. He was just makin' a point in your favor."

"That's right, agreed Johnson. "He don't talk much to folks. He was just lettin' you know he didn't want no trouble. Why, if he'd a wanted to kill ya, he'd of put that slug through yer heart."

Margaret Flitcher swooned. "I feel faint," she moaned. "I need to lie down." Supporting his wife, Flitcher stared at Coyler. "Well?'

"Yes, yes. Tomorrow. But at least come back after getting Margaret settled. These men have things of importance they wish to discuss with us. Matters we have a duty to listen to and give consideration as Indian Commissioners."

"Very well," snapped Flitcher, "but only because you ask it. I doubt anything they have to say will change my opinion and I assure you, when we make our report to Washington, the credibility of these...of these officers of the law will be duly cited."

As the couple approached the bottom of the hotel stairs, Flitcher stopped and spoke quietly to his wife as she began to whimper. Glaring back at Johnson, he said smugly, "And, Sheriff, your conduct in particular, I shall report to Governor Davis. You would be wise to consider the consequences if Bucklin is allowed to leave town. And when the United States Marshal arrives, and I give you my word he will, you had best have Sam Bucklin in your charge."

Swearing under his breath, the Sheriff watched Flitcher go up the stairs. Shaking his head in disbelief, he grumbled bitterly. "That cold-footed bastard don't know come're from sic 'em." Frowning at Coyler, he glanced at Wallace and Lanham. "Talkin' to them's gonna be like pourin' water on a drowned rat. You boys stayin' or comin'?"

"I'm staying, Nathan," answered Lanham, looking hopefully to Bigfoot.

"I'll stick around," said Wallace. "Might still do some good."

"Suit yourself," muttered Johnson, "I'm gonna fetch Sam and tell 'im what these damn Yankees are threatenin' to do."

Shaken, but still dignified, Coyler nervously tugged on his starched collar and twisted his neck as Johnson left the hotel. "Quite an exhibition," he protested with proper indignation, then unconsciously tossed down a full shot of brandy...But his shock drifted into childlike excitement and his pale lips curled into a faint grin. With a voice laced with awe, he whispered softly, "Quite an exhibition, indeed."

"I'm very sorry, Mr. Coyler," said Lanham, "but Sam believed Mr. Flitcher possessed a hidden pistol under his coat. He has learned, as many on the frontier have, that it is foolish to take unwarranted chances with one's life. He intended only to protect himself and perhaps even Mr. Flitcher."

"I seen the gun, too," added Wallace dryly. "And if he'd of gone for it, Sam would've been obliged to shoot 'im. But, be that as it may, Mr. Coyler, you done let loose the dogs. Sam's on his way and anybody tryin' to stop him'll have hell to pay."

Lanham glanced at Wallace curiously, but spoke to Coyler. "Despite what Mr. and Mrs. Flitcher apparently heard about Sam Bucklin, I fully stand behind him. There is no man in Texas more square than he and when Mr. Flitcher returns, I will put the record straight."

"Then you are still recommending him?" asked Coyler incredulously. "Even after this violent outburst?"

Lanham stiffened. With his face flushing, he said firmly, "You'll find no better man for what you have in mind, providing, of course, you fully understand what you are asking the man to do."

"What do you mean, sir?" asked Coyler.

"I mean, with all due respect, that you seem to poorly understand what it takes to merely stay alive in wild country. This is not the 'Smiling West' many believe it to be. Violence is a part of life more often than we care for, but nonetheless, an inescapable fact. What might be unthinkable in the East becomes the inevitable in the West and anyone unprepared for it will end up 'crossing the river' long before his time."

"So then, we should employ a common brigand then?" came a question from the stairs as Flitcher rejoined the conference. "I should think we could find more honorable men than Sam Bucklin...even in Texas."

Bigfoot Wallace gritted his heavy jaws, but managed a genial smile. "Have a drink, Mr. Flitcher. You'll feel better when yer nerves is soothed. And don't be troublin' yerself too much about hirin' Sam. He wouldn't take the job now fer love nor money."

Coldly returning the smile, Flitcher poured himself a drink. "Suddenly unavailable, is he?"

"Might say that."

Flitcher swirled the glass under his nose, inhaling the aroma of the brandy. "I can't say I'm surprised, but I understand the United States Marshals are quite adept at apprehending fleeing criminals, Mr. Wallace. And within the month, charges against him will be filed on behalf of the Indians he has killed and the murder of one Red McCarty."

"I believe," said Lanham, "that Mr. Bucklin is entitled to some defense before he is caused any more undue hardship."

Vincent Coyler nodded seriously and glanced at his son-in-law who shrugged indifferently. "By all means, Mr. Lanham," encouraged Coyler. "What is it you wish to say on his behalf?"

Lanham's eyes narrowed. "First of all," he said cautiously, "let me say that the accusations that he has killed 'untold numbers' of Indians is absolutely false. It is rumor, folklore, the essence of campfire storytelling.

"As a matter of fact, no one has ever seen Sam Bucklin kill an Indian nor can anyone prove he has done so. And he himself has never claimed to have killed any, either.

"As for his being a murderer, that is only the opinion of the teamsters. Mr. Wallace has been a Ranger for nearly three decades, and Mr. Johnson has been sheriff for nearly two years. I myself, as you well know, am a member of the bar. And the three of us, without debate, agreed the shooting of Red McCarty was well within the definition of self-defense."

Flitcher listened with an air of pompous boredom, but Coyler leaned forward intently. "But after witnessing his actions this evening I would have to conclude that further investigation into the charges is certainly warranted. Wouldn't you agree, sir?"

"What, Mr. Lanham," broke in Flitcher cunningly, "would your so-called Indian expert say were he under oath and asked how many red men he had killed?"

Knowing Bucklin as he did, Lanham hesitated. "If he'd killed Indians, he would answer truthfully. But, just as truthfully, he would explain the circumstances under which the deeds, if any, were done.

"In actual fact, Mr. Flitcher, along the entire Texas frontier it is not considered a crime to defend one's family and home against raiding bands of Indians, nor is it a criminal offense to pursue and punish them in the field."

With a suspicion of victory spreading over his white face, Flitcher said tauntingly, "Then you are saying it is the custom for Texans to make armed excursions into Indian territory and attack at will as long as they claim it is for self-defense?"

Bigfoot Wallace had taken out a pouch of tobacco and filled a paper. As he rolled his cigarette he said smoothly, "This country ain't been lived in long enough to have any customs to speak of." Pausing to lick the paper and close it, his eyes settled hard on Flitcher. "But one thing we don't abide is havin' a feller tryin' to put words into another feller's mouth ...tryin' to make him out to be a liar. Kind of a code, ya might say."

Flitcher glanced down as a large brown hand with heavily scarred knuckles dragged a match across the table in front of him, then illuminated a pair of old but threatening eyes. Instinctively retreating, he said quickly, "I intended calling no one a liar. I was merely attempting to clarify a point."

Poorly suppressing his irritation with Flitcher, Lanham resumed, "As to your question, Mr. Coyler, to understand what happened tonight, you must know more about Mr. Bucklin. I still maintain he is the man you are looking for."

Coyler waved a hand doubtfully. "Go on, Mr. Lanham. We are here to listen."

Thomas Lanham nodded solemnly and took a turn at his brandy, then settled back in his chair. "I met Sam in a Union prison in Illinois where we waited out the last year of the war. Conditions were poor and I was suffering badly from an infected wound. I am certain I would have died there if it hadn't been for his care.

"I was a school teacher before the war and he was an Arkansas backwoodsman, yet he knew more medicine than anyone imprisoned there. As I mended, I began to teach him to read and write as he was desperate to communicate his predicament to his dear family. A family he spoke of constantly, lovingly.

"Over the course of our internment, we talked of many things...our dreams, hopes, plans and our fears. We grew to know each other like only men in those conditions can. We became part of each other, so to speak.

"Even then, we knew how the war would end and tried to imagine how it would be for us afterward, what our lives would be like. Thinking I knew best, I continually encouraged him to come west, to Texas, where there would still be plenty of virgin soil, land for the taking for anyone willing to work with his hands and build a new home. And I told him there would be freedom here, even for Confederates."

Lanham paused remorsefully, then took a deep breath before continuing in a softer tone, "A year later he came. His family was with him, his father and mother, sister and brother, wife and baby. The child had been born on the way.

"They came, just as others like them came, hoping to find peace instead of war, and praying to find the liberty that would allow them to rebuild their lives. They came to build their homes and work the land and regain their independence, and thus their dignity. They wanted a chance to forget and start over in a new land.

"The Bucklins came because I urged them to, but hundreds of other families came that year, too. They were encouraged by Washington to move West, a Washington that was eager to see the frontier colonized and then moved farther and farther to the West. The land was there waiting for the country's citizens to settle it, clear it and plant it with crops and homes.

"What these good people found was everything they had expected, everything they had been told about was here. But the one most important detail that Washington left out, that even I failed to understand, was that the aborigines did not all reside on reservation land nor did those on that allotted land stay where they had agreed to stay.

"Within months, the family…along with dozens of others, had been massacred. The year of 1866 was the bloodiest in the history of the Texas frontier."

"Mr. Lanham," interrupted Flitcher impatiently, "we have read many of the letters your people sent to Washington, and as most were only semiliterate, we spent no little time in studying them. Were we to believe those many complaints of depredations, we would have to assume this country to be overrun with red men.

"As you apparently believe the reports, you may find it surprising, as did we, that throughout the course of our journey from San Antonio we counted not a single war party. In fact, Mr. Lanham, there was not a single Indian to be seen anywhere along our entire route."

Staring icily at Flitcher and turning his shot glass between his thumb and finger Lanham responded cooly, "How many catamounts did you see? How many wolves ran in front of your stage in the middle of the day? Did you even see a coyote?"

Coyler missed the connection and answered honestly, "We saw no panthers or wolves, but I believe we saw one or two coyotes. They could have been wolves, but they were off a distance."

"Exactly my point, sir," replied Lanham. "This country is thick with big cats and there are packs of wolves everywhere, but as these animals are as cunning as they are fierce, they are seldom seen by the casual traveler. Yet go into the countryside with the smell of fresh blood on your clothes, and you'll cease to doubt their numbers or their hunger to kill.

"The Indian warriors are like the panther in some ways, but most resemble the wolf in their habits. They kill in pairs or in packs. They kill without warning and then disappear into the wilderness from which they came. Those that witness these acts are the ones closest to the wilderness and most vulnerable to attack, the settlers and the movers.

"Should you have time and the will, I am sure a grand tour could be arranged so that you all could see the fire-blackened chimneys of scores of abandoned settlements and villages just to the west of where we now sit in relative comfort. We could show you dozens of piles of sun-bleached human remains that the wolves and coyotes dug out of hastily dug graves, many of them women and children. Or we might travel the trails and point out the charred planks of any number of wagons that stretch to the north and the south along the edge of the old frontier.

"You see, Mr. Flitcher, ten years ago the frontier was twelve miles farther west than where it now stands, and in that day there were twice as many people living in west Texas as there are now. A great number were murdered by the so-called Noble Red Man, and the rest of those that returned East were simply fearful of staying. And they were a breed of folks that did not scare easily, men and women that didn't show the white feather at the first sign of trouble.

"These brave souls, gentlemen, were *driven* back by the constant and unceasing threat of death. The Kiowa, the Comanche, and the Apache all are at work here and yet any one of the tribes would be sufficient."

A questioning eyebrow raised on Coyler's narrow forehead. "But is it not true that some of the actual occurrences are reported with, shall we say, some overzealousness and when retold, tend to grow in fervor until more fear is spread by rumor than by factual report?"

"Overzealousness," repeated Lanham slowly. After a moment of thoughtful silence, he turned to Bigfoot. "Mr. Wallace, would you please recount for these gentlemen what occurred four years ago at the Bucklin Massacre. And by all means, hold strictly to the facts. I believe the commissioners would benefit from an eyewitness account of but one of the many tragedies in the history of this conflict."

Wallace sucked the last smoke from the stub of his cigarette and dropped the butt into his empty shot glass. Blowing a stream of smoke into the heavy air, his eyes ran appraisingly over the commissioners.

"Like Thomas said, it was four years back, but I seen the same sort of thing plenty of times before and plenty enough since. They all bear a resemblance and the Bucklins' misfortune wasn't much different from the others.

"Onliest thing that keeps on surprisin' me is how many ways them red devils can think up to kill a man. I seen where men was skinned alive, burned alive, scalped alive, strung up like deer by their arms or heels or even hung on their own meat hooks. I seen a man staked out naked over an ant-hill where ants had eaten out his eyes and was crawlin' out thick and wide from his mouth and ears. I seen more'n one man tied to a wagon, with his tongue either cut out all together or with it havin' a stick poked through the end so's he couldn't get it back in his mouth.

"That was to stop a strong man from cussin' 'em before they roasted 'im alive.

"I even seen some men tied upside down naked and where a fire, a little one, had been built under their heads until their brains was boiled. And worse than all of it, I seen where women and children has been tortured to death, too. And let me tell ya, there ain't no sadder thing in this life than see'n a child done that way."

Wallace paused long enough to glance at the stunned and pasty faces of the easterners. As he saw the color drain from their faces, he shook his head and went on.

"Anyway, on that instant back then, me and a handful of Rangers was shadowin' a fair size raidin' party that had jumped the reservation and stole some stock north of the-Bucklin place. And we follered their trail right over 'cause we knowed where they was headed.

"When we got there, the Bucklins was scattered around a burning log house. Apaches burn what all they can't tote off, ya see.

"Old Man Bucklin was kilt and cut up. Most of his clothes had been took and he had four or five arries in 'im, one in his privates.

"The boy, Sam's brother, was done the same way, only they taken more time to cut 'im up worse than his pa.

"He musta fought good 'n hard to have 'em do that much to 'im.

"Sam's ma was lyin' in her door yard, shot and scalped. Only when we got down for a close look we saw she weren't dead. She was just then startin' to moan from the pain.

"Mrs. Bucklin, Sam's wife, died lucky. She was full dressed. She'd not been scalped, but her head had been bashed flat with a rock. And she had got shot twice in the stomach, too.

"We circled for tracks and found out our band had met up with another'n and had fought together, then took off in one bunch to the southwest. We found Sam's tracks too amongst 'em, which weren't no feat since his shod mule stuck out clear as plowed ground. And judgin' from the gait he was goin' hellbent fer leather after 'em, too.

"About five miles out we found 'im by hisself sittin' on the ground holdin' his dead baby girl. He had found her dead on a tree where them Apaches had hung her by stickin' a sharp branch through her little jaw...I guess maybe they got tired of her cryin'. Injun babies ain't allowed to cry none.

"If a captive child don't stop cryin' after they been on the trail a while, they kill 'em like they would swat a 'skeeter or pull a tick, without thinkin' twice about it.

"We took after them redskins and Sam was allowed to join in with us. About dark we come on 'em and they was gettin' liquored up from some of what they stole from the settlements. We didn't know it till the next day, but while we was watchin' from afar and waitin' to make our move, them savages was taking turns on Sam's kid sister. All of 'em...all fifteen of them bucks took her. We just couldn't see what was goin' on in them bushes down below us.

"Come that night, we got Sam's sister. I say we got her, but her mind was gone and to this day it ain't come back.

She lived a couple years with her ma back in Arkansas, but then Mrs. Bucklin died. I don't know what come of the girl, but likely she's with family back there."

Across the small table, Vincent Coyler and Rockwell Flitcher sat spellbound, their eyes branded with confusion, their faces suspended in disbelieving horror. In the deep silence, a suddenly conspicuous wall clock ticked away a ponderous half-minute of the commissioner's lives then, as if joined in thought, both men's expressions twisted with unspoken skepticism and disbelief. Glancing one to another, they began to toss and fidget until Coyler finally cleared his throat.

"Mr. Lanham, you spoke of the many depredations that this country has endured in the past and I have no reason to doubt your sincerity, but has it not been your experience to find that most of these acts have been committed by only a small number of hostiles? Is it not true that the great majority of Indians are peaceful unless provoked?"

"There is only one tribe in this area that is friendly to whites," replied Lanham, "and that is the Tonkawas. They never give us any trouble, but they are hardly peaceful Indians.

"They hate the Apaches as much as Texans do and they are our allies. Tonkawas do most of our difficult tracking of the Apaches and Comanches. They don't like whites much, but their hate for the other tribes is so great, they'll fight on our side and are anxious to help at any time."

"That there is a fact," joined in Wallace. "They like to eat a Comanche or 'Pache from time to time, too."

Flitcher blinked warily. "What do you mean, 'eat them'?'

"I mean they's cannibals. Ain't no secret around here. But nobody knows if it's fer food or fer religion. I came on a camp of 'em myself once, and sure 'nuff, they had a leg on the fire, but that 'tickler one was a Comanche."

Coyler took a deep breath and exhaled impatiently. "Go on, Mr. Wallace."

Aware of their growing agitation, Bigfoot squinted warily at the two commissioners. After a short pause, he began again, but spoke more carefully.

"Anyway, the rest of 'em, the Apache, Comanche, and the Kiowa, don't all live on the reservation land. Some bands of every tribe never agreed to no treaty and they keep on livin' like they always did. But them that do report to the reservation don't stay all the time.

"They show up to pick up their handouts, then go off and raid whenever the mood strikes 'em. Or most of the time--you can find 'em there in the winter since Injuns don't much like to fight then. But when they do leave, they go quiet. And the agent ain't none the wiser, neither.

"We seen a band of Comanches one day on the reservation and then three weeks later, caught the same ones comin' back crossin' the border of Mexico."

"But, Mr. Wallace," protested Flitcher, "that would be hundreds of miles from their homeland."

"Sure it was," snapped Bigfoot. "It ain't nothin' fer a Injun to ride three or four hundred miles to make a raid. These tribes has been raidin' into Mexico fer more'n a hundred years, probl'y two hundred.

"All the time though, them Mexicans not having guns, didn't fight back 'cept on occasion and them Injuns never took away all their women or livestock. They always made sure to leave 'em enough fer seed so there'd be booty the next time they come back that way."

Coyler squirmed in his chair, unaccustomed to the hard wooden seat. "Mr. Wallace, we have treaties, agreed to by the Indian chiefs, that assure us *the Indians will stay on reservation land.* I trust these leaders to be men of their word, more so than I would many white men. I believe them to be trustworthy."

"Some of 'em are, fer a fact. They do their best to hold to the white man's road and keep the young ones and the hot-blooded sub-chiefs at home. But the Injuns ain't like us.

"Just 'cause a chief says jump, it don't mean you gotta jump. A chief only leads. If you don't want to foller there ain't no penalty. It's their right to do as they please. The chief don't have no control like a army general does. If a warrior wants to make war on his own or to go off and raid, he'll do it and when he comes back to the village the peaceable chief ain't goin' to do nothin' to him.

"And then there's chiefs like Satanta that's as big a liar that ever lived on the Plains. Chiefs like him will put a mark on a treaty one day and break it the very next."

Flitcher placed both palms on his knees and leaned slightly forward. "So that we may completely understand your point of view, Mr. Wallace, are you asserting that these depredations are totally unprovoked? Have you ever considered the possibility that the Indians are acting defensively, only attempting to protect their sacred way of life?"

Bigfoot Wallace tipped his chair back to balance on the rear legs and thought for a moment. "Their way of life is sacred to 'em, like you say, and they don't like bein' told they can't behave the way they believe is fittin'. And mainly they don't like bein' put on a piece of land and told they can't wander no more. Can't say I'd like it neither.

"That part of it all is a sad thing and I s'pose lookin' at it like that could make a body feel sorry fer the whole damned race. But it ain't the whole story. Not by a large majority."

Somewhat surprised by Wallace's sentiments, Coyler seemed encouraged. "And what is the rest of the story, sir?'

"Well, let me put it this way. You recollect that bunch of Comanches I said we caught down on the Rio Grand comin' back from Mexico?"

"Yes."

"We stopped 'em there at the river and asked what they was doin' with stolen goods and why they was off the reservation."

Bigfoot stopped and smiled. With a chuckle he asked, "Know what they said?'

"What?' asked Coyler innocently.

"Said we'd no right to stop 'em. Got right frothy about it. Said they weren't raidin' no whites and that they were just goin' about their rightful business of stealin' from the Mexicans."

"I don't understand," said Coyler. "Were they perhaps at war with the Mexicans?'

Wallace snorted. "Naw. They was just puttin' in an honest day's work. There weren't no war. It's the way they live, the way it's been as far back as even they can recollect. To them, that way of makin' a livin' is their natural born right and it mostly don't make no difference if it's raidin' Mexicans, whites, or other tribes. They just don't understand nothin' else.

"Killin' a defenseless family of farmers and stealin' their property ain't a bad thing to an Injun. It's bragged about around their campfires, then told over and over how it was done while the scalps hang outside their teepees to dry."

Coming down on all four legs of his chair, Wallace was suddenly grim. "It ain't in defense of nothin', at least it didn't start that way. At first they was real happy to see white settlers 'cause they was easy pickins. But when the Americans started fightin' back, then is when they got riled. They was used to them Mexicans down south.

"They didn't know white folks could turn just as mean as they was. And that's just what happened, too. After they butchered and carried off a few too many settlers, they found out they was in fer a hell of a fight with people that could learn the ropes quick...just like Sam learn't."

Flitcher's eyes flickered with triumph as his thin lips curled upward into a victorious smile. "And precisely what...'ropes'...did he learn, Mr. Wallace? How to swindle the red man? How to invade and steal his land...or was it simply how to kill and take scalps?"

Suddenly realizing he had said too much, Wallace bridled an angry reply and waited for Lanham to take up the defense.

"Most of what Mr. Bucklin knows about Indians," countered Lanham smoothly, "was taught to him by the Tonkawas. From them he learned the trails, the location of the hidden springs and the habits of the hostiles. He was taught how to track and read sign as well as their patterns of movement across the frontier. But most importantly, and by far most difficult of all, he learned how to think like an Indian. Not act like one, mind you, but to actually think as one."

"Are you implying, sir," asked Flitcher tauntingly, "that the red man cannot think as well as a white?"

"I don't know if he can or cannot, sir," snapped Lanham. "I do know, however, that their customs and traditions, their beliefs and superstitions, are of utmost importance in determining how they act and react, what they will or will not do and when and where and who they will attack. To effectively fight the hostiles you either have to be an Indian or be able to predict them. Mr. Bucklin is the only white man I know of, that can do that and likewise is without question the man you need to solve the Navajo difficulties."

With smug satisfaction, Flitcher raised a single eyebrow and glanced across the table at Coyler's lingering skepticism. "It has been an exhausting journey, Vincent, and I am certain these good men are tired also."

"Indeed," agreed Coyler readily. "If there is nothing more, gentlemen, I believe we shall call it a day." Coming hastily to his feet he tipped his hat. "Thank you both for speaking with us. It has been most informative. Good evening."

Ascending the stairs together, neither commissioner spoke until reaching the top. In the lantern light they paused in front of their doors. For a moment they conversed in low, indistinguishable voices then stepped out of sight. A metallic click rattled from each keyhole, a board squeaked and then all was quiet.

Still staring blankly at the second story balcony Wallace asked uneasily, "What do ya make of *that*, Thomas?"

Lanham buried his face in his hands. After a long pause he looked up. "We gave them an earful, but I'm afraid we didn't change their minds about anything...including Sam's innocence."

"You sayin' they believe we was lyin' about all that? That we made it up?"

"Maybe. I don't know what to make of it. But I've seen enough juries to recognize disbelief when I see it. Might be they wouldn't... or couldn't believe any of it."

Turning back to the table, Wallace took a drink from what was left of the bottle, then wiped his mouth with the back of his hand. "Now that Flitcher strikes me as a small caliber man and he prob'ly figures we're lyin' for some reason 'cause it's what he's used to doin' hisself. But that other'n seems square enough. How come he don't believe us, do you reckon?"

"Damned if I know," scowled Lanham. "I agree with you about Flitcher, and Coyler seems serious about getting to the root of the problem, yet for some reason he's turned his back on the truth."

"Well now," said Wallace thoughtfully, "could be like a man when he gits belly sick. What he needs most to keep up his strength and git hisself well again is food, but he can't come to swaller none. Even the thought of eatin' makes 'im retch so he puts it out of his mind and don't allow hisself to think on it."

Lanham shrugged and reached into his vest pocket and removed a watch. Flipping open its gold cover he checked the time. "I understand Coyler's way of thinking, no more than I understand the mind of an Indian. He's after the truth, but can't let go of the myth. What he'll do with all he heard tonight I can't imagine. He's too smart to be able to forget it, so maybe it's like you said. Maybe he'll just bury it with more self-assuring fables of the 'noble red man.'" Shoving his watch back into place Lanham started to stand. "We better go warn Sam. If Nathan didn't convince him to leave Texas, we'll have to. Flitcher will have a marshal after him in no time."

"Hang on, Thomas," said Bigfoot calmly. "You don't have to worry none about Sam."

"Why not? I have no doubts he's going to be a wanted man. Flitcher has plenty of influence by himself and Coyler may even back him up. Either one of them can get a warrant issued."

"I don't doubt that, Thomas, but Sam'll be gone by mornin' and he'll be gettin' clean out of Texas alto-gether."

Thomas Lanham cocked his head to the side and cast a puzzled look at Wallace, who beamed with an air of fatherly pride. After studying him briefly, Lanham squinted with concern. "The New Mexico Territory?"

"Yep," replied Wallace crisply. "He's gonna take on that job whether them commissioners like it or not."

"What makes you say that?"

"'Cause I was there with Sam at the start and I know a thing'r two nobody else does about that time."

The thin walls of the hotel suddenly reverberated with hollow pounding as heavy boot heals hammered their way over the boardwalk outside. Swinging the hotel door wide open, Nathan Johnson rushed into the room and crossed quickly to the table. "He's lit a shuck," blurted the sheriff, then anxiously took a seat. Handing Lanham a folded piece of brown paper he added briskly, "Said to give you this."

Reaching for the paper, Lanham blinked in disbelief. "You mean Sam? Sam left town?"

"Just rode out and with lock, stock, and barrel in tow behind him on that second horse of his."

Unfolding the paper, Lanham stared at the message.

Deer Thomas plez tend to my land as you sade you wood. I will be back whin I kan make it. If I do not com back, sell it and sind the mony to my sisters keepers. Yur obedeyant sirvant, Samuel Bucklin

"What's it say?" asked Johnson eagerly.

"Sam wants me to take care of his land for him. It sounds like he'll be gone for a long time."

"Say where he was goin'?'

"No. But Bigfoot says he's off to the New Mexico Territory. He was just going to tell me why he thinks so when you came in."

Wallace smiled confidently, "Ya'll recollect the story of the massacre and the number of warriors that was there?"

"Sure," answered Johnson. "Fifteenteen. Ever'body knows that."

"Well, tonight, before this meetin', that is, Sam was all through huntin' 'em down."

Astonished, but relieved, Lanham asked, "You mean he finally quit?'

"Naw, sir, he was plumb finished...done! Took 'em the best part of five year, but he done it."

Johnson picked up a dirty glass and poured himself a drink. "Damn!" he whispered hoarsely, then gulped a shot of brandy. "Not nobody ever dreamed he could do it... or even stay alive tryin' to."

"But if he got them all," protested Lanham, "why New Mexico?"

Johnson scratched the back of his neck worriedly. "Don't suppose he's started to like it, the killin', I mean? I know some men that get as bad as a dog in a henhouse. Just kill fer the joy of killin'."

Bigfoot's chin wrinkled as he shoved his lower lip out. Shaking his head emphatically, he said, "Nothin' like that at all. What most folks ain't privy to is that there was *sixteen* of them devils at the house. But old Mrs. Bucklin seen one goin' fer her grandbaby right at the start and she grabbed up a shotgun and let loose on 'im. She shot his buf'lo shield and the lead went into his legs. He went down, she told me later, but he got up and took the baby anyhow."

"But what happened to him?" asked Lanham. "He wasn't with the others when you caught up with them?'

"No, he weren't. Sam always figured he died from the wound he got. And all along he had a feelin' this one kilt his baby out of revenge before he went off somewheres and died by hisself.

"But tonight he learnt that might not be the way it was. He heard enough about that Cabeza Blanca and his limp to make him set out after 'im."

"It sounded like just another renegade Apache to me," said Lanham doubtfully.

"That ain't much to go on," muttered Johnson. "Hell, we shot enough of 'em around here it's a wonder half of 'em don't limp."

"Yeah, it ain't much by itself, but Cabeza Blanca means white head or head of white and more'n likely is talkin' about his hair."

Thomas Lanham's muscles tensed. "And the Apache that took Sam's baby was white-headed?"

"Mrs. Bucklin called it gray. Said he was taller'n the rest, not as big as me, but a six-footer like Sam. And even though he was gray-headed he weren't old in the face.

"And Sam didn't need to hear no more than what he did to put it together in his own mind. I seen his face a changin' while they was talkin' on it. He'll find this Cabeza Blanca without too much trouble, but how he'll know he's the one he's been lookin' fer all these years, Lord only knows."

"Johosiphat," barked Johnson. "I got half a mind to go with 'im."

Lanham sighed heavily, wearily. "I only hope he has it in him to make sure...before he kills him. If he stirs up trouble out there they'll send the military after him for sure."

Wallace absentmindedly tapped his fingers on the table, then slowly touched them down one by one and then raised his thumb. "That's more'n five hunderd mile from here, closer to six."

"Which way do you think he'll go?" asked Lanham. "Up north to the Santa Fe Trail or south to San Antonio and over?'

"Neither one, Thomas. He's been clean into the Territory a couple of times already and knows his way. Likely he'll head west to Fort Defiance then turn north."

"But there's nothing out there from here to Santa Fe. It's all Indian country."

"Be safer," agreed Johnson, "if he'd stick to the stage roads."

"Take too long. When Sam makes up his mind to go, he wants to make tracks. He'll save a week or more by goin' on west from here. And he sure as hellfire ain't afraid of being in Injun country. Besides, them stage roads ain't all that much safer now."

Suddenly Johnson slammed his glass on the table and swore. "Know what I just remembered?"

"What?" demanded Lanham.

"Them Injun commissioners said they was headed fer Fort Defiance after leavin' here, remember what that old one said?"

"You're right," clamored Wallace as he sat up with a jerk. "When we was talkin' about the trouble at Fort Sill."

Suddenly wide eyed, Lanham's brow wrinkled as he glanced at Wallace. "How long do you think it'll take Sam to get to Fort Defiance?"

"Two, three and a half weeks, maybe."

Looking quickly to Johnson, Lanham asked, "And the stage, how long will it take?'

"Let's see now," mumbled Johnson, "San Antonio to El Paso to the Santa Fe wagon road is...and then to...I'd say right at two weeks, Thomas. Not so good for Sam."

The three men sat in silence, their minds racing ahead to an army outpost six hundred miles away. After a long moment, Wallace spoke slowly, "If they find out Sam's in the same territory, they'll have the army out after 'im."

Lanham nodded morbidly. "If they know he's there, they'll alert every station along the Santa Fe Trail, maybe even the trading posts. Flitcher had his pride stepped on. He won't stop until he's got Sam in jail... or worse."

Wallace tugged on his ear thoughtfully. "Do ya think Sam will recollect the talk about them three goin' to Fort Defiance? I sure didn't catch it."

"I don't know," sighed Lanham. "If he goes near that Fort...there's no telling what's going to happen."

CHAPTER FOUR

Riding from Jacksboro under a half-moon, Sam Bucklin kept the North Star over his shoulder until it faded into a dingy blue dawn. The sun was scorching the back of his neck when he slid down a sandy embankment and rode across the eastern fork of the Brazos River. After scouting up and down the river for Indian sign, he finally made camp at the water's edge.

Stripping the gear from the geldings, he rubbed them down with gramma grass then tossed his bedroll under a cottonwood deadfall. The horses needed rest and it would be foolhardy to push them too hard. He had survived more than four years in Indian country by taking his time and foreseeing danger, but above all, by being incessantly alert. But he knew when it was time to sleep.

With bloodshot eyes, Bucklin stretched out on his blanket. He was restless to move on, but forced his eyes closed and lay still. It had been two days since he last slept and his body ached from the long ride, yet his mind churned relentlessly.

The old wounds had been torn open by the description of Cabeza Blanca, but with the rekindled hatred came the resurrection of a nightmare that had all but faded into the tragic past.

He could smell the smoke and charred flesh once again and hear the painful groans of his mother. He saw his infant daughter dangling from a tree and felt the breeze that rocked her back and forth. Then, in his arms, he could feel the weight of her lifeless body. But worst of all, in the unsilencable reaches of his imagination, the sobs of a helpless baby constantly tore at his gut.

For over an hour he struggled against the memories and imagined horrors, but finally gave up his hope for sleep and made coffee over a smokeless fire. While the water heated, he climbed the riverbank to a point of high ground and studied the western landmarks he would follow. As he turned back, he paused and stared longingly at the far horizon. "This time, little darlin'," he vowed coldly, "this time, I swear."

Stopping through the rest of the day only long enough to switch horses or allow them an occasional bite of prairie grass, Bucklin headed west until the sun's blinding glare made it unsafe to go on. A half-hour before sunset he found a hidden draw and dropped into it and out of sight.

Pulling open a stained flour sack that Moses had packed, he grabbed a handful of biscuits and from the edge of the ravine watched his back-trail and waited for dusk. As far as he knew he had not been seen, but as the light dwindled he rode out of the ravine's security and didn't make camp until reaching the Salt Fork of the Brazos River. But there would be no coffee, no hot food, or warmth. Like the Texas Rangers that taught him, there would be no fires on this night nor any night, and his evening camp would always be made after dark.

Roughly following the Brazos for the next two days, Bucklin grew more wary as the trees became fewer and shorter and the air thinned with a dry heat. What green remained was dulled under a blistering sun until a day later he crossed Double Mountain River and headed directly into the heart of the Llano Estacado, the seemingly lifeless Staked Plains.

White men believed the country was something to be avoided, but Bucklin had stalked Indians over the forbidding plains too many times to be fooled by its harsh appearance. There was water, if you knew where to look, and herds of buffalo and antelope. And should these be in short supply, prairie dog meat was always at hand to get a man through.

From the Palo Duro Canyon in Texas to the Pecos River in the New Mexico territory the unmapped plains held thousands of empty square miles, but where there was enough water he had seen Indians gathered into villages, some with hundreds of warriors.

Avoiding the sharp-eyed Apache and Comanche, now Bucklin rode only in the early morning and late afternoon, but when the moon and clouds were right, kept moving through the night. Several times he crossed fresh sign, cutting his trail from north to south, and three times he spotted small bands of warriors with his army binoculars, yet so far he had passed through their land undetected.

Being careful never to skyline himself, he took shelter in the shadows of the low ground whenever he suspected Indians. Sitting motionless with his soiled buckskin clothes and grayish-brown horses he would blend into the rough tapestry of dried grass, sand, and yucca cactus. Bucklin had learned what those he hunted knew instinctively, and he too could vanish from sight in a land nearly void of cover and then reemerge to pass over the country in relative safety.

Having lost track of the days, but guessing it to be two weeks since leaving Jacksboro, Bucklin came to the Plains' western border and began a slow descent toward the green bottom land of the Pecos River Valley.

He had been to the isolated valley before, where the trees were tall along the river's banks and the water, cool and clear, flowed over a shallow bed of smooth rocks and sand. Deer moved easily in and out of dense thickets of willow and cottonwood and quail were plentiful in the tangled patches of blackberry. It was a fertile land with plenty of water, but there were no farmers or ranchers to work the ground or reap the harvest. And, except for a passing Mexican or white trader, it was home to no one.

To the southwest lurked the White Mountain, Mescalero and Sacramento Apaches and to the east the Western Apaches. To the north were the Chiracaua and the Comanches and all used the river for travel or to trade or for making war. The only inhabited outpost he had heard of was Fort Sumner, somewhere far to the north.

Stopping frequently to study the valley below, Bucklin took a half-day to reach the river and only then approached by means of a brush-choked coulee. After filling his canteen and giving the horses a short breather, he swung back into the saddle, crossed the river and worked his way to the foothills a half-mile to the west. Behind the hills stood a desolate range of mountains that bordered the valley to the north and south for at least a hundred miles.

He had tracked Apaches to the Pecos twice before but never had the need to cross it. One brave he left sprawled at the bottom of a ravine and the other he floated down river toward the Rio Grande, his heart blown to pieces by a.50-caliber buffalo slug.

But those Indians had left a trail, a faint one, yet readable. And those trails he had used to find the hidden waterholes, the springs and eventually the river itself. West of the river things were different. He was on new ground and with only a vague knowledge of the terrain to guide him he would follow the river north. At some unknown point he would have to turn west and, after crossing ninety miles of parched desert, hope to find the town of Santa Fe.

Continually looking to his left for a pass through the mountains and to his right for Indians, Bucklin rode until the afternoon shadows stretched long and dark over the baking sand. In the bottom of a dry wash he paused to check his back trail and take a sip from his canteen. As he reached for the cork, a breath of hot wind brushed past his ear and riding on it was the muffled rumble of trouble.

Without making any sudden moves, he pulled his Henry from its boot and slid off his saddle. Leading his horses behind a small rise, he picketed them near a few scant bunches of dried grass and eased his way to the top of a nearby knoll. With the binoculars hanging from his neck, he crawled under a knee-high mesquite bush and lay flat.

Heat waves rippled along the river to the east, but nothing else caught his eye. Pulling his hat down low to shield the binoculars from reflection, he methodically surveyed the river below, picking over it acre by acre. A half-hour passed, then another dull boom rolled up from the river but as Bucklin shifted the glasses toward the sound it too drifted into the stillness.

Taking the binoculars down only to wipe the sweat from his eyes, Bucklin stared at a bend in the river a mile ahead of him, watching for any sign of movement. For another half-hour interval there was nothing until, from a sandy bank, there came a flicker of sunlight. A moment later a third shot was fired but with a shift in the heated air the blast was crisper than the other two.

Bucklin swore. Someone was signaling from the river, but who would do such a thing and what were they doing here? No Indian ever wasted ammunition and only a fool would risk attracting their attention...unless he wanted them to come.

Only one brand of man was *that* safe. Somewhere down there a trader, a gun runner, was in trouble.

Smirking with disinterest, Bucklin backed carefully down the rise and started for the horses, but halfway there he slid to a stop. Swearing again, he scrambled back up to his vantage point. He had nothing but contempt for those who traded with Indians, but suddenly he wanted this one to stay alive, at least until evening.

The signaling continued throughout the hot afternoon, but the time between shots steadily increased and the short flashes that usually preceded them stopped all together. A few minutes before sunset, Bucklin made his way down to his horses. With the Henry across his lap and the binoculars at his chest he kept to the base of the foothills until he was opposite the sandy bank where he had seen the reflections.

The ground rolling out in front of him was empty, except for a few scattered yucca cactus, but near the river a stand of green prairie grass and small thicket of elderberry offered some decent cover. Other than that there was nothing over the last quarter-mile.

After searching the valley one last time, he stuffed the glasses into his saddlebags and levered a round into his Henry. Trotting the geldings into the open and toward the river, he spurred them into a gallop to cover the last two hundred yards. Whoever had been shooting would have the sun in his eyes for five more minutes and that was all he needed.

Engulfed in the last blazing moment of sunset and confident no Indians were within miles, Sam Bucklin rode straight for the bank but just shy of the river he veered warily to the left. Tying his horses behind the elderberries, he shoved his rifle into its boot and switched to the Long Tom shotgun. As the sun dropped below the mountains he crept quietly through the tall grass.

Nearing the river, he passed several trampled patches of grass where horses had stood cropping the tips off the long shoots and on the far bank he saw what had been a camp. There were tracks of several men, but none were in sight and no sound came from beyond the river. Whoever had fired the shots was either hiding, off dying, or already dead.

Wading across the knee-deep water, he paused to study the tracks. Next to a ring of fire-blackened rocks a pool of dried blood stained the sand and, leading away from it, a fifty-foot trail of drag marks pointed to a tangled pile of driftwood and logs. In front of the wood several bloody plugs of cloth were scattered about and a whiskey bottle lay empty on its side.

A twig snapped and Bucklin instantly dove to his belly, landing with the shotgun cocked and ready.

"Well, I'll be damned," boomed a raspy voice from behind a sun-bleached snag. "I'll be double-damned."

Rising unsteadily into view an old man with a sloping forehead and thin but prominent nose painfully worked himself into a sitting position.

Running front to back in his long, red hair were streaks of gray and behind his head, his hair was tied into a knot. His face, weather-beaten and brown, was wrinkled like pig leather, but under a drooping mustache a youthful grin showed a row of white teeth. Looking curiously at Bucklin from a pair of deep-set eyes, he snorted, "You ain't Injun. But you ain't Mex neither. Thought you was one of 'em come back to finish me."

Bucklin slowly came to his knees and lowered the shotgun. With the hammer still cocked he said flatly, "Heard your shots. Didn't figure you was Injun so I came to see if you was in need or just a plain fool."

"Guilty on both accounts," laughed the old man, "but you ain't much better off, son. What the hell are you doin' out here?" Glancing past Bucklin, he squinted toward the elderberries. "You alone, are ya?"

"Might ask you the same question," replied Bucklin, coming to his feet. "But first you bring out your weapon. You bled enough for one day and I'd hate to waste a load of buckshot on a white man."

The old man shrugged and laid an open-top Colt on top of the log. "I was out of powder anyhow. But you're right. A body can't be too keerful, 'specially if'n he's alone."

"How bad are you?" asked Bucklin as he took the pistol and slid it behind his belt. "Are you kilt?"

"Depends."

"On what?"

"My leg's shot up. Busted the bone in two. If I don't get blood poisonin', I got a good chance but I ain't got no horse to get help."

"You don't have much then," said Bucklin, then turned to walk away.

"You gonna leave me here?" bellowed the wounded man. "You can't just turn your back on a white man and leave him to die."

Bucklin stopped near the campfire and knelt down by a small set of moccasin tracks. "You got nothing I want, mister. I came out here to do some trading. Not to be no nursemaid to you."

"So you're a tradin' man?" perked up the old man. "I never seen you afore and by damn I know 'em all around here."

"Done my work in west Texas," answered Bucklin, still looking at the odd tracks. "Getting too crowded with the Rangers always prowling around, so I left."

Pulling himself up to sit on the log, the old man swung a blood-soaked leg over and down. "If you're lookin' fer Injun trade," he offered hurriedly, "I can set you up, get you in business right quick."

Walking around the camp and casting for sign, Bucklin glanced at the man's wound. "You a trader?"

"Reckon I'm the best in the territory," said the man, his head bobbing nervously. "I know all the tribes: Utes, Navajo, Apache, Comanche, Kiowa, and even them no account Paiutes. Been at it since the rendezvous ended in '38. Why near everybody knows old Harry."

Bucklin flinched, but quickly looked away to hide his surprise. It was the name the commissioners had mentioned, a name connected with Cabeza Blanca!

"Maybe you heard the name before?" continued Harry as the pitch of his voice grew higher. "I been around, I tell ya. Nobody knows me by sight hardly, but Harry is a talked about man."

Bucklin turned slowly and forced a sarcastic grin. "You don't look like the Harry I heard of. If you was him you ought to have a load of guns or stolen livestock around, at least some money, but you ain't got nothing that I can see. Now, for you being such a famous Injun trader, that's not much to show for thirty years work...That is, if you *are* him."

"I'm him, all right, and I got plenty cached away safe and sound. I'm up against it hard now, but I still got goods to trade, things you could use."

Bucklin pointed to the tracks. "They took it all. Whatever you had went with them."

Rubbing his stiff leg, Harry swore bitterly. "Don't never trust no Mexicans, 'specially one called Juan Garza. They got no honor, no decency a'tall. That's my advice to you...to you, ah..."

"Buck. Buck Samuels."

"Buck. Well, Buck, don't trust 'em. Leastwise, not out here. They took my outfit and my money. Took it all and shot me up to boot."

"Bushwhack?"

Sheepishly Harry shook his head. "Naw, not 'xactly. We was travelin' south together. Gonna get more goods for trade down near the border and take 'em back up."

"What went wrong?"

Harry thought for a moment, then ran a pointed tongue over his dry lips. Deciding to take a chance he cleared his throat. "Was on account of a woman, a white woman."

His eyes hardening with suspicion, Bucklin sighed heavily. Fighting the sickness in the pit of his stomach, he spoke evenly. "The one wearing the moccasins?'

"You read sign good," answered Harry with a weak smile, "damn good, I'd say. She's mine. Paid two repeatin' rifles for her. She'da brought a high ransom for the Mexicans if they'd a got her. I seen her up north before the braves got to her and the clothes she had on was fine ones, not like a sodbuster's wife."

"You trying to tell me she's still here, that the Mexicans don't have her?"

"They wanted her," answered Harry, "wanted her bad but I wouldn't trade her. Wouldn't let 'em have at her neither and after a while it made 'em mad. I kept on tellin' 'em I was savin' her for to get the ransom money my own self and had to turn her over in good shape. I'd get myself hung if she talked bad about me while I was tryin' to collect on her."

"That was right smart, Harry. Some folks value their women a lot more if they ain't been soiled none. White folks find out what happens to women captives and…well, sometimes they act mighty peculiar." Stopping to shrug his shoulders in feigned bewilderment, Bucklin added, "As long as they can still do for a man, what difference does it make?"

Harry chuckled agreeably, then with the tension draining from his face, he relaxed and shifted his weight to take pressure off the injured leg. "That's my feelin's on the matter too, Buck, but tryin' to reason with them people is like arguin' with a fence post so I learnt it's best to just bring 'em out and let 'em be. If a man needs a woman that bad he can always find hisself a squaw to oblige him."

"I take it you want to trade me this woman, seein' how that's all you got left?'

"I'll make you a good deal, Buck. You can have her for a horse, just one horse."

Bucklin laughed scornfully. "What kind of game are you trying to run on me? When was a woman ever worth as much as a horse?"

"It's not her," growled Harry, "it's the ransom money she'll bring. You could buy a string a horses for that much. All you gotta do is get her to a eastern town and put the word out you brought her in. Her kin'll be so grateful they'll pay plenty. I done it many a time. That's how it works, I tell ya. Easy money."

"I got plenty of money already and I'm headed north. When I get started going somewheres I don't let nothing stop me. I got no need of your woman, Harry."

"Take her with ya, Buck. You clean her up some and you'll see she's passable. Not more'n twenty. She's small, but I never seen a stronger woman...And them nights up that way can get cold for a man alone."

"Not for a horse, Harry. And like you said, there's plenty of squaws around." Laying the shotgun on his shoulder, Bucklin acted as if he were going to leave, then said indifferently, "Looks like your luck's running kind of muddy, Harry. If I wanted that woman I could track her down and just take her, but I got no use for her...or for you. I'm looking for a white-headed Apache that's wanting to do some serious trading. I got a load of Yankee guns and he's supposed to have more gold and silver than he knows what to do with."

"Cabeza Blanca," Harry said desperately. "You mean Cabeza Blanca."

Bucklin took the shotgun off his shoulder and walked closer to Harry, stopping a few feet in front of him. "What do you know about him? You know where he is?"

"I'm about the only white man that does. I trade with him ever' month up on the San Juan River. We got a rendezvous picked out nobody could find."

"And where might that be?' asked Bucklin coldly as he leveled the shotgun.

Smiling at Bucklin's sudden interest, Harry answered slyly, "You ready to make a deal now, Buck? Gimme that horse."

"Let's hear the deal then we'll decide on the trade."

"All right, but first you go fetch the girl before it gets dark and bring her back. Then you bring up your outfit and we'll have her feed us. You got any coffee? I'd admire a good strong pot of it along about now."

"I got coffee," replied Bucklin, lowering the 10-gauge. "Where is she?'

"When the shootin' started she run over the creek and down some. Crawled into some of that prairie grass and laid still as an Injun. Them Mexicans nearly stepped on her three or four times lookin', but they was cold-footed bastards and had no stomach fer a good fight so after a bit they took out without her. She ain't moved since. I think she figured I been shootin' at her all day."

"How far down did she cross?"

Harry turned and pointed. "Go down ta that last pile of tangled up limbs there on the bank and cut across. You'll see the bent grass where she fell tryin' to climb the bank and when you get about thirty paces in start lookin' down. The way you read sign you won't have no trouble findin' her."

A short distance from the camp Bucklin waded the river and easily found the trail. She had fallen, then crawled on her hands and knees, and finally slid along on her belly. He could see the depression where Harry had believed she would be found, but the trail went farther.

Going to one knee, Bucklin examined the tracks nearly hidden by the blades of grass. Digging in with her toes and fingertips she had moved along inch by precious inch, taking hours to go only a few feet. She had not panicked, at least, and for that he was grateful. Yet in the clawed ground he could see her desperation and in her relentless struggle he could sense her terror, her anguish, and her frantic hope of escape.

But escape to where? There was no place for her to go...unless she was hunting a place to die, a place to find permanent relief from her torment.

Grimly Bucklin came to his feet and for a passing moment painfully closed his eyes. His sister would be nineteen this fall. She would have been married already and had children by now. They would be old enough to play with his own...if only he hadn't been away from the settlement that day. They could have lived close by and Ma and Pa could have watched their grandchildren grow up... Sara, poor Sara. If only he hadn't been gone.

Reluctantly opening his eyes to face what lay ahead, Bucklin started on. Even in the fading light the trail was clear enough to follow quickly and in a matter of minutes he was standing over the young woman.

Pitifully trying to conceal herself, she had pulled the long blades of grass over her, then lay motionless with her moccasined feet in full view and her head buried in the fold of her arms.

"I'm not going to hurt you," he said gently. "I'm not going to let anyone hurt you anymore... You've tried real hard, ma'am, but it's over for now and you're going to have to come back with me. But ma'am, please don't stop trying. You're going to be all right, just don't let loose of your hope."

Reaching down, Bucklin slowly brushed aside the grass and put his hand on the woman's shoulder. She was dressed in buckskins that smelled of smoke, horse sweat, and animal fat. Her light brown hair was tangled in knots and matted with twigs and soot. Covering her skin was a layer of copper-colored paint that, from a distance, would have made her look as brown as any Indian. When he touched her she began to whimper softly.

Patting her shoulder as he would a child, he said, "You've come this far, ma'am, just hold on a while longer. It won't be long and you'll be on your way home."

Lifting the woman to her feet, Bucklin tried to steady her, but her legs buckled and he caught her. For an instant he held her tight against his chest then scooped her up into his arms. Tears streaked her cheeks, mixing with the dirt as they fell. There was a bloody bruise on her forehead. Her eyes were closed tight with grief.

"She ain't dade, is she?" asked Harry as Bucklin laid her in the sand near the stack of firewood. "She get herself shot?"

"No. She's not kilt. A little lifeless right now, but she'll come around. You keep an eye on her and I'll get my horses."

"Better tie her up, Buck. That's what she's used to or she'll run off."

Walking into the darkness, Bucklin waved a hand, "She ain't going nowhere. If she gets up, just holler."

Leading the horses across the creek, Bucklin staked them in the stand of grass and carried his saddlebags and guns back to the camp. When he returned, the woman was sitting up but hunched over with her hair shielding her face. Bucklin dropped a sack of coffee next to her and built a fire. As the flames grew, he arranged the stones to form a flat surface and took a large tin cup from his saddlebags. Holding it out to the girl he said firmly, "We need water."

Without lifting her head a small hand took the cup. For a moment the cup rested in her lap then slowly the woman got to her knees and finally to her feet. As she trudged to the river, Bucklin asked, "What do you call her?"

Harry shrugged. "Me, I just call her 'woman.' She don't talk a'tall so I never bothered askin'. The Injuns had a name fer her though, *Ojos Frios,* or Cold Eyes. Maybe it was their color or maybe somethin' else, but that's what they called her. Them Apaches speak Spanish pert near as much as their own tongue."

"What do you mean she don't talk? They cut her tongue out?"

"Nope. She just don't say nothin' ever, that's all. I seen 'em cut off a woman's nose before, but never heard of cutting out a woman's tongue, only men's."

As Cold Eyes returned with the water, Bucklin pointed to the flat stones. "There, put it there," he ordered. "When it boils put in the coffee."

Looking at the cup, Harry frowned. "You ain't got a pot?"

"Takes up too much room. I travel light."

"I declare," agreed Harry, then thumbing toward the horses, he said, "What happened to the other fella? You came in with a empty saddle and, if I do say so myself, ridin' two of the finest horses I ever seen. Got a lot of bottom, I reckon."

"I ride alone. There weren't no other'n."

Harry thought a minute then his brow wrinkled in admiration. "You swap mounts like the Injuns, don't ya? Well, I'll be damned, Buck. Bet you can make a hundred miles on a good day."

Bucklin tossed a stick into the fire as the steam began to rise from the tin cup. "On any day," he said, then nudged the woman. "Coffee?"

Reaching into the bag, Cold Eyes took a handful of grounds and let them trickle from her palm into the boiling water. Her face was hidden in the shadows of her dangling hair, but the curves of her body filled the snug-fitting buckskin dress. Scarcely over five feet tall, she weighed no more than a hundred pounds, but in the small frame was the indisputable body of a woman.

From another sack Bucklin pulled out a handful of dried buffalo strips and handed them to Harry. "That's supper," he muttered. "I wasn't expecting company."

After taking some meat for himself, he sat down cross-legged at the fire and laid the open sack beside Cold Eyes. "So what's your deal?"

"Coffee," mumbled Harry with a mouthful of jerky. He held out his blood-stained hand, took the cup, and swallowed hurriedly.

"North a here is a army outpost. It's about two day's ride and they got a sawbones there. You get me there and the girl's yorn. Then when I'm safe and sound I'll tell ya how to take up with Cabeza Blanca and not get yourself kilt doing it."

"I don't want the girl."

Taking a cautious sip of the scalding coffee, Harry savored the taste, then gulped it down. Smacking his lips, he cocked his head and grinned, "Ah, the simple comforts. That's all a man needs, Buck. Ain't nothin' can satisfy a man more.

"Now you get the woman 'cause I'm a man of my word, Buck and I always do right by my friends. Besides, you couldn't never find the rendezvous point by yourself even if I was to draw you a map. If you never seen that country up that a way, you might not believe me, but it's like nothin' you ever seen. Twists and turns like nowheres I ever been. And red, ever'thin's red. Looks like hell with the people moved out. Cliffs, blind canyons, walls a thousand feet straight up. You need the woman to show ya, Buck, believe you me!"

Stalling for time to think, Bucklin stared at Cold Eyes and swore. Pausing for a moment, he turned to Harry. "If she knows the way, maybe I'll just take her and leave you here."

After another gulp of coffee Harry answered unperturbed, "No. You need to know what I got to say or you'll never get close enough to talk to him. You'd be dead right quick unless I tell ya how to save your hair. Cabeza Blanca stays alive 'cause he don't take no unneeded chances.

"You want to do business with him, you gotta go through me and take the girl, too. I'm just trying to do right by ya for saving my life. I'm a grateful man, Buck. Mighty grateful."

"She'll fight me all the way, Harry. And what makes you think she'll guide me in there? Likely she'd just soon die as go back."

Shaking a stick of meat at Cold Eyes, who hadn't moved, he said, "Not this 'un. She's left somethin' back there she wants more than anything on God's green earth and she wants nothin' worse than to go back."

Slowly, knowingly, Bucklin turned his head toward the young woman and gazed at her in amazement. As he did, she timidly reached into the sack and took a piece of meat, then reluctantly put it to her mouth.

"Only one thing a woman can love that much," said Bucklin solemnly, "and that's a baby. Is it white or red?"

"Oh, he's white. A little boy about two, three maybe. Come from her dead husband. Them Injuns prize a strong boy child. Don't matter if he's not red. They turn 'em into good warriors all the same as if they was born of a squaw and a buck. And a few of the whites are the best men in the village and the funny thing is, they hate the white settlers as much as the Injuns. I never could figure that 'un out, 'course it's none of my business no how."

Thinking quickly, Bucklin asked, "I imagine the ransom money would be some higher if the boy was included in the bargain."

"Well, that might be right," agreed Harry, surprised at the idea, "I never give it a thought. But now that you bring it up you could be onto…Naw. You'd have to pay too much fer the boy child to get 'em to let loose of 'im. That won't be none of my business when you get there, but I'd say fergit the boy. You done got the girl free."

Still looking at the girl, Bucklin grew curious. "Do you think she listens, that she hears what we're talking about?"

"She understands fetch and cook good 'nough. She gits by, but sometimes I seen them eyes of hers a-watchin' and I wonder. Seems like maybe she still has her mind, but could be she's just plumb crazy. It happens to 'em."

Bucklin twitched and gritted his teeth. "You say she wants to go back?"

"Don't seem to care about nothin' else," replied Harry, then he took another bite of jerky. "Serve her right if they keep 'er."

Reaching for the bone-handled knife on his belt, Bucklin drew out its nine-inch blade and held it over the fire. Watching anxiously, Harry blurted, "What's that fer?"

"Gutting mostly. Sometimes skinning. Once in a while killing. But right now it's for looking at your leg wound."

"What are you aimin' to do with that pig sticker? The bullet done gone on through."

Walking to Harry's stiff leg, Bucklin paused. "You be still, do you hear? You jump around and you'll get cut up." Sliding the blade under the blood-caked pant leg, Bucklin slit the cloth to the knee and removed a crude bandage. Bending low, he smelled the wound.

"What do ya think, Buck? You seen many gunshot holes?"

"Wore the gray for four years. Patched up more'n…yeah, I seen plenty."

Harry nodded. "Figured you for a southern boy from the way you talk. Too bad about the way that war ended and all them folks dead for what? Fightin' over slavery when it's been goin' on fer thousands of years. Damnedest thing to fight about if you ask me, 'cause it's still goin' on and always will be."

Going to the firewood, Bucklin began shuffling through it. "We weren't fighting for slavery. That had nothing to do with the war." Finding two inch-thick branches that were relatively straight, he turned to his saddlebags for some rawhide straps. "They say we lost a quarter-million men on the field. Not one in a thousand had a slave or ever wanted one."

"Then what the hell did they fight about? That's an awful lot of dying fer nothin'."

Bucklin began carving off the sharp barbs from the branches. After a long minute of silence he said, "We fought the Yankees because they come after us on our own land, hunting us, going to tell us what for. We never let nobody do that, none of us. So we fought."

Harry scratched his head, pondering Bucklin's answer, then shrugged, "I s'pose ya got a point, Buck. Kinda goes along with what the Injuns say 'bout their own situation. I guess it ain't much different."

The whittling slowed suddenly then gradually came to an end. Bucklin stared into the fire briefly, then glanced at the girl. "It ain't quite the same."

"What about my leg?"

"You need a doctor or you'll lose it, but you got a good chance for now. I'm going to mend it with these sticks so you can ride. You'd have been better off if you hadn't a put them dirty rags into the holes."

Cutting a short strip of leather, Bucklin handed it to Harry who placed it between his teeth and braced himself. As Bucklin positioned the sticks and tightened the leather thongs, Harry's jaws clenched and sweat beads sprouted on his forehead, glistening yellow-orange in the reflected fire light. A deep growl of pain broke the silence, but there was no scream. Cold Eyes looked up slowly, her pale blue eyes drifting toward the sound, then coming to rest on Bucklin.

After the last knot was tied off, Harry groaned in agonizing relief then sprawled onto his back gasping for air. Wiping the sweat from his face with a dirty shirtsleeve, he swore bitterly as his chest heaved up and down. "I shoulda... saved...some a...that whiskey."

"You'd of bled less if you hadn't drunk it. Now you best drink as much water as you can hold."

"What about my bandage?" asked Harry as he sat back up. "Ain't you gonna wrap it?"

"It's crusted over on both sides. Might as well let the air at it. It'll do more good than what you put on it. We'll prop it up on something while you sleep and find a cover for it in the morning."

Bucklin squatted by the fire and passed the blade of his knife back and forth through the flames then dropped it into his sheath. Feeling the stare of the woman he carefully slid the sheath's thong over the brass tang then glanced up. Her face was expressionless and hollow, but her eyes held a vivid clarity, a clarity his sister had lost and never regained.

"I'll be damned," said Harry. Looking closer at Cold Eyes, he said again, but more quietly, "I'll be damned."

"You'll get no argument about that from me, Harry," replied Bucklin dryly, "but why you bringing it up now?"

"The woman. I never seen her look at nobody before, I mean not like she's lookin' at you. You better tie her up tight tonight, Buck. I tell ya she's actin' mighty peculiar."

"Whatever you think, Harry. You been around her long enough to know."

Studying the girl more closely, Harry curiously turned his head to the left then to the right. "There's somethin' else I jest now seen. Even though she's as dirty as a flop-eared hound, she's kinda purty."

"You're not wanting to go back on the deal, are you?" asked Bucklin.

"No, sir. I keep my word. It's just funny I never seen it afore. Like she just come to life of a sudden. But maybe I'm jest gittin' old. Them Mexicans likely seen it all along and that's why they wanted her so bad."

"How many of them were there?"

"They's three of 'em. But after I burnt one of 'em they went skallyhootin' outa here like a pack of scalded dogs."

"You figure they might circle around on us tonight?"

"Don't think so. They'd be afeard the Injuns would find out what they done to me and skin 'em alive. They know I'm favored by the tribes. Likely as not they's half-way to Santa Fe by now."

Letting the fire burn low, Bucklin went to his gear and returned with his blanket. After unrolling and spreading it onto the sand, he grasped Cold Eyes by the upper arm and lifted her to her feet. Tying her hands behind her back, he led her to the blanket. "Sleep," he said firmly, then eased the pressure on her arm.

After a short hesitation, the woman dropped to her knees and then rolled onto her side. She lay still as Bucklin tied her feet, but when he covered her with the rest of the blanket she flinched and buried her head into her shoulder.

Easing the blanket down, Bucklin said, "Seems like she's had some rough treatment."

"Ain't easy fer a slave in a Injun camp, 'specially a white woman. The squaws is the worst on 'em. Always beatin' and pokin' at 'em. Their way of havin' fun is to torment the captives."

Hiding his sympathy with a frown, Bucklin scowled at Harry. "You sure you can't draw me a map? This woman's going to slow me down and I don't like wasting time."

"Can't be done, Buck. You'll see when you get there. You'll be glad you got her then or," Harry paused and grinned roguishly, "or maybe you'll warm up to 'er on the way."

Bucklin swore under his breath and tossed Harry the second bedroll.

"Could be you ain't worth the trouble."

Harry caught the blanket with one hand and snickered, "You'll see, son. You'll see soon enough ole Harry's right." As Bucklin walked into the darkness he crassly raised his voice, "Where you goin', boy? Your woman's over here."

A moment later Bucklin returned with two horse blankets and dropped them next to the fire. Using his saddlebags as a pillow he laid down and pulled them over himself the best he could. "If what you say ain't true, Harry, I just might come back and hunt you up."

Harry laughed out loud as he struggled to the ground and wrapped himself in the heavy wool bedroll. "Pull in your horns, Buck. This here's been your lucky day."

CHAPTER FIVE

The Big Dipper was already down and the eastern horizon glowed with a hint of sunrise, but Sam Bucklin had not risen nor had he moved for ten minutes. Moments before, something had awakened him. Had it been a dream, a sound of someone near, or even a smell? Listening, smelling, and waiting, only his eyes moved in the faint light.

From the woman's blanket came a muffled crunch of sand as she restlessly shifted her weight and curled her legs closer to her body. She moaned then spoke in a soft agonizing voice. "Tommy."

The woman had been talking in her sleep and with heart-sinking realization, Bucklin rolled onto his back and stared wearily at the stars. "She's crying for her baby, Sara," he whispered. "What do I do now? What am I gonna do?"

Cold Eyes stirred again and Bucklin got up. After tucking her bedroll closer around her shoulders, he laid his horse blankets over her for more warmth, then took his bow and two arrows and went upstream. When Harry and the woman woke up the fire had been burning for an hour and fresh meat was roasting over it.

Propping himself up on an elbow, Harry wiped the sleep from his face then sniffed the air. "Venison," he said hungrily. "Got us some camp meat, eh?"

"Figured you needed some on account of you bleeding so much," replied Bucklin as he untied the woman. "And Cold Eyes here runs a might on the skinny side. Needs some rounding out, I'd say."

Harry scratched his beard and ran a hand through his hair as he looked around, "I didn't hear no shot."

"Wasn't one," said Bucklin, cutting off a piece of meat and handing it to Harry. "Been using a bow since I was a boy back in Arkansas. Used to hunt with the Caddos."

Slicing more venison, Bucklin handed it to Cold Eyes who now sat cross-legged with the bedroll wrapped around her. A small, dirty hand accepted the food without hesitation and she began to eat. But unlike Harry, there was an element of grace in her manner and some of the matted hair had been pulled out of her face and lodged behind her ears.

"You ever been shot before, Harry?" asked Bucklin as he examined the leg wound.

"Once. In my side."

"Then you know what you're up against riding on a horse?"

"I got a good idee. But I'll make it all right. You may have to tie me on, but I've lived through blizzards, snake-bites, and jealous husbands. I ain't about to let a little scratch like this put me under."

"What do we do with the girl? You want her behind you or me?"

"She's yores, Buck, and besides I'll have my hands full jest keepin' myself forked proper. I don't need her a tuggin' on my backside."

Turning to the woman, Bucklin cupped her chin in his hand and raised her head to look into her eyes. Their color was unlike any he had ever seen. "Ma'am, you're gonna be riding behind me. You behave yourself and we'll go get Tommy. You fight me and you won't see him again, do you hear?"

Her pale blue eyes widened with fear, then she nodded weakly. As Bucklin dropped his hand she took the blanket from her shoulders and rolled it neatly, then placed it by his saddlebags. Walking to the edge of the fire, she poured out the coffee grounds from the cup and headed for the river.

Harry glanced curiously at Bucklin, but before he could ask a question, Bucklin said, "She talks in her sleep, said her kid's name."

"Tarnation," snorted Harry in amazement. "If that don't beat all."

"Surprised me, too," agreed Bucklin as he tore his old shirt into strips. "And she understands better'n I thought she did."

Chewing on a slab of venison, Harry's eyes filled with concern. "Wonder how much she'll talk when you turn 'er in for the money. Think she'll recollect what we was talkin' about with the Injun tradin'?"

Wrapping the strips of cloth around the broken leg, Bucklin scoffed, "She won't talk for months, if she ever does. By then I'll be long gone. Talking in her sleep is one thing, but facing up to a bunch of white folks' meddlesome stares and prying questions is another altogether. She'll mostly keep to herself for a spell then maybe come out of it later."

"Just the same," muttered Harry, as Cold Eyes neared, "we best watch what we say."

"We'll play it safe then," said Bucklin, finishing the bandage. Reaching down for the two saddle blankets, he pointed to the washed cup Cold Eyes held in her hands. "I want coffee when I'm done packing!" he ordered.

Hoisting the saddle over his shoulder, he went to the horses and didn't look back until hidden by the backs of the animals. The young woman was kneeling by the fire, her attention entirely consumed with the chores at hand, but she had understood him perfectly. Had she understood the day before? Could she grasp what he planned to do, that she was finally safe? Or was she merely one step above his sister, able to handle only the simplest tasks and respond to the most basic commands? Bucklin saddled and loaded the horses, pausing often to glance at Cold Eyes. After cinching up the slack in both saddles, he picked up the reins and took a long look at the tragic figure. "God, help her," he said, then, wiping the compassion from his face, led the mounts out of the grass onto the sand.

Throughout the morning and into the afternoon, Bucklin let Harry take the lead with the buckskin and set his own pace as he gingerly selected the best route for his broken leg. Each time the horse stumbled over the rough terrain the old trader grunted painfully, but whenever Bucklin suggested a rest it was refused with a barrage of swearing.

In the beginning Cold Eyes balanced herself by holding only to the cantle of Bucklin's saddle, but as the day wore on and her fingers began to cramp, she latched onto the sides of his buckskin jacket. Occasionally, she fell asleep and wearily leaned into his back, then suddenly awoke and shoved herself erect only to repeat the process a few minutes later.

It wasn't until late afternoon that Harry pulled up and even then it wasn't to dismount. Taking his battered hat off his head, he held it high to better shade the sun from his eyes. As Bucklin rode up beside him, he grumbled, "Better get her down. Got Injuns comin' and it wouldn't be fittin' fer 'em to see her ridin'. Squaws of warriors should be afoot, not on a war pony."

Sliding Cold Eyes to the ground, Bucklin asked, "What kind?"

"Just barely caught sight of 'em, but they seem to be Comanches. You best be thinkin' of somethin' to trade with. They'll be expectin' it of a white man."

"I don't have much to trade, Harry. Nothing I want to do without, anyway. I carry only what I need."

"That may be, but if you don't come across as a tradin' man they may up and decide to kill us all. They got no reason to let us pass lest we's traders. You best get ready to give up on them guns you're totin'."

While Harry watched and waited for the Comanches to appear, Bucklin rode a few yards to the rear and stepped out of the saddle. From his saddlebags he took a box of .44 shells and dumped a half-dozen into his hand. Drawing the Henry from its scabbard, he rested the butt in the sand and braced the barrel between his legs. With his back to Harry, he stuck the lead bullet into the tip of the barrel and pried it loose from the casing. After dumping out the powder, he carefully replaced the lead and rolled the casing shut.

As he quickly finished the last shell, he glanced up to find Cold Eyes standing a few feet in front of him, a spark of curiosity in her otherwise blank stare.

"To jam the rifle barrel," he whispered. "To tear it up." Hearing the pounding of hooves, Bucklin replaced the emptied bullets, lining them side by side in the front of the box, then closed it and tucked it in the saddlebags. Dropping the Henry into place, he grabbed the saddle horn and slung himself onto the roan and trotted up to Harry.

Looking pleased, Harry said, "They're Comanche, all right, and they got horses."

Bounding out of an arroyo that crossed a hundred feet in front of them, a lone Comanche jerked his pony to a dusty stop. The horse reared slightly and then fought the tight reins as the Indian glared at the two white men blocking his path.

Hanging down his back like the matted tail of an unkempt mustang was a growth of coarse black hair. His feet were covered to the knee with moccasins and from his hips hung a ragged breechcloth. Red and yellow stripes of colored clay lined his face and forehead effectively distorting any expression of surprise he might have had.

Both ears of the bay gelding he rode had been split in the Comanche custom and there was no saddle. The only means of securing the rider to the horse was a braided loop that had been woven into the horse's mane.

Bucklin's lips thinned with a knowing smile. He had fought the Comanche when he could not avoid it and had seen them hang an arm through that loop and shoot from under the horse's neck at full gallop. But he had learned early on that the Sharps rifle shot through their horses and on through the hidden riders as well. Their skill meant nothing to a well-placed buffalo slug.

Raising a hand in recognition, Harry called out in Comanche, "Osolo." Then, switching to Spanish, he added, *"Amigo."*

The warrior grunted. As he started forward, a herd of a dozen horses rose out of the arroyo behind him, followed closely by five more Comanches.

"You talk Mex?' asked Harry under his breath.

"Some."

"Good. Most Comanche and Apache use it if needs be. Them Navajos up where you're headed know it, too. You'll need it anywhere you go in this territory."

Osolo stopped in front of Bucklin looking first into his steady eyes, then at Harry. *"Quien es?"* he demanded, pointing to Bucklin.

"Wants to know who you are, Buck. This here is Osolo or Big Wolf. Important man with his band...and a hothead."

Making the sign for trader, Harry said strongly, *"Amigo. Buck es amigo."*

Four of the braves rode closer, leaving the youngest with the herd while Osolo circled slowly around Harry and Bucklin. When he had completed the round and the others had drawn near, he spoke in Comanche. After a short pause he looked hard at Cold Eyes.

"He says we ain't got much to trade with and he's braggin' how they just stole them horses from some soldiers upriver."

"Then tell him we'll catch him the next go around when we've stocked up on supplies. We need to keep moving if you want to keep that leg of yours."

Harry nodded and, with a mongrelization of Spanish and Comanche, explained to Osolo pointing occasionally to Bucklin and then to Cold Eyes. When he finished speaking he nudged the buckskin with his good leg, but Osolo suddenly reached out and grabbed the throat latch of the bridle. *"No mueve."*

Making the sign for trade with his other hand, Osolo paused to look at his men. Proudly he turned back to Harry. *"Un caballo para seniorita."*

Harry's eyes flared unexpectedly. "We got trouble, Buck. He wants to trade for the woman. I don't know why, but he must want her bad. He's offerin' to give a horse fer her."

"Tell him no. The woman is mine. She's my woman and she's not for trade."

Harry answered Osolo speaking briefly, uneasily. Then Osolo's eyes filled with indignation. Holding up two fingers, he said angrily, *"Dos caballos."*

"He's uppin' the ante, Buck. Two horses. He ain't gonna give it up."

"Seems amight upset," returned Bucklin, deciding Osolo would be the first to die if the situation exploded. "Tell him I got something worth three horses that I'll trade and it ain't the woman."

Reaching down to his saddle scabbard, Bucklin slid out the Henry repeater and held it high. As the sun caught the polished brass frame and long barrel even the painted mud could not hide the Comanche's awe.

"Tell them it shoots fifteen times before a reload and fires as fast as you can work the lever."

Harry sighed with relief. "You're a-learnin' son," he said, wiping sweat from his forehead, "had me worried there fer a time."

Holding up both hands with fingers spread wide, then only one hand, Harry bragged of the rifle's fire power, *"Dies e cinco, diez e cinco."*

Osolo grabbed the rifle from Bucklin's hands and threw it to his shoulder. Levering the action, he fired into a rocky slope then levered and fired three more times in quick succession. Proudly rubbing his dirty hand over the brass finish, he grunted his satisfaction then scowled, *"Cuantos balas teine?"*

"Wants to know how many cartridges you got fer the rifle?' asked Harry. "These Comanche got more rifles than most other Injuns on account of them raidin' so many whites, but what they's always short of is ammunition. They ain't many of them Henrys around, but I seen them figure out how to reload them little rim firecases even so. How much you carryin'?"

Pulling the box from his saddlebags, Bucklin answered, "Fifty shots."

Harry smiled as he took the box, "Comanches can't count but to ten, Buck. When you trade with 'em everything is tens. You go five tens of bullets."

Seeing the box of shells, Osolo called back to the warrior guarding the horses and a moment later he brought up two geldings and a dun mare. Each had a military brand on the left flank.

Handing the shells to Osolo and taking the lead ropes in exchange, Harry smiled at Bucklin, "You're off to a good start, Buck. He's a hard man to swap with and you done made a happy Injun outa 'im. He'll put a dog on the fire tonight and they'll have a way up time over this."

Raising the Henry high overhead, Osolo screamed triumphantly then charged away, taking the other warriors and herd of horses with him.

As their dust settled, Bucklin dismounted to separate the dun from the bays, which were considerably taller. After looping its lead rope into a war bridle, he motioned to Cold Eyes.

"You take this one," he said harshly. "That Henry was damn hard to come by."

Bucklin felt her hand brush solidly over his own as she took the rope. Watching her hop belly first onto the dun then throw her leg over and sit up, his eyes narrowed keenly. Had she gently squeezed his hand or was it his imagination? Was she aware of his predicament and his desire to help, or was it just an awkward bump? As he wondered, Bucklin found himself staring at a shapely but dirty thigh that had been exposed by the short leather skirt. Flushing suddenly, he turned away, but as he settled into his saddle he glanced at her again. Under all the grime and filth…she was still a woman.

"She done caused me to get a busted-up leg," said Harry as he looked shrewdly from Bucklin to Cold Eyes, "and she cost you a good rifle, but by damn the more I take notice of her the more I'm sure she's worth the bother. Somebody's goin' to pay a high price to get hold of her."

Bucklin shrugged indifferently. "You see the brand on these horses?"

"Yeah. They's army hosses. Likely from them boys up at Fort Sumner."

"What do we do if they catch us with them?"

Harry shook his head. "We best not let that happen, Buck. We can hide 'em out. They'll be wondering what we was doin' out here in the first place, but I done got a idee to take care of that part of it. We go ridin' in there with them mounts though, they're gonna get mighty suspicious."

"There might be a patrol coming our way right now trailing those Comanches," said Bucklin as he rode near the two bays and slipped the lead ropes from their necks. "One horse we could say we come across along the way, but having three would get us hung."

"S'pose yer right." agreed Harry, but as Bucklin sent the horses running with a slap on their rumps, Harry groaned. "But them's fine animals. Fetch nigh on to fifty dollars apiece in Santa Fe."

Turning to Harry, Bucklin disgustedly cocked his head to one side and leaned forward on his saddle horn. "I'm going a hundred miles out of my way to nursemaid a cripple, I got a woman traipsing along to slow me down, I lost my best rifle, and now you got to remind me I just threw away a hundred dollars that I could've picked up in Santa Fe where I was headed in the first place... Don't tempt me, Harry. Don't tempt me."

"Oh, now don't mind me," shrugged Harry as he hurriedly nudged his buckskin back onto the trail. "I was just talkin' to hear my head rattle. Runnin' off at the mouth, that's all."

Holding her head low and slumping at the shoulders, Cold Eyes clutched the rope bridle tightly with both hands. Greasy strands of hair hung down past her face, nearly concealing it with streaks of shadow. For a moment she trembled, then was still as the heat of the day beat down on her.

"Ma'am," spoke Bucklin softly, "I want you between me and Harry. I'll drop back a ways and take the rear so you two can set the pace...and I hope you know, ma'am, I didn't mean what I said about that rifle. I wouldn't have let them take you...no matter what."

As the dun walked past, he thought he heard her voice, a single word or even two, but the sound was hardly more than a whisper and he couldn't be sure. Curiously watching her ride ahead, he again forced his eyes from her legs, then shamefully cursed himself for looking. Pretending to check his back trail, he waited until Cold Eyes was nearly out of sight before going on. Then he swore again.

A half-hour after the afternoon shadows had melted into dusk, Bucklin caught up to the lead horses. Both had been tied to a mesquite bush and the buckskin had already been stripped and rubbed down. Harry, his face paled with pain, lay on the ground, resting his head on a saddle seat while Cold Eyes blew gently into the small flames of a camp fire.

Swinging stiffly to the ground, Bucklin glanced at Harry. "You dead yet, old man?"

"Well, ain't been buried yet."

"How'd you get off your horse?" asked Bucklin as he pointed to Cold Eyes. "Had the woman help you?"

"I asked her, but she didn't get the drift of what I wanted, I reckon. I done all right by my ownself till my good leg give out and I fell."

"Who took care of the horses?" asked Bucklin. "You?"

"Hell no. Apache women do all that kinda work. That there Cold Eyes is a might on the puny side, but she can toss off a saddle as good as any squaw I seen. Went right to work, she did. That'n'll take good care of you, Buck, if ya decide to keep holt of 'er."

As the flames grew brighter, Bucklin took a closer look at Harry's leg, a leg that had swollen to twice its normal size. Saying nothing, he turned to Cold Eyes. "The camp meat's hanging on my saddle. Fetch it and start cooking."

Casually taking out his knife, he passed it over the flames as Cold Eyes went to the roan. "That plug of venison's some crusty on the outside, but this dry air's nearly cured it. Gonna taste fine after a long day on the trail."

Allowing the knife blade to cool, Bucklin held it low and out of sight. Harry's eyes were closed tightly as he fought off his pain and he hardly noticed when Bucklin sat down near his feet. "You shouldn't of poked them dirty rags in that bullet hole, Harry. You got the blood poisoning now."

Harry groaned. "You sure?"

Reaching for a burning brand, Bucklin said, "Well, sort of. Let me take a better look. Now hold still so I can see."

Bringing the flame closer, Bucklin hunched over the leg smelling the fetid odor of infection. Without warning, he brought the knife up then and plunged it two inches into the bulging flesh wound.

Harry screamed and tore at the sand with his fingers as his body jerked then crumpled into unconsciousness.

With a twist of the knife blade, a thick stream of yellow pus gushed out and Bucklin began milking the leg with his other hand until blood began to flow in its place. A moment later he pulled the knife out and wiped it clean on Harry's pant leg. When Cold Eyes returned he sat cross-legged at the fire holding the blade in its cleansing flames.

Stopping several feet away from the two men, Cold Eyes stood at the edge of the fire's light, her eyes open wide. Not until Bucklin put the knife away did she come closer and even then she came warily.

"If you're thinking I kilt him, ma'am, you're wrong. He needed some doctoring on that leg that's all. He's passed out and if he's lucky he'll sleep for a long while."

Cold Eyes studied Harry for a long count of ten then slowly relaxed and knelt down across from Bucklin. After shoving a stick through the slab of crusted meat, she wedged it between two rocks to hang over the fire, then sat with her legs beneath her, staring into the flames.

Only the crackling fire broke the calm as stars began to fill the darkening sky and the smell of sage grew steadily stronger. The air was still, but the day's heat had gone with the sun and in the sudden coolness, the fire's warmth was a welcome comfort.

"It's been a long time since I had company around a cook fire," said Bucklin as he looked kindly at Cold Eyes. "It helps more than I recollect just having somebody close by... Sometimes the long nights can close in on a man alone."

Leaning forward, Bucklin turned the stick of venison. "'Course it's good to have somebody to talk to. Or maybe just to listen. Keeps you from thinking on your problems too much, especially the ones that set you to brooding.

"Sort of like me whistling past the graveyard back home when I used to come home after a Saturday night dance. 'Course I never was much for dancing, but my wife Sara..."

Bucklin's voice drifted into silence then he too stared into the coercive flames. After a long pause, he somberly went to his saddlebags and returned with two dried-out biscuits and laid them carefully on top of a flat sandstone rock bordering the cook fire.

"They're a couple of weeks old, but when they get hot they taste all right. I like to see them heat up and smell the bread. Reminds me of Ma and how she used to bake a pan full ever morning before we'd go to the fields. She'd put some in a tin for us and send us off with Pa. It was a good time, a fine time. Only I didn't know it so much then."

Looking up from the biscuits, Bucklin gazed at the unblinking pair of blue eyes. As reflections of yellow flame flickered in their emptiness, he said softly, compassionately, "Don't fret about Tommy, ma'am. They prize boy children too much to do him any harm. I give you my word I'll fetch him for you, and I'll get him back before they can make an Injun out of him." Dropping his eyes, Bucklin gritted his teeth. "No Injun will ever take a white child and keep it if I got any say in the matter. It's the least I can do for you, ma'am.

"I know your grief. And I understand, ma'am, I *know* what it is to lose a child."

Taking a deep breath, he fought off a wave of sadness, then halfheartedly reached for a biscuit. As he picked it from the flames he heard a fragile voice struggling to speak "Plea...please...Help me."

Bucklin's head snapped up, his eyes full of surprise, but Cold Eyes had not moved. Her chest rose and fell with her gentle breaths, but her hands were clenched into fists.

"I will, ma'am," said Bucklin. "I swear I will."

With the tension slowly draining from her, Sam Bucklin held out the biscuit and waited. The small, grimy hand that finally took it was stained from countless hours of forced labor and above the wrist, torturous scars attested to the savagery of the Apache squaws. The Indians had taken everything from her and she had suffered far more than his poor sister, yet contrary to what Harry believed, he was certain she had not been broken.

Easing back on his elbows, Bucklin stared curiously at the young woman huddled across from him. Virtually speechless and filthy from head to toe, she was a tragic figure. But even in her weakness, he could sense a remnant of dignity and strength. And as much as he tried to deny it, there was an attractiveness about her he could not explain.

Because of his sister he had felt a deep kinship toward her from the beginning and that he accepted. Now, however, in the mellow firelight and with only a vague awareness of something unseen, he studied her closely but could only wonder at his growing admiration.

A light breeze stirred the flames and from the hills a coyote yipped. The venison sizzled and popped while the night grew steadily colder. When the meat was done and they had eaten, Cold Eyes curled up in her blanket and in a matter of minutes was asleep.

She had spoken. She had asked for help, but were her words meant for him? Did she realize he was a friend or was she merely delirious? Bucklin had seen too much in the war, too many men calling out in agony not to wonder, and as the coals faded into ashes his ray of hope languished into wistful despair.

The night seemed unusually long and Bucklin had not slept well, but knowing the effects a festering wound could have on a man's strength, he let Harry rest as much as possible. It was well after sunup when the old eyes finally opened. From a wounded man he expected as much, but what encouraged him was seeing Cold Eyes sleep nearly as long.

Throughout the evening hours Bucklin had gotten up to check on Harry and, unlike the night before, the young woman had not stirred. There were no moans and no rest-lessness. She had slept soundly, perhaps for the first time since being captured.

The swelling had gone down in Harry's leg and after ruling out the need of a travois, Bucklin loaded him onto the buckskin and again let him take the lead. With stub-bornness and grit he held himself in the saddle until mid-afternoon when finally he motioned for Bucklin to ride up alongside him.

"'Bout five mile up there's a bend in the river," he said hoarsely, his face gray with pain and clammy with sweat. "It opens up considerable up yonder but has lots of trees for cover. The Mexicans call it *Bosque Redondo* or Round Woods, but to you and me it's Fort Sumner. It ain't no real fort, but it's got soldier boys a-plenty in it. They's officer's quarters and a barracks and a passel of out buildings, but no walls or nothin' around none of it. That woman's gonna have to be hid out till you git back or you'll lose her and more'n likely get our necks stretched. They see her being a white woman and dressed like she is they're gonna ask questions. If she don't an-swer 'em they'll git mighty curious as to why not. And if she does up and start to pallaverin' she'll turn us in for tradin' guns to the Injuns."

Bucklin hesitated, then thought of the Comanche and the Henry rifle he had traded for horses. How much did she understand about that? Was her mind sound enough to reason out what he had tried to do or was she more likely to confuse him with someone like Harry? He had treated her badly to keep up his facade, but was it clear to her that it was only an act? She needed to be off the trail and cared for by her own kind as soon as possible, but trying to help her too soon could get him killed. There was no other way. She would have to wait a while longer, at least until Harry told him the secret of

Cabeza Blanca. Once he knew that he could come back and send her in alone, but for now she would just have to hold on.

"We got no choice about that," agreed Bucklin. "I reckon she'll do all right while I pass you off to the sawbones...or you could go in alone."

"Thought about it," grimaced Harry, "but I ain't gonna make it sittin' up, son. I'm takin' you up on that travois, I'm pretty much scalded."

Bucklin swung down quickly, just in time to catch Harry as he crumpled over and started sliding off the saddle. As the broken leg banged against the cantel on its way over, Harry groaned feebly, his head spinning from the wrenching jolt of pain. "He'll kill you," he muttered deliriously, "Bay...Chen... You can't...leave me...You'll never..."

Laying Harry down in the shade of a yucca, Bucklin helped him with a drink from his canteen, then propped his head up on a bedroll. Looking to Cold Eyes, he said, "You'll have to look after him while I hunt up some poles along the creek. He ain't been drinking enough water and he's got a fever from his leg."

Still sitting astride her horse, Cold Eyes looked down listlessly at the old man, but as her eyes focused with comprehension, they gradually filled with a repressed hatred.

Sliding off the dun, she walked slowly for him until stopping beside a jagged stone the size of a small melon. There she stood, waiting patiently for Bucklin to ground hitch the horses and then leave the two of them alone.

After securing the buckskin and roan, Bucklin went to Harry who was groggy from the pain and fatigue. Picking up the canteen, he took a few steps toward Cold Eyes and held it out to her. "You'll have to pour it down him, ma'am," he said hurriedly, but then noticed the venom in her ice-blue eyes.

Glancing down by her feet, he saw the rock, then took another step and pressed the canteen into her hand and closed her fingers around it. Holding her hand tightly, he said, "We need him alive, ma'am. He's got information we need yet to get to Cabeza Blanca...and little Tommy...After that...it don't matter. But for now we've got to go along with him. The both of us."

Cold Eyes hesitated, then turned her head away. A moment later she took the water and grudgingly started forward. As she squatted next to Harry and uncorked the canteen, Bucklin lead his buckskin to the creek's bank before turning back for a quick look.

Seeing her working diligently on a man she would have rather killed, he nodded in admiration. "Good girl," he said quietly. "Good girl." Then, with a faint smile, he headed upstream.

A quarter-mile to the north in a stand of young cottonwood trees, he chopped down two of the straightest saplings, then cut off the branches, tossing the largest into a pile. After trimming the poles, he tied the narrow ends to the pommel of the buckskin's saddle and began stripping the leaves from the branches. Weaving them into a crude lattice-work, he lashed the seven-foot-long platform onto the lower end of the poles, using up the rest of his rawhide strips and one of the bridle reins. When he returned with the completed travois, the sun was an hour closer to the horizon.

Hearing Bucklin's approach, Harry leaned up on his elbows and grinned with relief. "There you are, boy. I knew you'd be back. You're not the kinda man that'd leave me out here to die, no, sir. And when we get to the fort I'm gonna make it worth your trouble, you'll see."

"She treat you all right?" asked Bucklin as he brought the travois along side Harry.

"Her?" scoffed Harry. "Them Injuns learnt her real early not to cause no trouble to a man. She knows better'n to do anything to old Harry."

"That so?" said Bucklin taking the bedroll from under Harry's head. "Could be them Injuns know something you don't. Maybe that's why they traded her."

"What are you sayin'?"

"Nothing in particular," replied Bucklin innocently, "but I'm a cautious man and try not to take chances I don't have to. I don't trust her. I think them Injuns knew she wasn't broke to harness 'cause it showed now and again in her look. That's why they named her Cold Eyes. I'm thinking there's something going on behind those eyes, more than she lets on. Something vengeful.'

Harry squinted at Cold Eyes, who sat dejectedly in the shade of her pony. As he studied her for a moment, a sneer of disbelief twisted his face. "Not this'n, Buck. They beat all the fire outa her. She won't cause you no trouble. She knows her place."

After spreading the blanket over the lattice, Bucklin slid Harry onto the travois then ran the remaining rein across his chest and under the arms, strapping him to the wooden frame. As he tied a lead rope onto the horse's head stall, he said, "These poles are green and full of spring. You best hang on tight."

Holding the rope, Bucklin swung into his own saddle then turned to Cold Eyes. As she hopped onto her mount, he said flatly, "You ride behind, woman, and keep up. If he falls off, you let me know right off or there'll be hell to pay."

Moving out at a slow walk, Bucklin skirted the spiny yucca and mesquite bushes, ponderously winding his way across the desert floor. A half-hour before sunset he spotted a grove of trees a mile ahead. Situated in their midst were several white buildings arranged in typical military fashion. Surrounding the trees were hundreds of acres of abandoned farm land.

Turning to his right, he led the horses into a shallow arroyo that was bordered on the north and south by tall mesquite. Dismounting, he went to Harry. "It's up there about a mile," he said, then squatted down and took a closer look at the haggard old man. "You hear me?"

Wearily, Harry's eyes rolled to a stop, then cleared. Blinking heavily, he asked, "What? You say somethin'?"

"We're here. Just up yonder is the fort. We got to get us a story to explain what we're doing out here so far from nowhere. We don't want them getting suspicious and they're gonna want to know how you got yourself shot up."

"Done figured that out yesterd'y, Buck. And some today. And matter of fact it ain't even much of a lie."

"Keep talking."

"We leave the woman here. Tie her up so's she can't get to the fort and ruin us. Then we ride in and tell 'em we was after white captives to take back to their kinfolks that hired us out. That's why we's out here where no self-respectin' white men would go...less'n they was tradin' with them red devil Injuns.

"Then we was come on by Mexican bandits that shot me up and took off with all our gear... and we seen 'em with a herd of army horses, too."

Bucklin tilted his hat back on his head. "You been busy, Harry. That there is a professional job of lying if I ever heard one."

"Comes with the job, Buck," Harry said weakly. "You'll get the hang of it by the time you're old as me."

"I'm going farther up this draw and hide the woman," said Bucklin as he wrapped the lead rope around a mesquite branch and began removing his weapons from the horse. "And I'm leaving my horse here, too, along with all my gear."

"What for?"

"You never know about army officers, especially them that look after Injuns. They might take a look at all I'm totin' around and figure I'm out here starting trouble, taking scalps to sell to the Mexicans. Like I said before, I'm a cautious sort."

"Got a point," agreed Harry, "got a point. But hurry it up. This here leg's worser than a ulcerated tooth."

Leading his second horse over to Cold Eyes, Bucklin took the rope from her hands and worked his way up the sandy wash until he was sure Harry could not see or hear them. After tying both horses to a yucca spine, he finally glanced up at the pale blue eyes.

"You can get down now, ma'am," he said politely. "You'll be safe here."

As she dropped to the ground less than an arm's length away, Bucklin involuntarily took a step back and averted his eyes as hers came up. "We been coming on an army fort all day and now it's just up ahead of us. I been thinking today, ma'am, long and hard, and I don't rightly know what to do with you or what's best. Maybe it ain't my place to decide what's right so...so from here on it's up to you.

"Harry claims I can't find Cabeza Blanca without you coming along to point out the way, but I can't see where that could be so. I reckon I can hunt him up like I done the others and I'll get your boy back, too.

"Them at this fort or maybe Fort Defiance will know where to send him. You just leave word with the army where you'll be at, and Tommy'll get there. If you're feeling up to getting back to white folks you're welcome to go on to the fort up ahead, but I got one big favor to ask you.

"Just don't ride in until we been there a while. If Harry sees you there afterward he'll figure you got loose on your own. I don't have that secret he keeps promising and I need him to believe I'm an Injun trader till I can get it out of him.

"All I'm asking is that you leave my horse and gear here where I can get at it... and that you find it in your heart to forgive me for the way I been treating you." Bucklin paused awkwardly. "There's one more thing, ma' am... Just in case there's any reason you might want to stay on, to come with me and show me the way to Cabeza Blanca, I wouldn't mind at all if you did. And you'd be safe as any lady I ever met."

Taking one of the pistols from his belt, he laid it inside his saddlebags within easy reach. "That's loaded and capped, ma'am. Stay close to it or hold onto it if you're a mind to."

Before turning to leave, he looked up once more, but this time his eyes met hers...and they held. Bucklin's throat tightened as he gazed into a face of unspeakable sorrow and before he was aware of it, he had spoken again.

"I'm sorry for all that's happened to you, ma'am. I know the hurt you feel inside. I know because they took my sister...like they took you."

Reaching out, he touched her shoulder gently. "The suffering never seems to end," he said, "but someday...maybe it won't pain you so much as now. When it's over, all over, maybe then the both of us can try to forget.

"If it can be done at all, I'll get your boy back for you. And while I'm at it, them Injuns'll reap the whirlwind, ma'am. An eye for an eye, a tooth for a tooth...and then some."

Slowly taking his hand from her shoulder, he added, "One way or the other I'll try to be back by morning or thereabouts. Then I'm headed for Santa Fe and then to Fort Defiance. It'll be a long, hard ride, ma'am, and you been put through a terrible time already."

As Bucklin walked away, he paused to look back. "My name is not Buck, ma'am. It's Sam Bucklin. And if I don't get the chance later, I want to tell you I'm proud of the way you're holding up. Takes more courage than most women got, to get as far as you have. But either way, what you're gonna do from here on out will take pretty near as much...So long, ma'am."

CHAPTER SIX

E xcept for the trees shading the white-washed buildings ahead, the land surrounding the military outpost was a scene of desolation. Evidence of laboriously dug trenches scarred the land in every direction, but nothing save a scattering of yucca sprouts survived in the scorched soil. What brush there once was had been uprooted and piled into hundreds of flimsy shelters, then covered with scraps of canvas that now hung twisted in the gnarled branches like bleaching bones.

Passing by the eerie deserted huts, Bucklin glanced back at Harry.

"What kind of place is this?"

Half-raising his head from the travois, Harry took a quick look around.

"This here's what the army calls the white man's road. It's how they like to have kilt eight thousand Navajos trying to show 'em how to be farmers. Cold winters with nothing to burn but mesquite roots and them hogans out there couldn't turn a light breeze on their best day. Cut-worms and floods in the summer, alkaline water to drink, and reservation Mesquleros raidin' 'em to boot. It's a wonder any of 'em got back alive."

"They brought the Navajos all the way down here?'

"Shore they did. After Kit Carson rooted 'em out they marched nearly all of 'em out here. Three hundred mile. The Injuns called it, 'The Long Walk.' Still do."

"Where'd they take them to? They sure ain't here now."

Harry laughed snidely, "Back where they got 'em."

Bucklin shook his head. "Union officers. How'd we ever get whipped by the likes of them?"

With no sentry posted, Bucklin led the horse to within one hundred yards of the fort before he saw two riders coming out to meet them. Keeping a steady pace, he said, "We got two soldiers coming at us. The fort's just ahead."

"Don't be sayin' no more'n you have to, Buck. The less we talk, the better off we'll be. I'll do most of the pallaverin' if you don't mind, seein's how I got a better feel for the yarn we're gonna spin on 'em. Some of these soldiers is green uns. Some's just the bottom of the barrel, really the scrappin's, but once in a while you meet up with a smart one. It's them we got to watch our step with."

Approaching at an easy walk, the two soldiers drew up a few feet in front of the travois and watched it come nearer. Suddenly a lanky sergeant with a drooping mustache sat up, his attention aroused. "Hell, that ain't no Apache, Corporal," he said, "he's white."

"Yeah, Sergeant. I can see that now," replied the corporal lazily, "coming out of the desert like he done and wearing them skins a body could make a mistake. And he's about as black as one."

Bucklin ignored the comment. "Got a wounded man on back. You got a sawbones here?"

"We do," answered the sergeant, riding back to inspect the travois. "What in damnation are you doing here? And why're you coming in from the south?"

"Evenin', Sergeant," offered Harry pushing himself up on his elbows. "We're mighty glad to see you. Been traveling for two days with this busted leg."

"Who are you?" demanded the sergeant.

"Colby, John Colby," answered Harry freely. "Me and Buck Samuels here came up the Pecos a while back looking to ransom some white captives that was tooken out of-Fredricksburg, Texas. You han't seen no German-speakin' captives amongst your Mesqueleros, have ye?"

Riding parallel to Bucklin, the corporal eyed him suspiciously. "You two's traveling awful light. You say you was going to ransom whites?"

"Shore we was," nodded Harry agreeably, "but some Mexicans we come across stolt all our trade goods and shot me up doin' it. We was lucky to come out of it with a horse or we'd be dead sure enough."

"What was you fixin' to trade?" questioned the sergeant pointedly.

"Hold on now, Sarg," said Harry. "We ain't no pilgrims. We know better'n to give guns to them bloodthirsty devils. We had a few knives, but ever'thing else was just trinkets and sugar and coffee. But them three Mexicans took it all anyhow."

"Rough," replied the sergeant. "But that ain't none of our affair. We got enough to do without chasing after greasers."

Harry feigned a scowl of disappointment, then mumbled just loud enough, "Then you ain't goin' after your horses neither."

"What horses?" snapped the sergeant.

"They was driving a dozen army horses. Figured they was some of yours."

"What'd they look like?"

"Bay geldings mostly. But they was one small dun mare in the bunch."

The sergeant swore and the corporal turned in his saddle to listen. "How far south did you see them? That mare was the captain's favorite."

"Day, day and a half of long riding," answered Harry. "Be nigh impossible to ketch 'em now, but they was likely headed for Santa Domingo or Santa Fe...judgin' on the way they took out that is."

"You notice anything else?"

Licking his lips thoughtfully, Harry said, "Oh yeah, come to recollect it. One of 'em called the other Garza."

"Juan Garza?" blurted the sergeant.

"Don't know, but he had silver conchos on his belt and pants. And his horse's breast collar had 'em, too."

"That's the bastard," sneered the sergeant. "Thief and Injun trader, damn his hide."

The fort's buildings stretched long and low around a rectangular parade ground with a flagstaff in its center. Some had been built with logs, but most were adobe and all had flat roofs covered with a six-inch layer of reddish-brown dirt and a feeble sprinkling of brown grass. On the east and west were rows of soldiers' barracks and on the north end were the officers' quarters. They had ridden in from the south, passing between a guardhouse and a small hospital.

"Hang me fer a fool, boys," remarked Harry amiably, "but seems you just overshot the hospital."

The sergeant grunted. "We don't do nothing here without the say-so of Captain Bennet. Ever since he was transferred here, he's been sullen as a sore headed dog. Anybody steps outa line he gets ugly as galvanized sin."

Guided by the corporal, Bucklin halted in front of a singular log building with small windows and a covered porch. Stepping out into the last rays of sunlight was a short, hard-faced man in his mid-forties. Growing along the sides of his face were bushy gray sideburns that accentuated a perpetual scowl.

"Let's have your report, Sergeant Willkins," ordered the captain as his eyes ran disapprovingly over Bucklin's appearance.

"Names are Colby and Samuels, sir. Said they come up the Pecos looking to trade ransom goods for white captives. Met up with three Mexicans that must have stole our horses because they were driving a herd with your dun mare in it. They say they got robbed and shot by the bandits and made it here looking for a doctor."

Walking off the porch, Captain Bennet stopped in front of Bucklin. "'No pen can portray the agony of a child lost in the wilderness,'" he quoted mockingly. "Such a noble undertaking...this retrieving of wretched captives. Wouldn't you say, Sergeant? Or should I use one of your own vulgar expressions and compliment these brave men for 'having sand in their craw'?"

"Such bravery indeed," continued the captain sarcastically, "with the Staked Plains to the east and unexplored desert to the west. Why, even Santa Fe is one hundred and fifty miles off to the north and God only knows what lies to the south."

Glancing down at Bucklin's feet, Bennet said mildly, "I see you wear Indian moccasins. And you are?"

"Buck Samuels," answered Bucklin, taking an immediate dislike to the officer.

"Mexicans generally wear boots, Mr. Samuels. But we found only moccasin tracks where the horses were taken. We assumed that Indians had stolen them...or at least someone wearing moccasins did."

"Injuns'll steal anything," answered Bucklin blandly. "Especially poorly guarded livestock."

"Them three Mexicans," offered Harry nervously, "musta traded with Injuns fer them horses before we come on 'em. One of them greasers was Juan Garza."

His keen eyes lingering on Bucklin, the captain strolled casually to the travois. "And you must be Mr. Colby."

"Yes, sir, Cap'n. John Colby."

"And you say one of the Mexicans was Juan Garza?"

"Well, I heard 'em call the name and from what I told the sergeant, he figures it was him, too. You know 'im?"

"He's a known man in the territory," answered Bennet shrewdly. "A name that's easy to come by. I have no doubts he'll end up at the end of a rope, but perhaps...perhaps he is blamed for more crimes than even he can commit."

Walking thoughtfully back to his porch, the captain stopped and turned.

Folding his hands behind his back, he smiled coldly. "Sergeant, take Mr. Colby to the infirmary and have his wound tended. Corporal, you may show Mr. Samuels his quarters for the evening...in the guardhouse. He will be our guest this evening. In the morning we'll send Apache scouts out to cover their back trail. When they return...we'll decide how long their stay with us will be.

"If you'll be so kind, Mr. Samuels, carefully hand your pistol and knife over to Corporal O'Mally. When the scouts return and all is as you say, you'll have my apologies. Until then, make yourself at home."

O'Mally dismounted and held out his hand. As Bucklin removed his weapons, he said, "My horse could use some grain and a rubdown. He's wore out from the ride. I don't want to break him down."

Bennet sighed. "Very well, Corporal. Escort the two of them to the hospital and then Mr. Samuels to the stables. When he's finished, take him to the guardhouse and feed him. Otherwise don't disturb me with this until morning. My supper's getting cold as it is."

After the captain went back inside, Bucklin led the travois across the parade ground. Near the flagstaff, he paused. "Mind if I talk to Colby, Corporal? He's a mighty sick man. We been together for a while...and, well, you never know about these things."

"Make it quick," snapped O'Mally. "I ain't eaten yet neither."

While the corporal and Wilkins rolled a cigarette, Bucklin bent over Harry and spoke softly. "I got to go tonight before they send out their scouts and find the woman. But me leaving will make it look bad for you. Like maybe it was us that stole the horses after all, and I'm making a run for it."

"Damn that Bennet," snarled Harry. "Just our luck to get a spit and polish man way out here in the middle of this cactus patch. But don't you fret none, boy. I can talk my way out of it. You best go on."

"All right then, Harry. I kept my end of the deal and got you here, now what about this Cabeza Blanca, what is it you got to tell me?"

"It ain't about him," whispered Harry. "It's me. Don't nobody but a handful of folks know my Injun name, the name the Apaches give me years ago. When you get close by Cabeza Blanca or any of his bucks, you just tell 'em Baychen-day-sen sent you. Means 'Long Nose.' Not even that no account Garza is privy to my Injun name. It'll get you started off on the right foot with 'em, but the rest of it's up to you."

Repeating the name to himself, Bucklin straightened up, then paused thoughtfully. Glancing over his shoulder at the soldiers, he looked back down, his face suddenly filled with contempt.

"I don't know that you deserve this, Harry, but you at least brought the woman out and kept the Mexicans from her. I'm going to say this once, so listen good. You get out of the Injun trading business. If I catch you at it, I'll kill you."

Harry's mouth dropped open. "What the hell?"

"Shut up, Harry, and listen or you might get yourself hung right here for horse stealing. I'm wanted in Texas, for murder most likely. My name's Bucklin, Sam Bucklin. You tell them that's why I escaped and lit out tonight. Say I was afraid of being found out and sent back to Texas so I lit a shuck. You tell them after I'm gone that I just now told you tonight *who* I really am. That way you're off the hook and don't look guilty. The rest of it you can lie your way out of. You got all that?"

His eyes wide with shock, Harry choked hoarsely, "You…Sam Bucklin? I'll be damned. And you're after Cabeza Blanca? Hellfire, I'd give my eye teeth to see that ball open... So you're Sam Bucklin!"

"All right, you two," interrupted the sergeant, "break it up and let's move."

As Bucklin started to go, Harry grinned. "You ain't never kilt a Injun like him, Bucklin. They say you tooken a hundred scalps, but this here one, this is one Injun scalp that can't be took. Not never."

"Maybe he's the one I'm after, maybe not," replied Bucklin. "But I plan to put it to the test before I'm done."

"So you will, Buck," mused Harry with a hint of admiration. "I think I owe you one more favor for savin' my life... and givin' me that Texas story. And this may save yores."

"Don't go up the river tonight. Due west from here, if you foller the lay of the land, you'll hit a lake after a two-day ride. But keep an eye out for the Apache scouts. It's them the army'll send after you if you got the nerve to cut across that desert."

"Then we're even-up, Harry," nodded Bucklin. "But you mind what I just said."

Harry shrugged with resignation, "Was gettin' ready to cash in and settle down anyhow. So I'll give you one more piece of advice. Don't let loose of that woman. If you want Cabeza Blanca you got to keep a holt of her. You won't never find him otherwise, not never."

After helping Harry into the hospital, Bucklin was directed behind a row of barracks that formed the eastern edge of the fort, then down to the stables that lined the river's edge. While Bucklin unhitched the travois from his saddle, O'Mally lit a coal oil lantern and found an empty stall. When Bucklin passed by he handed him a feedbag filled with grain. "Fine looking mount you got there," he said amiably. "Looks to be sixteen hands."

Bucklin untied the cinch and hefted the saddle and blanket onto a sideboard. "Closer to seventeen."

Holding the lantern high, O'Mally studied the animal curiously. "Funny he don't look broke down none."

Leaving the bridle on, Bucklin casually laid the feedbag aside and picked up a brush and began currying slowly. "Your captain's a hard man to go and accuse us of horse stealing. He treat everybody that rough or just us strangers?"

"Bennet," exclaimed the corporal. "I swear that man was weaned on a sour pickle. I don't know how he come to be stationed here, but ever since he took over he's had one frothy spell after another. Been wound up tighter'n a two-dollar watch."

"What was the captain talking about back there when he said he had Apache scouts? He have many of them?"

"Well now, there's where he do know what he's doing. He's hired a half-dozen Mescaleros to work the reservation like a police. Pays 'em good, too. Sometimes he uses them for regular army, sends a pair of them out with a patrol. It's the smartest thing he done yet. They can track a lizard over a rock."

"Yeah," agreed Bucklin, switching the brush to his left hand. "Most Injuns can read sign better'n any white man."

Brushing steadily, Bucklin gradually turned his back to O'Mally, then bending down as if he were checking a loose shoe, he slid the Whitney hideout pistol from its shoulder holster and stood erect. But before he made his move, Sergeant Wilkins appeared in the flickering yellow light.

"Keep your distance, O'Mally," Wilkins said sharply. "We got us a couple a gunrunners. One of the Apache scouts just recognized that Colby fella. Said he's a trader they call Harry. Been tradin' guns to Injuns for years."

Stepping back, O'Mally swore. "You told the captain yet?"

"Nope. Came right over to make sure this one got to the guardhouse. After we lock 'em up we'll git Bennet. He'll be happy as a bunch a free niggers."

"Damn right," smiled O'Mally, drawing his pistol. "Maybe then things'll ease up around here."

Holding the small pistol in the shadows, Bucklin glanced at Wilkins who held a carbine in the bend of his elbow and stood a few feet to the left of O'Mally. "Since when did you take the word of a lying redskin over a white man's?" he asked scornfully then eased down for the feedbag as the two men briefly pondered the question.

"That Injun's got no reason to lie," answered Wilkins, "And it makes more sense than the cock and bull story you two give us."

Grasping the feedbag tightly, Bucklin spoke easily, "Well, then how'd Colby get shot? You know Injun traders are big medicine to all the tribes and no harm comes to them. And besides..."

Without warning, Bucklin swung up and around with the heavy bag, slamming it full force into O'Mally's right shoulder throwing him off balance and sending Wilkins fumbling for his rifle. Before either could recover, the Whitney was cocked and pressed against the back of O'Mally's head.

"Drop the carbine or you're both dead men," ordered Bucklin savagely.

Instantly the rifle fell to the packed-dirt floor. Bucklin took O'Mally's pistol and then retrieved his own along with his knife. "Now you boys listen and listen good. I could cut your throats and you'd die without so much as a whimper, but I ain't gonna. You recollect that when the time comes." Pointing to a coiled rope, he said, "Wilkins, you tie up the corporal here and do a good job or I'll string you up miserable tight when it's your turn. I seen how the Comanches do it enough so, don't call my bluff."

Without hesitation, Wilkins went to work on the corporal, hog-tying his ankles and wrists behind his back as he lay on the ground. As he finished Bucklin cut the excess rope from O'Mally. "Pick it up and tie a loop around your neck."

Swallowing hard, Wilkins took the loose end of the rope. "You...you ain't gonna hang me? I done like you said."

"Just tie it and shut up."

After Wilkins made the loop, Bucklin ordered him against a post. With the pistol trained on the wide-eyed sergeant, he walked the rope around the post, lashing him tightly from his neck to his feet.

From Wilkins's trouser leg he cut two long strips of cloth and gagged each man then quickly resaddled the buckskin and hung the bag of grain over the horn. Before blowing out the lantern, Bucklin held it close to Wilkins' face. "The name is Bucklin. I'm no gun runner and I got no argument with the army. But I kilt plenty of Yankees and more'n my share of Apaches, so a few more of either'n won't bother me none too much. You tell Captain Bennet to leave well enough alone."

At a trot, Bucklin rode eastward for a quarter-mile before breaking into a gallop and veering to the southwest. Returning to the Pecos, nearly a mile below the fort, he paused on its banks, listening for any sound of pursuit.

In the stillness, the gelding's heavy breathing seemed deafening, but as it began to subside the fragile calm of evening returned. A hot gust of wind stirred the night air, raising a few grains of sand and rustling the knee-high sage. Downstream a faint chorus of frogs croaked lazily in the tepid water while overhead the beating wings of an owl caught the silver-blue hue of a crescent moon.

Keeping to the edge of the river, Bucklin rode further south until finding the cottonwoods where he cut the branches for the travois, then followed his tracks. As he drew near where Cold Eyes was to be waiting, he reined in and called out softly. "Ma'am, it's Sam Bucklin. If you're still here and able to, I'd be obliged if you'd show yourself."

For a long minute there was no movement, then the buckskin's ears came forward and it blew. Bucklin could see nothing, but the horse's attention was fixed on the shadows directly ahead. A moment later the horse jerked his head higher and blew again.

With the hairs on the back of his neck bristling, Bucklin grabbed a Colt and leaned forward to conceal himself in the animal's silhouette. As his thumb slid over the hammer, he saw movement and instinctively swung the barrel in line with the unknown target. Sand crunched under a light footstep. The hammer clicked back, but betraying his better judgment and bracing himself for the worst, he spoke once more.

"Step out of them shadows or I'll start shooting."

As if floating over the desert, a small form appeared from the blackness then came forward to stand in the moonlight. Bucklin hesitated and glanced around warily. "You alright?" he whispered, knowing she would not answer.

Swearing under his breath, he reluctantly dismounted, keeping a firm grip on his reins and the pistol. Reaching out, he tilted her face upward, bathing it in the soft light. Peering into it he asked urgently, "Trouble?"

Even though she made no attempt to nod or shake her head, her expression reassured him. Sliding his hand down her arm, he felt the pistol hidden in the fold of her skirt and knew they were alone...and he knew, that if she had wanted to, she could easily have killed him.

With his hand on her shoulder, he turned her around and started for the other horses. "There was trouble at the fort," he said softly, "and they'll be after me."

Stopping next to the tied roan and dun, Bucklin took the Colt from her hand and dropped it into his holster. Glancing down at Cold Eyes's shadowed face, he said, "You might as well wait here. They'll find you and take you back to where you belong."

After saddling the roan, he paused uncomfortably. "I was just hoping... it would've been... No. No. It's better this away, ma'am. I best git."

As he gathered the reins of both horses, he felt a small hand grab his sleeve. "No," pleaded the young woman, then straining to form the words, she continued in a weak, raspy voice. "Please, no...I must come...I...*must* go...with...you."

Surprised by the words, but shocked by their meaning, Bucklin froze.

A moment later, shielded by the darkness, Sam Bucklin smiled faintly. Taking both her hands as he would a child, he felt their trembling warmth as well as the leathery calluses that covered her palms and fingers. "I don't want to put you through any more hard times, ma'am. And what's ahead is gonna be... well, you know better'n me. You seen it all before. The question is, do you really want to go across that desert and back into who knows what kind of trouble and suffering?"

Cold Eyes merely squeezed his hand and looked up. Seeing the moonlight in her eyes and the smooth outline of her face, Bucklin asked, "Are you sure? It'll be dangerous to come along now. If they get close, there'll be shooting, and with them using Apache scouts that'll be likely."

This time there was a faint nod.

"Then it's settled, ma'am, we go it together."

Handing her the reins, his mood quickly changed. "Hold these," he said grimly, then untied the mare. "Stay here. We'll need more water."

Leading the horse down the shallow ravine and back near the river, Bucklin flipped the rawhide thong from his knife. Stepping behind the right shoulder of the unsuspecting dun, he reached under its neck and slit the throat to the bone.

Hardly flinching as the razor sharp steel passed through its neck, the mare's head began to drift from side to side as blood gurgled from the gaping wound. After struggling to stay on its feet, the small dun's legs buckled. Crumpling to the sand, it rolled on its side, the last breath of life hissing back into the desert from which it had come.

Opening the horse's belly, Bucklin cut out the stomach and a long piece of the lower intestine, then waded into the water. Squeezing out the contents of each organ, he flooded them several times to rinse out the acids and as much of the taste as possible. When they were clean, he tied off one end of each with a two-foot leather thong, filled them with water, then used the other end of the strip to close them off.

With the water bags hung over his shoulders, he returned to the other two horses and surprisingly found Cold Eyes mounted on the buckskin waiting.

Hanging one bag over her saddle horn, he said, "She was a good little mare, but this country's got no pity. There just ain't no room."

After looping the other bag on his saddle, he walked his roan to the river as Cold Eyes followed close behind. Avoiding the fresh kill, he stopped at the bank and filled his canteen, then handed it to the girl. "Drink as much as you can hold. Before this is over we'll have to prime ourselves to spit."

When she had finished, Bucklin followed suit, then refilled the canteen and swung aboard. "We're headed due west," he offered solemnly. "After two days of desert riding, if we're lucky, we'll find a lake. If not, it'll take another day to reach the Rio Grande. But somewhere out there, if they keep coming after us, I'll have to let them catch up."

CHAPTER SEVEN

C utting a clear trail to the west, the hooves of the roan and buckskin pounded steadily through the night, but as the sun cast its first shadows, Bucklin slowed to an easy walk and angled northward in a wide arc. Several minutes later, with Cold Eyes close behind, he rode into the sun for a half-mile, then in a meandering course, worked his way back to the northwest.

As the sun grew hot on their backs, the flatness of the desert floor gave way to a gentle rolling and the vegetation, though still sparse, began growing higher. Cresting a small rise that overlooked his back-trail for several miles, Bucklin reined in and stepped down.

"We'll lay by here, ma'am," he said, uttering his first words since leaving the Pecos. Handing her his canteen, he pulled the cork. "This'll taste better'n the other as long as it lasts, but go easy on it. We'll be sharing what's in the bags with the horses."

Cold Eyes took a short drink, then stiffly dismounted and took another before returning the canteen. Bucklin nodded and smiled, then drank himself. Shoving the cork in with a squeak, he said, "You'll do, ma'am. You're one to ride the rivers with."

Gathering the reins of both horses, Bucklin took out his knife and gave it to Cold Eyes. Pointing to the scattered mesquite and sage, he said, "Chop some good-sized branches and stack them up here. We'll need a passel of them to make shade while we sleep."

Without hesitation, Cold Eyes was off, but Bucklin stood for a moment watching as she went to work. It had been a long, tiring ride with no sleep, yet even in the burning heat, she was swinging the heavy blade with all her strength. Had the brutality she endured as a captive given her such endurance or was it something else, something she had always possessed? Or was she more like his sister than he wanted to admit? Had she suffered so much that her mind had been damaged?

After leading the horses to the far side of the rise, Bucklin tied them to a pair of six-foot mesquite, allowing enough lead rope for them to move to any shade that might develop. From the nosebag he fed a few handfuls of grain, then loosening the rawhide around one of the makeshift canteens, he poured each a hatful of Pecos water.

Going to the saddle Cold Eyes had been riding, he removed the bedroll and his binoculars, then from the roan he took a second blanket as well as the Sharps .50-caliber rifle and two cartridges. Walking the sixty paces back to the top of the hill, he dropped the bedrolls and with his heel dug two parallel lines into the sand six feet long and five feet apart.

"Pile the branches along these lines," he said to Cold Eyes as she approached with her arms full. "Stick them in natural like, but don't build the sides more'n waist high. When you're done, lay those blankets from side to side for a roof and crawl in and stretch out. I'll be back directly."

Cold Eye's face, though void of any readable expression, was red with heat and streaked with grimy sweat, but her gaze held on the long rifle.

"They're not out there," offered Bucklin. "Not yet, anyhow. You just get some rest."

With the heavy Sharps resting on his shoulder, Bucklin followed their own tracks as they had ridden toward the rise until he found the spot he wanted. Thirty yards from a half-acre of open ground, he turned briefly to see what the piled branches on top of the knoll would look like through army binoculars. Then, keeping his eyes on the shelter and paralleling the horses' tracks, he walked backward until he stood in the middle of the clearing. With the tip of a yucca he pricked the end of a finger and sprinkled blood onto the sand. When the bleeding stopped, he took two steps to his right and started back. But this time, his stride was even and slightly longer than normal and each one was counted.

As Bucklin reached the brush pile, he muttered to himself, "Six hundred ninety-three," then swung the rifle from his shoulder. Flipping up the rear Vernier sight, he added, "Make it an even seven."

After making a few careful adjustments, he eased the sight down then glassed the clearing where his blood now stained the trail. With his advantage in elevation, there were no obstructions. There would be nothing between the .50-caliber muzzle and his target more than two thousand feet away.

Stooping down to enter the shade, he saw Cold Eyes lying on her side already asleep. She had gone on her own to the horses and brought back the saddle blankets to lie on. It was something he had forgotten, something only a rational person would have done.

Taking off his hat and pistol belt, then pulling the binoculars from his neck, he crawled into the cramped space next to the young woman. Carefully placing the rifle between the two of them, he put the pistols to the far side. From her half-opened palm he retrieved his knife then double-checked his line of fire before rolling onto his back.

They wouldn't catch up for at least two hours, but more likely it would be closer to sundown and he was exhausted. For now he would have to settle for a couple of hours of sleep, but later on, if he could trust her, perhaps the woman could be of use in keeping watch...maybe tomorrow...maybe the next day...he could get enough sleep.

Closing his drooping eyelids, Bucklin listened comfortably to the soft, rhythmic breathing next to him. She had fallen asleep to one side of the blankets and must have understood the shelter was meant for both of them, yet she lay there sleeping soundly...And less than a day before, she stood poised over Harry, waiting for her chance to take his life.

Suddenly Bucklin rolled his head to the side for a second look at Cold Eyes. There was no doubt she would have killed Harry, but she appeared to trust him and the night before had chosen to stay with him instead of going to the fort. For that he had admittedly felt a wave of relief, but today she had not spoken a word or even made a sound. How long had it been since she had talked with anyone and why wouldn't she speak to him now that they were alone? She had ridden throughout the long night and part of the day in total silence and had kept her eyes averted from his. What could she be thinking and why did she constantly avoid his eyes whenever he looked her way? Easing his right hand down to the top of his moccasin, Bucklin pulled the knife from its sheath, slid it under his blanket, and quietly buried it in the sand. With his hand resting cautiously on the rolled gun belt and pistols, he drifted into a light, uneasy sleep.

In what seemed only a few minutes, he awoke and glanced outside to see the meager shadows of midday now stretching several feet across the blistering sand.

Rubbing the dryness from his eyes, he sat up sluggishly, then shook the sleep from his head. After squinting into the heat waves for any sign of movement, he looked down at Cold Eyes, who hadn't moved in the few hours he had slept. Her tangled hair hung over her sunburned face and he could see several nits and a few lice crawling between the strands. On her wrists and neck were the unmistakable marks left by rawhide thongs that had been pulled tight and left too long.

Bucklin sighed heavily, then carefully brushed the hair back on her neck, allowing a faint breeze to cool her skin, then leaned back on his elbows.

Enjoying her closeness, he waited several minutes before moving again, but when he felt his eyes growing heavy, he dug up the knife and grabbed his pistols.

Leaving the Sharps in the shade but taking the binoculars, he strapped on the guns and went to the saddlebags for coffee. After gathering a small pile of dried twigs, he found a patch of shade where he could glass the back trail. He then built a smokeless fire no bigger than his cup.

They needed the water, but he needed the coffee more. He couldn't risk nodding off to sleep now. The Apache scouts would be coming soon.

With the battered tin cup balanced over the fire on two flat rocks, Bucklin restlessly scoured the desert for any sign of pursuit. He was not used to taking risks and not having the horses saddled and ready made him uneasy.

If all went as planned, though, there would be time enough later to pack up, and Cold Eyes needed the rest anyway. But he had always made allowances for the unexpected... always. Swearing to himself, he dropped a palm full of coffee grounds into the simmering water and set the cup aside to steep. He had no quarrel with the army, but they would never have believed his innocence or that he had come for Cabeza Blanca. There was no time to clear his name, no choice but to run.

Had Harry told them he was Sam Bucklin? Had he tried to set them straight or had he, being a friend of the Apaches, claimed he was guilty in hopes of getting him killed? Had Harry told the army about Cold Eyes and if he had, *what* had he told them?

Perhaps the old man would do him one last favor and convince the army not to come after him, but considering what Bucklin had seen of Captain Bennet, he quickly dismissed the thought. If he judged the man correctly, neither the loss of a prisoner nor of his favorite horse would be tolerated. And with Apache scouts to guide his patrol of regulars, there was no doubt they were closing in.

"Should've left him for the coyotes to fight over," sneered Bucklin as he reached for the cup and took a sip of the scalding coffee. "Could've been to Santa Fe by now with no blue bellies on my tail and nobody to slow me..."

Abruptly ending his train of thought, Bucklin nursed the coffee, his eyes occasionally drifting to the company of the shelter then returning to the bleakness of the desert.

A few moments later his eye caught a flicker of light two miles out and he raised the binoculars for a better look. Riding single file over his tracks were eight men and even at that distance he knew the two in the lead were Apaches.

Swirling the dregs in his cup, Bucklin took a last mouthful and sucked the coffee from the grounds, then packed them in a wad against his cheek and gum. Circling around behind the rise and staying low, he crawled to the shelter and shook Cold Eyes's shoulder. "They're coming, ma'am," he said firmly. "We need the horses packed and saddled."

Cold Eyes was instantly awake and swiftly gathered the two saddle blankets. "Stay low," said Bucklin, handing her his cup, "and when you're done, mount up. We'll be leaving soon."

As Cold Eyes obediently hurried off, Bucklin slowly pulled down the bedrolls. Rolling both of them in front of him, he rested the forearm of the Sharps across them, opened the breech and slid in a cartridge. With the binoculars, he watched the patrol until they came to a halt in the clearing and the two scouts dismounted for a closer look at the blood sprinkled on the trail.

Flipping up the rear sight, Bucklin brought the front bead down on one of the Indian ponies and pulled the set-trigger. An easy breath later, he touched the second hair-trigger, exploding the desert silence with a smoke-bellowing blast. Before the smoke cleared, he touched off another round no more than three seconds behind the first.

Without making any sudden movements, he took the blankets and backed down the rise until it was safe to stand, then went quickly to the horses. There was no need to see what he had done. One horse would die, maybe two, and that would slow them down as well as warn them. They would know he could shoot accurately to a half-mile; in wide open country with little cover, only a fool would come after him on those terms. Hopefully they would also realize that this time, only horses had been shot.

Riding northward in a shallow arroyo and with the sun in the eyes of the army patrol, Bucklin and Cold Eyes carefully walked the horse for a half-hour before climbing the western bank and glassing their back trails.

"Them Apaches can keep after us afoot as good as they could on a horse," said Bucklin as he lowered the binoculars, "but I think them soldier boys got the drift of what's ahead of them. Likely they'll head back, circle north and try and find us along the Rio Grande, Santa Fe, maybe."

Glancing back at Cold Eyes, he half-smiled with relief. "We'll keep an eye out for them, ma'am, just the same, but the thought of a buffalo gun and what it can do generally makes a man jump, even an Injun. I'll wager we're safe enough for a while."

Nudging his horse forward, Bucklin started in the lead then dropped back and kept pace with Cold Eyes. "Harry recalled there was a lake up ahead. When we get closer to them mountains, I'd say 'bout forty miles away, there should be a lake. I've heard the Mexicans call it *Laguna del Perro,* or Lake of the Dog.

"Anyway I figure to make it by sun up if you're able. We'll rest along the way a time or two, but it's best to push on. We got to get west of the Rio Grande before them soldiers come in from the north."

For several minutes there was only the creaking of saddle leather and the shuffling of hooves over the yellow sand. The white-hot sun gradually tempered with color as it neared the horizon. The cloudless sky, baked by the day's heat, cooled into a deeper shade of blue. A quail called from a gnarled pile of dead sage, but hearing no answer, called again.

"When we get to the water," offered Bucklin gently, "there'll be time to wash up. I got some lye soap I use for shavin', and you're welcome to it. I got an extra shirt and one of the bedrolls could be fashioned into a dress or some such. You could get rid of them buckskins and when we get to one of them towns on the Rio Grande we can buy something more fitting. 'Course that might mean britches if you're going to ride clothespin style, but that might be best anyhow. There'll be lots of folks in town but nobody where we're headed will care, no how. But at least you could shuck them Injun clothes for good. And it'd be nice to sleep in a town for change. Would you like that, ma'am?"

Cold Eyes despondently raised her head. Staring at the horizon, her brow wrinkled with some hidden thought then her face darkened with hopelessness.

Watching her from the corner of his eye, Bucklin saw the spark of interest suddenly vanish. Without thinking, he spoke again, but this time there was a tone of harshness in his voice. "You hung on too long to give up now, lady. Remember whatever it was that's kept you going, that's given you the courage to live, and think about that. Don't be afraid to face what's coming next."

Bucklin's voice softened, but he continued with a sense of urgency. "You ain't alone in your misery," he began solemnly. "This here is a hard land and it don't care who it hurts, good or bad...Ma'am, Injuns took my little sister. She was thirteen, as gangly as a half-growed pup. Innocent as a child, but full of wonder and proud as could be at what nature had done for her. She was like...like springtime itself, all the time chattering like a squirrel and you never saw a girl giggle so much...But that was five years ago." Bucklin paused and looked away. Then his eyes returned to the young woman.

"They used her like they used you. She don't laugh no more. Not at nothing.

"She wasn't strong as you. I wish to God Almighty she was, but she couldn't bear the hurt. You got to come out of it. You got a chance where Ruthy didn't. She couldn't understand nothing I said to her, but you catch every word and I know it. Fact is, you ain't lost your mind, but you could still turn out near as bad as her if you start trying to hide now.

"Nobody's going to blame you for what them Injuns done and not nobody out here's going to find out from me. We'll get you some clothes and just you and me will know."

Bucklin paused and stared at Cold Eyes as the two rode side by side in the setting sun. A dry gust of wind passed by, cooling the sweat on his back and forehead. Taking off his hat, he wiped the headband then tugged it on tight and set his jaw.

"I know full well what you been through, ma'am, and this is the last time I'll bring it up. I just want you to know that you got no secrets to hide or be ashamed of with me. I know Injuns and I know as much as any white man about captives.

"One thing I want to make sure of, something I don't want you to have no doubts about, is that it don't matter to me. It don't change who you are. You won't never forget, but in time you can learn not to think on it and go on with your living. Now, one way or the other, when we get to the lake I'm gonna burn them clothes you're wearing and you're getting cleaned up."

For several minutes Bucklin was deep in thought, then broodingly he leaned forward and to the side and spit out the black wad of coffee grounds. Roughly wiping his mouth with the back of his hand, he straightened up in the saddle, glaring at the trail ahead.

"You got your child to be thinking about and what kind of life you can give him...just as long as you put all this behind you and let it be. Your boy's safe, ma'am, and will be till we get him back. The Injuns'll raise him like one of their own and their children is the only thing, man or beast, an Apache is kindhearted to in this world. No matter where he is right now, be thankful your baby is alive and well."

With his mood darkening, Bucklin paused. "When you have him back," he said, "you'll be able to rest easy. You'll be able to hold him in your arms and rock him to sleep at night. In the morning he'll be there when you wake up and he'll open his little eyes and smile at you. Then you can pick up your child and hold him close and give him all the love you got inside that's just busting to get out... A child, ma'am. There ain't nothing more precious, and you're going to get yours back."

Out of habit, Bucklin checked his back trail, then warily searched the desert to the right and left for Indians. "I ain't never going to see," he continued bitterly, "nor hold mine again. Stealing a child from its ma and pa is a terrible crime, but killing...murdering a baby is another thing entire. Ain't nothing, nothing more cruel and full of black-hearted evil as that. And for them that did such a thing, I swear, there ain't no place on God's earth they can hide."

Spurring his horse to take the lead, Bucklin did not see the eyes of the young woman as they followed him nor did he see them fill with confusion and fear as he rode farther and farther out in front of her.

"Jenny," she whispered hoarsely. "I'm Jenny."

Frantically kicking the buckskin into a trot, her blue eyes filled with tears. "I'm Jennifer Lee Mason."

For hours the pair traveled in darkness, but stopped frequently to give the tired horses a breather and to listen to the night sounds. They had been climbing gradually since sundown and by midnight, Bucklin stopped on what appeared to be the summit of a low range of hills. Before starting the descent, he stepped down and grabbed his Sharps. Handing his hat to Cold Eyes, he said, "We need to water the horses before we go on. Use the hat for a trough and give them everything that's in your water bag and then let them have some grain. I'm going back down the trail about a mile or so to see if we got any company." Pointing to the shotgun in the saddle boot, he added, "And I'd keep that handy if I was you. It don't pay to take chances. You carry it with you all the time. You hear, ma'am? I'll be back shortly."

On moccasined feet, Bucklin vanished without a sound, leaving Jenny Mason alone in the darkness. A moment of uncertainty passed, then she slid the scatter-gun from the saddle and dropped to the ground. Hanging the weapon over her shoulder by a leather thong, she gave each horse two hatfuls of water and then a double handful of grain. After replacing the empty belly pouch and nose bag, she backed away from the horses and sat down next to a small boulder with a yucca growing up from behind it. She took the shotgun from her shoulder and laid it on her lap. After resting her palm on the mule-eared hammers, she joined the moonless night, now just a shadowy form huddled in the dim starlight.

Returning half an hour later, Bucklin stood several paces from the two horses, his eyes and ears searching the darkness. He expected a sound or even movement but, except for the animals, he could detect nothing. Easing up to the geldings, he put his hand on their necks and then their shoulders. They were standing at ease and he knew the girl must be nearby or at least that no Indians had come near. In that respect, the geldings were as good as any watchdog, having long since learned the smell of Indians meant trouble.

"Time to go, ma'am," he said softly. "And wherever you're at, don't forget my hat."

Secure in her hiding place and shielded by the black veil of night, Cold Eyes gathered her courage. "My name," she confessed hesitantly, "is Jennifer, Jennifer Mason."

Stunned by the words, Bucklin glared into the shadows from which they had come. For a moment he was dumbfounded, then, sensing her apprehension, he hurriedly spoke the only words that came to mind. "Pleased to make your acquaintance. My name's...Samuel Bucklin."

From a small boulder came the rustling sound of someone moving, then the sand crunched lightly under delicately placed feet as a small figure timidly approached and stood quietly before him.

"Everything's going to be fine, Jennifer Mason," he said compassionately. "The worst of it's behind you now. There's more ahead, but it'll be different from before. And after we get to the lake, you'll feel a whole lot better. Then, if you're feeling up to it, we'll talk more...but you're gonna be just fine!"

By the first light, the trail had again leveled out and the scattered cactus and mesquite were growing more dense. To avoid another string of rolling hills, Bucklin angled to the northwest until the dingy gray-blue horizon lightened enough to reveal the jagged spine of a mountain range directly to the west.

They had traveled for two days in an almost straight line and, with the mountains rising steeply ahead and hills to the south, Bucklin turned northward. They would run out of water by the end of the day, but if Harry was right about the lake, it would have to be nearby hidden in a low-lying basin, likely the result of runoff from the mountain snow.

Taking Harry's advice, Bucklin studied the lay of the land around him and how the flood-waters would drain. When the sun's rays hit the mountain peaks to the west, he watched the developing shadows cut into the range and darken a network of water-worn canyons. A few minutes later, with the scarred terrain pointing the way, he led off to the north, angling slightly to the west.

Without stopping, they rode for three hours and, with the day's heat already bearing down on them, Bucklin spurred his roan down the dusty bank of a large arroyo. Coursing down its center was a streak of dead algae, but farther on there was a tinge of green. After another mile a trickle of water flashed under the horses' hooves and a half-hour later Sam Bucklin and Jennifer Mason rode out of the desolate creek bed and onto the sandy beach of a shallow blue lake.

At most a mile wide, the water pooled for several miles to the north, but the shoreline was nearly void of trees and dotted with rocks and small boulders. Where the arroyo emptied into the lake, a small stand of willows had taken root and Bucklin turned in under the meager shade and dismounted from the jaded buckskin.

"We can rest up now," he said as Jennifer slid to the ground then held onto the stirrup leather to keep her knees from buckling. "Harry said there was wagon ruts west of the lake that'd take us over to the road to Santa Fe. There's lots of little towns up and down that road where we can get you some…well, things you might be needing."

Jennifer slowly let go of the saddle and hobbled a few painful steps to the water's edge, then waded a few more feet and sat down with only her head above the surface. A moment later it too submerged for several seconds then re-appeared, her matted hair hanging in drenched clumps that clung tightly to a sunburned face.

Watching her as he untied his cinch, Bucklin smiled. "You go right ahead, ma'am," he said quietly. "Wash it off. Wash it away the best you can."

After removing the gear from both horses and rubbing them down with a handful of dry leaves, Bucklin laid his pistols and moccasins on the sand. Wading into the cool lake, but keeping a good distance from Jennifer, he said, "In a little while I'm going to hunt up one of them mule-eared rabbits we been seeing and I'll roast us some fresh meat. I rode you purty hard getting here so you just set here as long as you want. When you get out, my extra shirt'll be there and, like I said, one of them blankets can serve as a dress."

Jennifer pulled her thick brown hair away from her eyes, but couldn't bring herself to look at Bucklin. She started to speak, but turned her head away, clenching her hair in both fists as if tugging on the straps of a wind-blown bonnet.

"I got one more thing you might want to consider," offered Bucklin. "There's a plug of lye soap that'll nearly take your hide off. That I'll leave out, too." Wincing with uncertainty he added, "If you was to use it in your hair, your head'd be some sore afterward, but begging your pardon ma'am, it'd wash out anything... dead or alive."

Seeing Jennifer shrink away from him, Bucklin cut his bath short and started for shore. "I'll be gone for an hour or two, I reckon. Not too far out so I couldn't get back in a hurry, but out of sight. I'll leave the shotgun like before, just in case."

Bucklin slipped on his moccasins and, while tying them tightly below the knee, be watched Jennifer's trembling hands gradually loosen their grip. A moment later she timidly ran her fingers over the wet, tangled knots.

A woman's hair was always important to her. It was important to his wife Sara and to his sister Ruthy...when she was younger. Bucklin glanced once more at Jennifer then reached down and picked up a foot-long piece of driftwood that had washed down from the mountains. Brushing the sand from the sun-bleached pine, he thoughtfully tucked it in his pants.

After belting on his pistols and setting out the soap and shirt, he half-turned toward the water, but kept his head low. "Unless there's trouble, and that ain't likely, I'll make it a point not to be back for about two hours. You can rest easy on that and take the time for yourself. Take all the time you need."

Without looking back, Bucklin started up the arroyo they had come down and in a matter of minutes was beyond sight of the lake. Slowing to an easier pace, he found a tall mesquite and sat down cross-legged in the shade. It would only take him a short while to find and shoot a rabbit and he did not want to go far from camp. But, more importantly, he also needed the time to whittle. And for nearly two hours he did just that.

When the carving was finished he looked it over carefully, then blew the shavings from it and nodded with satisfaction. "That'll do'er," he said and dropped the wood into his shirt.

Coming to his feet, he drew one of his navy Colts and worked his way up the arroyo following the water and the scant green grass that grew along its edge.

He had gone no more than two hundred yards when a black-tailed jackrabbit jumped up from the base of a spiny yucca and loped up the side of the narrow arroyo. As it reached the edge of the bank thirty paces away, it stopped and turned for a better look at what had flushed it. Sitting up on its hind legs with long ears erect, it was an easy shot and a .36-caliber ball knocked the rabbit into the bank and sent it tumbling back into the wash.

Before Bucklin could take a step toward it, a flash of white flickered through the scattered sage to his right and he spun and fired at the running cottontail. The rabbit rolled head over heals then slid to a stop forty feet away.

The target was half the size of the jackrabbit and running at full speed through cover, but the Colts were accurate and Sam Bucklin was alive because he had learned to shoot with any weapon, from any position, and without warning.

A short distance from camp, he skinned and cleaned the rabbits, then tossed the flea-infested pelts away. In the Apache rancherias the squaws and captives did such work but when he returned to camp, he wanted nothing to remind Jennifer of what her life there had been like. For a while, at least, he hoped she could block it from her mind.

As he came into view of the willow trees, he stopped. "Hello, the camp," he called, then walked on, but more slowly. "I'm coming in."

Under the shade of the trees the stones and sticks had been cleared away and the sand had been smoothed flat. A bedroll was laid out neatly with the saddlebags laying on top and a few feet away was a circle of rocks with a small stack of twigs placed alongside. Next to it, spread out to make a pallet, was half of the second blanket and the two saddle blankets. On them was the tin cup filled with fresh water and his sack of coffee.

Standing amazed at what he saw, he hardly heard the rustling of the new wool skirt as it brushed against some sagebrush just beyond the drooping willow branches. Glancing up, his eyes opened wide and for several heartbeats he did not take a breath.

Coming out of the desert carrying an armload of firewood was the woman he had ridden beside for two days, a woman his eyes had seen, his hands had touched and his heart had pitied but, until now, a woman he could not possibly have envisioned.

The filthy buckskin dress had been replaced with a dark blue skirt that wrapped tightly around a small waist and hung just below the tops of her knee-high moccasins. Tucked into the skirt was his gray calico shirt which drooped loosely around her shoulders and even with all the buttons fastened, exposed a smooth neck and the soft white skin of her chest.

Having freed most of the tangles from her hair, it now flowed in gentle waves down her back. With each step she took, it caught the harsh glint of the desert sun and changed it into a reflection of yellow silk. And her face, blushed by the heat and no longer masked by months of neglect, was fresh, vibrant, and beautiful...disturbingly beautiful.

With her blue eyes self-consciously cast downward, Jennifer Mason stepped into the shade then uneasily crossed to the fire ring and carefully placed the bundle on the ground. Taking a step backward, she rubbed her palms on her skirt, then stood still, her body poised in quiet anticipation.

Unconsciously removing his hat, Bucklin stared in disbelief. "How are you feeling, ma'am?" he inquired politely then continued, only half-aware of what he was saying. "It's hard to believe you're the same... I mean to say I'd not hardly recognized you 'cepting your eyes. I declare, ma'am, I never seen the like."

Fidgeting nervously, Jennifer glanced around the camp. Catching sight of the rabbits she started for them until Bucklin put out his hand. "No, ma'am," he said sternly, "you just set. You need the rest and I'm used to doing for myself anyway."

Suddenly, as if she were lost, Jennifer began searching desperately for something she could do. As a look of panic spread over her face, Bucklin reached inside his shirt and pulled out the comb he had carved from the driftwood. Holding it out to her, he smiled encouragingly, "It's only got six teeth, but you done such a nice job already that ought to be enough." Taking her hand and placing the comb in her palm, he added, "I'd be honored, ma'am, if you'd just set and let me fix supper."

Slowly releasing her hand, he turned to his saddlebags and knelt down. As he unbuckled a flap, he heard Jennifer try to speak then clear her throat. "Thank you," she managed weakly, then knelt down on the half-blanket holding the comb with both hands and clutching it to her breast.

Bucklin paused, but did not face her. "You're welcome, ma'am," he said then took out a match and lit the dry twigs she had gathered for kindling. "Got two rabbits. One of them tough ole jackass rabbits that I've got used to eating and a nice cottontail for you, ma'am."

Jennifer Mason raised her head. As Bucklin watched the flames and occasionally added more wood, her eyes secretly followed his every move, embracing him with unspoken gratitude. When the fire was right and he stood up to get the rabbits, she stared down at the comb. "I don't... I can't remember your name."

Freezing suddenly, Bucklin looked at the distraught figure at his feet. Kneeling close beside her, he impulsively lifted her chin. Her eyes resisted meeting his own, but she made no attempt to turn away. "My name is Sam. Samuel John Bucklin. But I would be pleased if you'd call me Sam."

Gently letting her chin go, he leaned back slightly, "I'd be honored, ma'am, if you would."

With her head beginning to sink, Jennifer nodded. "Sam," she said softly. "Thank you... Sam... for the comb."

Bucklin nodded. "It was my pleasure," he replied, "and it's nice just to hear your voice."

Standing and walking away quietly, Bucklin found two forked sticks and, after securing them at the edges of the fire, cut a green branch from the tree and ran it lengthwise through each rabbit, then hung them over the flames. With his tin cup in place to heat the water, he stretched out on the remaining bedroll to wait for steam, but in a matter of seconds his eyes grew heavy.

Blinking sluggishly he strained to focus on Jennifer. "If you want coffee, ma'am, that's yours there," he said, pointing to the cup. "I ain't going to make it to supper. When the rabbit's done, go on and eat yours and set mine aside. Then you get some sleep your own self."

Jennifer nodded faintly. After Bucklin had closed his eyes, she leaned her head to one side, grasped a thick strand of light brown hair with one hand and, after a moment of hesitation, brought the comb up with the other.

Bucklin did not move for hours, then awoke with an abrupt jerk. With every sense alert and his heart pounding, his eyes opened into darkness. The air was cool and held the smell of charred wood and cooked meat, but there was no firelight nor glowing coals. A nearby horse shifted its weight and kicked a pebble with its hoof. Next to him was breathing, soft, and easy.

The Big Dipper was below the horizon and judging by the rest of the stars it was only an hour before first light. He had slept more than he thought possible and in Indian country to sleep so soundly was inviting disaster. It was a mistake and the thought of it made him angry. Then realizing what it could have meant to Jennifer Mason, he swore under his breath.

Sitting up cross-legged, he rubbed the sleep from his face and eyes. Under the branches of the willows even the meager starlight was blocked out and he could see nothing. As he felt for the fire circle and searched for the rabbit, he heard Jennifer stirring. Suddenly a hand took hold of his wrist while another placed the rabbit into his palm.

"Would you like coffee?" asked Jennifer, her voice clear and calm. Startled by the hands and then the question, Bucklin glared vainly into the pitch-black shadows. "Surely would, ma'am, but we can't chance a fire," he answered. Then, after a short curious pause he asked, "Can you see?"

"Yes."

"How?" asked Bucklin incredulously.

"I've always been able to see at night," she answered, then began scraping a layer of sand from where the fire had burned. "They say it is due to the color of my eyes."

A moment later a cloudy bed of coals appeared, then, after being stirred with a stick glowed red hot. Placing the tin cup on the embers, Jennifer said, "You slept well."

With her face barely illuminated, Bucklin looked comfortably into her eyes as he spoke. "Too good, ma'am. I don't know what come over me."

"But you were tired. You had not slept for two days."

Bucklin sighed heavily, shaking his head. "I been tired before. It won't happen again, ma'am. Can't, not out here."

Taking a bite of the stringy meat, Bucklin worked it between his jaws, then swallowed. "How are you doing, ma'am?"

There was a long pause then avoiding his question, she said, "You called me Jennifer yesterday. Now you stopped."

"Yes, ma'am," answered Bucklin thoughtfully, "I did."

"Why?"

"Well," began Bucklin slowly, "after coming back from hunting it was...like seeing you for the first time. Like all of a sudden we just met. Somehow or other it didn't seem proper for me, who hardly knows you, to be calling you by your first name."

"Is that...was that the only reason?" asked Jennifer.

"Yes... And the fact that I've never seen a handsomer woman in all my life. That sort of thing puts a kind of fear into a man."

For a moment there was a warm silence, then Jennifer spoke softly.

"You know me better than any man ever will. I would not consider it improper if you...if you called me Jenny...My closest friends do."

With the coffee water simmering quietly, Sam Bucklin gazed across the fire ring. Unsure of what he was seeing in the nearly hidden eyes of Jennifer Mason, he smiled. "Then Jenny it is."

CHAPTER EIGHT

R iding over rough terrain, it was almost midmorning before Sam Bucklin and Jenny Mason found the wagon road Harry had described, but an hour later they reached the settlement of Tajique. While graining the horses at a makeshift livery, they took a seat inside the village's only cantina. After ordering a plateful of tamales, Bucklin questioned the pot-bellied owner using a blend of simple English and broken Spanish.

The route ahead was lightly used and usually free of Indians, but recently there had been reports of bandits and no one was considered safe until reaching Albuquerque, a half-day's ride to the northwest. There they could find lodging and purchase what supplies they might need.

After paying for the meal and an extra canteen that hung on a peg behind the bar, they rode north on the wagon road, Jenny with the shotgun across her lap and Bucklin with his Colts positioned in easy reach. At dusk, without incident, they entered the adobe-walled plaza of Albuquerque.

Several flat-roofed haciendas lined the crude streets and masking the mud bricks of each was a drab coat of whitewash paint. Over their front doors and windows a pole framed porch held up a woven mesh of dried sticks and often a thick growth of grape vines.

Three cantinas and a row of stores bordered the south side of the square while on the north, standing alone and fronted with a thirty-foot bell tower, was the massive San Felipe mission. Several horses were tied in front of each saloon and lights flickered from every window in the plaza except the abandoned church. Just past the largest cantina a half-dozen men were lounging in front of three freight wagons as a pair of Mexicans hitched up the teams. A few of them raised their heads to look briefly at the two strangers, then went on with their business.

Finding an empty hitching rail in front of the *Cantina del Camino,* Bucklin swung down then helped Jenny to the ground and held her until her legs steadied. As she forced herself onto the boardwalk and bravely took a step forward, a booming round of vulgar laughter sent her cringing back into the shadows.

"It'll be all right, Jenny," assured Bucklin. "You look fine and nobody's going to know anything 'cept that you're with me."

After a long pause, Bucklin peered inside the cantina then indecisively rubbed the side of his jaw, "Well, maybe you should wait out here. I can go in and see if they have a room and then have the food brought to us."

Gathering her courage, Jenny shook her head. Sweeping her hair over her shoulders to shield the sides of her face, she took Bucklin by the arm and pulled herself close to his side determinedly. "I'll come," she said and with a tug urged him forward.

The large open-spaced room was crowded with people and buzzed with a caterwaul of Spanish. The high ceiling, held up by well-spaced, rough-cut beams, was clouded with the smoke of cigarettes while the heavier air smelled of liquor and cooked beef. Most of the men and all of the women were Mexicans, but the bartender was Anglo and with Jenny at his side, Bucklin crossed between the tables to speak to him. As they passed through the crowd nearly everyone glanced their way once and some looked twice, but beyond that their presence seemed to be of little interest.

Leaning over the planks that served as a bar, Bucklin waited for the bartender to come his way. "Need a room," he said raising his voice over the rumble of voices. "And food sent in if you can."

The bartender, a tall wiry man with a wide, flat nose and drooping mustache, eyed Bucklin for a moment then took a closer look at Jenny who held her head low. "Got a room, but won't be ready till the teamsters clear out. Oughta be soon, but one of 'em got hisself a senorita so it might be a while, so best let me brang your supper to you out here. You never know with a teamster."

"All right," agreed Bucklin as he searched the cantina for a remote table, "bring us whatever you got, but make it double. We'll have coffee to drink."

Looking again at Jenny, the bartender grinned. "We got good corn whiskey if you don't cotton to that damn tequila. Make it my ownself right out back."

Bucklin smiled appreciatively. "If I was back home I'd take you up on it, but not tonight."

Turning an ear toward Bucklin, the bartender asked, "Where might home be for you, boy? Tennessee, Arkansas, maybe?"

"Texas by way of Arkansas," replied Bucklin.

"Can tell by the brogue," offered the bartender, then, in a friendly tone, added, "The name's Otis Crebs from Tennessee myself before the late war. Nice to see a home boy way out here. You two go set and I'll get the grub."

Taking the table in the corner nearest the front door, Sam sat with his back to the wall and Jenny sat across from him, her back to the bustling people. A few moments later she brushed her hair behind her shoulders and with a faint smile of relief slowly raised her head.

"You did fine," encouraged Bucklin as he savored her smile and the warmth it brought to him. "I'm happy for you, Jenny. Proud and happy at the same time."

Taking his eyes off her long enough to scan the room he glanced back, his face now stiff with regret. "I been thinkin', Jenny," he said, "that it might be better if you were to stay in Santa Fe where you could…rest up. Being on the trail ain't no place for a lady like yourself. It's a hard ride and dangerous even in the best of times…I'd feel like I was doing you wrong by taking you along, and…"

With her smile melting away, Jenny covered her face with both hands then crumpled forward until her forearms rested on the table. Bewildered by the sudden turn, Bucklin stopped in mid sentence, then resumed urgently, "But I would still get Tommy, I would never think of leaving him with Injuns. I'd fetch him to you, Jenny. I swore I would."

With no response from Jenny, Bucklin found himself at a loss for words…and struggling with the impulse to take her in his arms and hold her. But before the idea could take root, it was abruptly swept aside.

Weaving around the jumbled tables, but steadily coming closer, were two Mexicans and with their attention locked on Jenny, there was no mistaking who they wanted to see.

They wore the dirt of a long trail and under their straw sombreros black eyes stared with suspicion. Each wore a short leather jacket and a sash around their waists. Belted over the sash was a pistol and long-bladed knife while in their hands both men choked the neck of a half-emptied tequila bottle.

With his back to the wall and Jenny sitting opposite from him, Bucklin was pinned tightly in the corner. There was not enough space nor time to get Jenny out of the way if the Mexicans made trouble. And from the looks of them, they had seen more than their share of it.

As they drew within a few feet of the table the taller of the two men mumbled something in Spanish to his partner then flashed a toothy smile.

"Hey, *Amigo*," he said almost singing the words. "You have no tequila and we have no one to share ours weeth. Maybe you and your woman would like a leetle drink with us, *Señor*?"

"Some other time, maybe," answered Bucklin as Jenny's hands slid down past her eyes exposing a horrified glare. "Been too long since we ate good."

Taking a few steps closer, the Mexicans came alongside the table, trying for a better look at Jenny.

"Maybe we wait for you to eat, *Amigo*," said the taller Mexican as both stooped and stared hard at Jenny. "But this *senorita*, she don't look so very hungry to me."

Bucklin glanced at Jenny and for the first time saw the shock in her eyes. "You boys'll have to excuse us," he said sharply. "The lady's had a long day and don't want company right now."

"Ojos Frios," blurted the second Mexican, then burst into laughter.

Bucklin's stomach plunged violently, then twisted into a knot. No one would call Jenny Cold Eyes, no one but the three Mexicans that had shot Harry while trying to take her.

Unable to help Jenny for the moment, Bucklin suppressed his rage and smoothly reverted to the cold-hearted Buck Samuels. "If you two know Cold Eyes here then you must ride with Juan Garza."

The two drunks sobered instantly. The second Mexican, a squat, but powerfully built man with a pock-marked face, glanced nervously over both shoulders as the taller intruder hunched over the table. "Don't say that name so loud," he warned in a scathing whisper. "You wan' to get us hung?"

Sliding up two chairs from a nearby table, the Mexicans sat down on opposite sides of Jenny. Leaning forward with both elbows on the table, the tall Mexican demanded, "Where you get this woman? You buy her from Harry?"

"Traded," said Bucklin then added, "his life for the girl. Now she's mine and I plan on keeping her. And I'm taking over his trade…if you catch my drift."

"I think maybe Juan Garza want this one," warned the squat Mexican with a menacing smile. "Want her bad. I think maybe you sell her to us…or maybe you have some troubles sooner than you know."

Bucklin paused as if in thought and casually reached for one of the tequila bottles. "Sounds like a hard man, this Garza," he muttered then took a drink. "I might be willing to sell her... for the right price. But she ain't for sale just yet. Like I said I'm taking over for Harry and I need her to show me a thing or two first."

The Mexicans grinned knowingly at each other then looked back at Bucklin. "Sure, sure, *Amigo*," assured the tall man as his black eyes danced with cruelty. "But Juan Garza will pay much for her. We can take you to him to-night. After you bring her, he can tell you about Harry and his trade. You don' need the woman for that."

"Maybe we'll talk tomorrow," answered Bucklin, still holding the thick bottle.

The squat Mexican's eyes narrowed threateningly. "To-night," he growled, then, shifting his weight to the back of his chair, he grabbed the handle of his knife.

Biding his time, Bucklin shrugged and smiled without humor. "You want it to be tonight, then we'll go after sup-per," he said easily while his eyes ran from the bandit on his right to the one on his left.

The instant the Mexicans relaxed, he made his move. In a sweeping backhand he smashed the bottle against the thick forehead to his right and while making a cross-draw with his left hand, sprang to his feet.

As the first Colt cleared leather and Bucklin reached for his second pistol, the heavy-set Mexican fell backward, but before hitting the floor, spun out of the chair landing on his knees with a gun already in his hand.

The Mexican turned to fire, but the table flipped sud-denly and crashed into him, deflecting the bandit's shot into the roof of the cantina.

Instantly lunging behind the tall Mexican who was struggling to get out of his chair, Bucklin shoved one gun barrel against the back of his head and pointed the other at his partner. "Hold it," he roared. *"No mueve nada."*

From the corner of his eye, Bucklin saw Jenny moving in behind him and realized it was she that had overturned the table. "Take this one's pistol and knife, Jenny," he said quickly. With his eyes riveted on the upturned table and the enemy behind it he added, "Use either one you want, but kill him if he so much as twitches."

As Jenny disarmed the seated Mexican, Bucklin stepped aside, then grabbed a leg of the table. "Let me hear that pistol hit the floor or I start shooting."

The dull thud was heard throughout the cantina, now smothered in heavy silence. "Now, mister," resumed Bucklin icily, you got a hideout, you just let it be. You make a play for it and you'll both die right here and now."

After a short pause, he slid the table away, exposing a face streaked with blood, but one totally devoid of fear. Staying clear of the knife, Bucklin kicked the pistol out of reach then stood back to let him stand. "You two best pull in your horns. But if ya feel like putting your chances to the touch you can go tell your master to let loose his dogs. Either way, you bother us again and I swear the ball's gonna open."

"What about our *pistolas*?" sneered the pock-marked Mexican.

"Tomorrow," snapped Bucklin, "now git."

As the two bandits turned to leave, Otis Crebs began easing through the crowd holding a pot of coffee and two cups. "All over, folks," he said calmly smiling to those nearest him. *"No mas la noche, no mas.* Go on and enjoy yourselves, folks."

Setting the pot down on the floor, he waited until Bucklin holstered his pistols before he uprighted the table. "You handled yourself good, boy," he said with a grin that showed several missing teeth. "Word is, them two is bad 'uns. Nobody'll say it to their faces, but it's believed they's working fer Juan Garza. Nothin' but cutthroats, all of 'em."

"Sorry about the trouble," replied Bucklin, then he glanced at Jenny. "They just had too much tequila."

Crebs set the pot down on the table and pulled the chair out for Jenny, whose colorless face betrayed her brave facade. "My apologies to you, ma'am," he said and calling on his best manners bowed clumsily. "It ain't often we get such a fine lady as yourself down here in Albuquerque."

As the roomful of people lost interest in the corner and went about their business, Jenny stiffly took her seat then laid the Mexican's huge pistol in her lap. With the barrel pointing toward the wall, she held onto it, cradling it with both hands.

Nodding toward the pistol, Crebs squinted thoughtfully at Bucklin. "Not a bad idee, son. The lady havin' a gun, I mean. 'Course not that hogleg Dragoon there, but somethin' smaller. Somethin' small and fittin' fer a delicate hand that can be..." Crebs paused awkwardly, his face flushing a faint red. "Well, you know, that can be hid-out private-like. Under the clothes so's it don't show, but makes her feel safe all the while."

Bucklin poured himself and Jenny a cup of steaming coffee then leaned back in his chair and took a sip. Shoving his hat back, he said, "You're talking about a Derringer. A good idea, but I don't own one."

"Well, sir," smiled Crebs proudly, "I got just the ticket. A genuine silver inlaid Derringer, not a cheap copy neither. It's a .45, but the lady here could hold it easy enough and it'll do the job at close range. I hear it's the self-same make and caliber that kilt President Lincoln."

Bucklin nursed his coffee and kept an eye on the front door to the cantina. "How much?"

"You say you was from Arkansas?" asked Crebs, scratching the gray stubble on his chin.

"I did."

"Seems to me I recollect that state was split in the war," said Crebs as he observed Bucklin from the comers of his eyes. "Some fit fer the North and some the South. What color did you wear, son?"

Glancing warily at Crebs, Bucklin said clearly, "I wore the gray. I was with the Arkansas Seventh and I got no apologies to make to nobody for it and if that..."

"Hold on, hold on," chuckled Crebs, holding up both hands. "I was just makin' fer sure certain. I wore the gray myself and I heard of the Bloody Seventh. You boys took a beatin', but you always held up your end of the bargain."

"You didn't say how much," muttered Bucklin.

"Well," began Crebs slowly as if the whole matter were suddenly of no importance, "I got no use fer it and since we both fit under Lee I was figurin' to make it a gift to the lady. In fact I'd be comforted knowin' what I done to help keep her safe. Women's too scarce as it is out here. Least-wise white women."

Bucklin looked across at Jenny who stared rigidly at some ill-defined point on the wall behind him. "In that case," he said, "I'd be much obliged. And I'm sure the lady would rest easier on account of it."

"Good 'nuff," returned Crebs cheerfully. After taking another admiring glance at Jenny, he spun eagerly on his heels and disappeared into the crowd.

For a moment Bucklin said nothing, then, raising his cup with both hands, he rested his elbows on the table and peered through the steam at the tragedy in front of him. "I'm sorry, Jenny," he offered sincerely, "sorry this had to happen at all. But I need to know who they were...and how they came to know you."

Surprisingly, Jenny answered without hesitation, although her eyes remained riveted on the wall.

"The big one was called Ramon. The ugly one was Juan Garza. They were with Harry before you came."

"Had you seen them before, before Harry took you down the Pecos?"

Jenny's stare grew icy, lethal. "Yes," she answered then paused as her eyes came to meet Bucklin's, then welled with tears. "They came to Cabeza Blanca's camp. They stayed...for days."

With her lips trembling, Jenny strained to get the words out. "Garza... bought me...for the nights he slept there."

Sam Bucklin felt his gut twist and his face flush with heat, yet he sat still. What Jenny needed now he would give her now. What the Mexicans deserved now...he would give them later.

Setting his cup down calmly, Bucklin reached over and touched Jenny's arm. "I know that was hard on you, Jenny, but it's important to know for the both of us. Anything that can get us close to this Cabeza Blanca is in our favor. And to do that everybody's got to believe I'm an Injun trader like Harry and Garza. If we convinced Garza, I'm taking over for Harry it'll likely get around to Blanca and help get us in to where Tommy is."

With her half-expectant eyes beginning to waiver, Bucklin added quietly, "And as far as I'm concerned what was done back then is over and done with. It don't make any difference to me in the way you might think. My sister is no less my sister than she was before...or is now in my heart.

"You don't blame a man for losing his crop to a drought or to a plague of locusts or a flood. He's the same man come hell or high water. Nobody thinks less of him on account of his misery and that's how I look at it. You're as good a woman as you ever were and nothing can change that unless you want it to."

Leaning back in his chair, Bucklin waited until he saw Jenny blink and heard her short breaths even out. "One thing has changed, though," he began casually, yet keeping a close eye on Jenny's response. "I was thinking before, it would be safer to have you wait in Santa Fe, but now with Garza knowing you're..."

"You can't," broke in Jenny as tears began slipping down her cheeks. With her voice torn with frustration and anger, she continued, "You can't leave me behind. You'll never find Tommy without me and I won't risk losing my son for any reason. You've never seen that country and you can't imagine what it's like."

Pausing to clear her eyes with the cuff of her shirt sleeve, she peered at Bucklin for several seconds. "And if you want to avenge your family…you'll need me to get the one you're after…Cabeza Blanca."

For a long count of ten, Bucklin stared back at Jenny as a frown grew on his face and his eyes darkened with morbid memories.

"That's a private matter," he said, "I've got no call to bring you into it or to use you to get what I want. I wouldn't be much different than Cabeza Blanca or Garza if I did."

"I don't want you to use me, Sam…I want you to need me… like I need you. If we help each other, if we need each other, it's nothing to be ashamed of. I would go with or without you to find my child, but you are an uncommon man, Sam Bucklin, an honorable man, and I don't think I could ever find another like you…please, Sam, take me with you to find my Tommy."

"Have you thought this through, Jenny?" asked Bucklin. "I mean all the way through. Where you'll be, what you'll see…who you'll see. Can you face all that again?"

"If it were your child," asked Jenny, "would you do any differently?"

"No. But it's different for me."

"Is it, Sam? You hunt the Apache alone and in his own land, and now you're trying to go after Cabeza Blanca. No one would do that unless they valued something more than their life, no one would risk the kind of torture the Indians enjoy. You know the Apache and what they would do to you if they caught you alive and yet you go on. And for what do you offer your life? Is it so different for you and your child as it is for me and mine?'

Rubbing his temple, Bucklin glared at his coffee. "There won't be much chance of turning back once we get into the thick of it. And the closer we get, the harder it's going to be on you. I may have to do things, act different about you, maybe even be awful to you when we're around other people and Injuns. And I guess it don't need to be said but once, that we both may end up dead."

"Everyone dies," replied Jenny. "But only a few die for anything worthwhile. I would rather die trying to save my son than live knowing I could have done more to get him back, to save his life. And I know he won't live without me. I know it."

"Steaks and frijoles," announced Crebs, suddenly coming alongside the table with two large plates and sliding them into place. "And if that ain't 'nough we got plenty more where that come from."

After handing a tarnished fork and knife to Bucklin and a set of ivory handled utensils to Jenny, he pulled a small leather pouch from the sash around his waist. Loosening the draw-string, he lifted the Derringer out with his thumb and finger then held it in his palm for Jenny to admire. "She's a beauty, ain't she?" he boasted. "Won it on the Mississippi playing cards, but never had no use fer it till now."

Easing it back into the pouch, he added, "Just be sure and hang on tight when you cock the hammer 'cause she's a might tight and when you pull the trigger have a good holt."

Daintily taking the pouch from his open hand, Jenny said graciously, "Thank you, Mr. Crebs. I shall ever be in your debt."

Bucklin glanced at her curiously noticing the subtle change in her mannerism then looked at Crebs, who stood blushing with gratification. "Can you get somebody to grain and board our horses, the roan and buckskin out front and bring the gear to the room you got us? Might not be too healthy for me to stick my head out your door for a while."

"Sure, young fella. Got a boy that'll take 'em to the livery down the street. And you can get to the room without goin' outside. It's behind the bar and through the door. There's only one window and it's covered with a rag and the back door's bolted shut from the inside. You can rest easy in there."

Bucklin nodded thankfully. "We could use the sleep."

"Well, if'n there's nothin' else, I'll go straighten up a little before you get settled in."

Waiting until Crebs was out of hearing range, Bucklin turned to Jenny. He started to speak, but decided against it and the two of them ate together, each engulfed in the privacy of their own thoughts.

The room Crebs had prepared was scarcely more than a ten-foot square, but the door had been built with heavy timbers and the floor was clean and made of stone. A single coal-oil lamp burned on a crate next to a frame bed and feather mattress. On top of it were several extra blankets. His long guns, saddlebags, and bedroll had been neatly stacked in the corner.

Taking his own blanket and two from the bed, Bucklin made a quick pallet on the floor. "I'll stretch out down here," he said and tossed his hat in the corner. Without thinking he added, "I imagine it's been a spell since you slept in a feather bed."

As Bucklin wearily lay down on his blankets, Jenny sat down slowly on the bed. Rubbing her hand gently over its linen surface, she asked wistfully, "What month is it, Sam?"

Bucklin scratched his head blinking sleepily, "I don't know. I been figuring it to be July. Don't think it's August yet."

After a short silence, Jenny spoke almost to herself. "If it's July, it's been a year and three months. Tommy was only nine months old."

Rolling onto his elbow, Bucklin looked up at Jenny only then realizing what she had asked. "That's a long time, Jenny. I didn't mean to bring it up."

"He's beginning to talk now," she sighed. "His first words were Apache. They wouldn't let me speak to him in English... My baby speaks Apache."

"He won't remember any of it, Jenny. Don't fret over it."

"And if we don't get him back," returned Jenny, "he'll soon forget me. My child won't know me."

"Just a few more days, Jenny," encouraged Bucklin, "and we'll be back there. But you got to know one thing from here on out. You got to remember one word and that's *patience.* When you're dealing with Injuns you can't think like a white man. Time ain't the same to an Injun as it is a white.

"We'll get Tommy back, but it'll have to wait till the time is right. To deal with Injuns you practically got to be one. Just as patient, just as tough, and just as cold-blooded as they are. Acting white will get you kilt quicker'n anything I know."

Leaning to the lamp, Jenny blew out the flame. In the blackness, she said, "Whatever it takes, I will do it."

The thick adobe walls of the bedroom held the night's coolness and under its heavy red-tile roof, the air was still. With the window covered, the darkness lingered until well after sunup and without the instinctive arousal of first light, Bucklin slept until midmorning when he kicked suddenly and threw off his blanket.

Swearing under his breath, he went to the window, raised the cloth and swore out loud. Turning in disgust he took a step then froze. "Beg your pardon," he said, seeing Jenny sitting on the edge of the bed. "I didn't mean for you to hear that."

"What happened?" asked Jenny. "Is something wrong?"

"Slept too long, way too long, and it don't set well. Can't do that too many times and expect to get away with it, and this's the second time."

After belting on his Colts and checking his hideout gun, Bucklin opened the door to the cantina just wide enough to see beyond the bar. Seeing no one present but Crebs, he said, "I'll be right back, Jenny," then stepped through the door and up to the bartender.

"Those two Mexicans around?" asked Bucklin sensing something in the bartender's eyes.

"Nope. They left earlier," drawled Crebs wiping his hands on a dish towel, "just after the army patrol rode in. Guess them bandits decided to high-tail it."

Bucklin looked around warily. "You get many patrols down this way?"

"Lately they's been more'n reg'lar on account of the bandits, but these here Yankees ain't lookin' fer no Mexicans."

"No?"

"Nope. They sent a courier, Pony Express like, all the way from Fort Sumner to Santa Fe to get after this feller. Then they come down here lookin' fer him."

Tossing the towel over his shoulder, Crebs leaned against the bar, looking at Bucklin from the corners of his eyes. "You know they's only one thing I hate more'n a blue-belly Yankee. Only one thing lower'n that and that there is what they're a lookin' fer."

"Injuns?" asked Bucklin casually.

"Worse. Them that trades guns to Injuns. And the peculiar thing is, you fit the bill down to your eyeteeth. You're even riding a buckskin and wearing moccasins. Hardly nobody does that and them horses of yores has been wore out."

"They been here yet?"

"Yep. Askin' all sorts of questions about you. Didn't say nothin' about the lady, though."

"And you didn't tell them I was here?" asked Bucklin. "Why?"

"Didn't want to jump the gun. Wanted to hear your side first on account of the lady. I can't see her riding with a no account gun runner."

"All right then," sighed Bucklin. "Reckon I got to trust you. Got any coffee?"

Walking into the kitchen, Crebs pointed to the stove and Bucklin took a cup and filled it. "They're after me sure enough, but for no good reason…except they believe I traded with the Injuns."

"And you're sayin' you don't deal with 'em at all?"

"I got my business with some of them, but it ain't of a sociable nature."

Crebs stared hard at Bucklin. "What are you gettin' at?"

"You ever hear of Cabeza Blanca?" asked Bucklin as he worked on his coffee. "Or a man by the name of Harry that runs with the Injuns?"

"Heard of both of 'em, damn their hides," snarled Crebs. "So what?'

"I'm after Cabeza Blanca," said Bucklin, then, after a long appraising look at Crebs, added, "and part of the reason is to get that lady in there's baby back to her."

"Baby," blurted Crebs incredulously. "What in hellfire is Cabeza Blanca got to do with her baby? You sayin' he's got her child?'

"Afraid so. And I don't intend to let him keep him."

"How'd he get her baby," drilled Crebs angrily, "take it on a raid? Damn their thievin' hearts."

"I don't know exactly how it came about and I ain't asked. Only she asked me to get him back and that's what I intend to do."

"But that army patrol's after you, boy. I mean they're hell bent fer leather to get at you. Hadn't you oughta to tell 'em your story?"

"No. It's better they think what they do. I want to let it out that I'm trading with the Injuns. That's how I'm going in after him. I'm taking Harry's place. That ought to get me in close, right into his camp."

"But how you goin' to get the child back without bein' kilt?"

"Buy him, likely. They all understand ransom. If not I'll steal him out."

Running his fingers through his thinning gray hair, Crebs shook his head.

"You're a bubble off plumb, boy. You ain't goin' to get out alive. One mistake and they'll tie your heels to a tree limb and build a fire under your brains or maybe stake you stark naked on top of a ant hill and let 'em eat you to death. I seen men kilt both of them ways...or seen what was left of 'em.

"That Cabeza Blanca bunch is the worst in the territory. They's mostly Apaches, but they's Comanche, Kiowas, and Utes, too. A white man'd be loco to walk into that. You'd be better off takin' your chances with the army and tell 'em what you're after. They might even go with you, send a patrol to lend a hand."

"Them," snapped Bucklin. "There's not an Injun west of the Mississippi that's afraid of the regular army and for good reason. When it comes to hunting down renegades they couldn't hit the ground with their hats."

Crebs frowned and scratched his head, then glanced at Bucklin. "Well, son, you got plenty of sand, that's fer certain. But them mounts of yores is broke down from long ridin'. If you're headed out soon you'll be needin' fresh mounts. Even with grain yours'll be a week on the mend."

"You any good at horse trading?" asked Bucklin. "I need two of the best, but with the soldiers in town, I better not show my face around trying to hunt up what I want."

'I can judge horse flesh as good as any man," answered Crebs dryly. "And I know whose got the best stock around here, too. I'll fetch 'em and tie 'em out back of your room. Take me about an hour."

"Much obliged, Mr. Crebs. We're anxious to get on with it."

Crebs nodded and turned, but after taking two steps stopped and spun.

"We? You don't mean to say you're takin' the lady with you...out there?"

With his brow hardening over a cold stare, Bucklin spoke slowly, "It's her child they got and she's the only one that knows how to find Cabeza Blanca's hideout."

"How could she know such a thing?" scoffed Crebs. "Only somebody that's been there could..."

Creb's eyes flared wide open then after a few seconds began blinking sluggishly as the impact of Bucklin's statement took effect. "Those filthy, rotten savages," he muttered, then swore in disbelief. "This country won't be no good to nobody till all them wild Injuns is kilt. I mean ever' last one of them bastards and tomorrow wouldn't be soon enough. Damn them all to hell's fire fer what they done. Damn them."

"An hour then?" asked Bucklin calmly.

"Or less," replied Crebs angrily as his worn boot heels banged heavily across the cantina floor. "And two of the best."

In the rented room, Jenny had folded all the blankets and sat quietly on the edge of the bed with her hands in her lap. When Bucklin walked in, she did not look up. "You told him," she said painfully. "You told him about me."

Bucklin paused in the doorway looking down at Jenny. "How much did you hear?"

"I heard you tell him and then I heard his reaction...and he had been so courteous."

"Jenny, I had to trust him. The army's in town looking for me and he can get us fresh horses without me being seen. I've come too far to be arrested by Yankees for something I didn't do and if I'm in jail...well, it wouldn't do for neither of us."

Taking a few steps to his saddlebags, Bucklin knelt down beside them. Pointlessly unbuckling one of the straps, he added sincerely, "But I'm sorry for the grief it caused you just the same. It wasn't my intention you should've known anything about it."

Lifting a hand from her lap, Jenny rubbed each eye with her palm. Gazing at Bucklin, she whispered, "I believe you, Sam, but...but will it ever stop? Won't someone always find out, somehow? Can it ever be like it was before?"

"I don't know, Jenny. But I do know you and me can't get too far 'till we can put it all to rest...And we're a ways from doing that. No wound can heal till what's causing the festering is dug out. But there's always the scar left and nothing can get rid of that."

Opening his saddlebags as if looking for something, Bucklin waited for Jenny's reply, but hoped there would be none. When she didn't speak, he glanced up at her drawn face.

"Are you hungry? There's a kitchen next room over and Crebs is out buying us horses."

Jenny raised her head and steadied herself with a deep sigh. "Then I will do the cooking," she said, forcing a faint smile. "A man should know what he's getting himself into."

The wood stove was still hot, the kitchen well-organized and in a half-hour a breakfast of eggs, bacon, biscuits and gravy was on the table. As the two sat down to eat, their eyes met and for a moment they held. Steam rose from the speckled coffee pot and the smell of baked bread and bacon filled the air. Under their feet was a wooden floor and over their heads a solid roof. The room was quiet, the chairs comfortable, and they were alone. And, perhaps for the last time, they were free from the constant threat of attack.

"The only thing west of here that's anything like a town is Fort Defiance and that's two hundred miles out. When the horses get here, I'll be wanting to hit the trail...and it could be a rough one."

Jenny's pale blue eyes were unflinching. "I'll be ready to go, Sam Bucklin. I've been ready since the day Harry took me away and I'm well aware of what's ahead."

Nodding respectfully, Bucklin replied, "Then I won't bring it up again. If you change your mind along the way it'll be your place to come to me. Otherwise, there'll be no turning back."

"Then the matter is closed," said Jenny. "There will be enough to do without worrying about me. Cabeza Blanca is as cunning as he is cruel and you'll need all your wits about you just to stay alive. Put me out of your mind, Sam, and think only of him."

Pulling his eyes away from the beauty across the table, Bucklin fought down the urge to swear. "That's the way I figure it, too," he muttered. Then with nothing further began to eat.

With his mind distracted, he was nearly finished with his breakfast before he realized how good it tasted. As he started to offer compliments, Crebs entered through the bar and after tipping his hat to Jenny hurriedly took a seat at the table.

"Got your horses tied out back and done fair on the trade, considerin' the hurry. A sorrel and Appaloosa, all black feet. Them soldiers is still asking around about you since they heard you was in here last night on account of the ruckus and all. As soon as you can, boy, you best hightail it out of here. They seem bound and determined to root you out."

"Thank you, Mr. Crebs," said Jenny. "You've been very gracious, as well as helpful."

"Least I could do, ma'am. But I got me one more piece of advice to give and that's if you're thinkin' of takin' the Old Spanish Trail, forget it. I heard them sayin' they was sendin' men out that way already."

"Is there another way?" asked Bucklin as he found himself admiring the older man. "I've never been this far west."

"Shore is. Ain't used much no more, but the Beale wagon road is open all the way to the Zuni Pueblo. It's a tradin' post and the Injuns there is all friendly. From there the trail heads due north, passes by Fort Defiance and goes on to the San Juan River."

"We'll be following the Rio de Chelly for a day," said Jenny flatly, "then we'll come to the San Juan."

Bucklin glanced surprisingly at Jenny as Crebs averted his eyes and his face flushed. For a moment there was a heavy silence, a cumbersome, awkward silence.

"We'll do it," said Bucklin finally, then reached into his pocket. Bringing out a twenty-dollar gold piece, he added, "Will this cover what I owe?"

"No, sir, it won't," replied Crebs, waving a hand sternly. "Your money ain't no good here. You keep it fer when you really have need of something."

"Neighborly of you, Mr. Crebs," said Bucklin. "Maybe we'll see you on our way back through."

"Will you be coming this way again?' asked Crebs with genuine interest. "It'd be a comfort knowin' what come of you two now that I think on it."

Bucklin pushed his hat back on his head, suddenly realizing he had given no thought to what might come after Cabeza Blanca. For five years he hadn't looked beyond the next horizon or the next Apache, nor had he cared to. But now there was Jenny. "We'll make it a point," he said thoughtfully. "We'll do just that."

CHAPTER NINE

Following a brief, but convincing conversation with Nathan Crebs, the unshaven and saddle-weary troopers galloped out of Albuquerque confident Buck Samuels was just in front of them and headed for Santa Fe. When the dust beyond the village square cleared and the patrol disappeared to the north, Sam Bucklin and Jenny Mason slipped out of town to the southwest, at first riding in the sand-covered bottoms of shallow ravines, then onto the sage-covered remains of the old wagon trail. By nightfall they crossed the Rio Puerco and camped on the west bank of a second river, the name of which Crebs had not recalled. Two days later and ninety miles further west they found themselves at the Zuni River and walked their horses halfway across the ankle-deep water before stopping to stare at the Indian pueblo.

Across the shallow river, dozens of mud walls, two to three feet in height, checkered the bank with terraced gardens. Beyond them on a slight knoll sat what resembled a crude adobe fortress.

Around its irregular base, the walls had been built ten feet high, but toward the center of the sprawling structure a second and third story of rooms had been added. In these, there were doors and windows.

On the flat rooftops of nearly every house, smoke swirled from chimneys made of stacked red clay pots. Scurrying about each, at every level, hundreds of Indians busied themselves with tasks and in the fading light of day the entire complex took on the bizarre appearance of a monstrous human anthill.

"Got to be the Zuni Pueblo," said Bucklin in awe. "I ain't seen nothing like it before. Must be the Mexicans built it up."

Jennifer gazed at the pueblo for a moment, then her eyes grew distant.

"No, the Zunis built it. The Spanish built a church in it, but the pueblo was here before the Spanish ever saw this land. Coronado thought it was one of the seven cities of gold."

Bucklin's head turned slowly toward Jennifer, his eyes squinting curiously at her blank expression. "You been here before?"

"No. My husband…my husband was to be employed by the Board of Indian Affairs. While we were still in the East, we studied as many tribes as we could before leaving for Santa Fe…but we never made it."

After a grim pause, Bucklin looked back at the pueblo. "I don't know that Coronado fella, but that over there is a far cry from gold. Looks like a bunch of mud shacks all piled on top of each other. The Caddo Injuns built something like it back home, only not so close together."

As the two rode closer to the pueblo, the Indians searched them briefly with unreadable eyes, then continued with their work. Only the children seemed to show any signs of interest in the approaching strangers and, gathering in small groups, they looked down from the edge of the outer wall.

After riding several hundred feet along the southern wall, they turned into a narrow passageway that led to the interior of the pueblo. In a matter of seconds the seemingly solid collection of mud houses opened up into a plaza of several acres. In its center, built of adobe bricks but lacking a roof, was a large Spanish mission. Two bells hung thirty feet from the ground in a partially completed bell tower while a walled courtyard of nearly an acre formed the entryway to the abandoned church. In the front of the courtyard stood a weathered cross surrounded by a thick growth of greasewood and an array of spiny yucca cactus.

Just outside the courtyard wall, a rectangular stone building had been built onto the side of the mission and above its door a crudely painted sign said TRADEGOODS.

Dismounting in front of the trading post, Bucklin helped Jennifer off her horse and set her down gently, although her legs were rapidly growing stronger. "Looks more like a regular town from in here," he said with a hint of bewilderment. "You say these are Injuns?"

"Yes. They were here, had been here for years, before any European ever saw this land. They could be nothing else."

"I don't know," muttered Bucklin as a squaw peered down at him from a rooftop. With wide set eyes and black hair tied neatly to the sides of her head in what resembled a pair of twisted buns, she sent a chill down his spine. "The Comanches tell of trading way off down in Mexico and bringing back all sorts of bright-colored feathers and such. The people down there was said to live in rock houses that reached up to the sky. Up on top of the biggest one they killed people and took out their hearts. Them Comanches, as mean as they are, said they wasn't real people like themselves, but was bad spirits."

Bucklin looked over his shoulder and studied the plaza carefully. From where he stood the passageway they had used was barely visible and might easily be missed if he were in a hurry to get out. Crebs had said the Zuni were peaceful, but still they were Indians and that, at least to a white man, made them unpredictable.

Just as he started toward the trading post door, Bucklin glimpsed two sets of fresh tracks that cut the packed sand street. Two shod horses had ridden up, but only one man had dismounted to enter the store while the other had led the horses somewhere out of sight.

Before Bucklin reached for the door latch he flipped the leather thongs off the hammers of his Navies. Shod horses either had been stolen or belonged to whites or Mexicans, and Sam Bucklin trusted no one he could not call a friend. And those were few and far between.

With only two small windows to let in light, the inside of the trading post was a patchwork of shadows and dark musty corners. To the right, shelves covered the entire wall and cn them were several stacks of Indian blankets, canned and dried foods, bags of salt and an adequate array of other sundries Bucklin was surprised to see.

To the left were two card tables separated by a few feet. Sitting at the one nearest the front window was a small man dressed in a wool shirt. Wearing a headband around his gray-black hair, he sat easily smoking a clay pipe. At the second table furthest from the door was a Mexican who held his head low as if half-asleep, his sombrero covering his face. Along the back wall a smaller shelf, half-filled with whiskey bottles, stood just behind a crude bar that consisted of three roughhewn planks on top of two large wooden barrels. Next to the shelf a second door opened into a back room.

As Bucklin walked slowly up to the bar, he maneuvered Jenny to his right side while his eyes darted back and forth between the two men to his left. The Indian's eyes met his briefly, but the Mexican didn't move except to nod slightly.

"Welcome, strangers," said a short, round-bellied man as he suddenly appeared from the second door and walked eagerly behind the planks. "Welcome to Zuni," he repeated taking a second unbelieving look at Jenny Mason. "My name's Burns, Noah Burns, and this is the best and last place to stop over on your way to anywhere. What can I do

157

you for? Got all the comforts and supplies a tired body could ask for. Hot food, hot bath, and warm beds. You name it."

Looking the trader over carefully, Bucklin said flatly, "You seem to be well supplied for being so far west, so deep into Injun country, I mean."

Noah Burns waved a hand and shook his head. "Traders always get along with everybody. Treat folks square, red or white or Mexican, and you got no worries."

"You ever trade up to the north of here?" asked Bucklin, glancing to his left. "Figured on doing some of it myself."

"Well, now," answered Burns, enjoying the company and the conversation, "I was up on the San Juan for a spell before Kit Carson took up fighting the Navajos. Then I came down here and took over this post. Things has settled down up there now and I hear there's a lot of posts starting up along that stretch of river. But if you're headed up that way you ought to buy a couple of Navajos. It's going to be getting into the rainy season and they'll be worth the money."

"You mean for guides?" asked Bucklin.

"No, no," said Burns with a smile. "I mean to say a blanket. The Navajos make the best blankets you ever saw. It's wove so tight it's waterproof and warm as can be. Folks in this part of the country just naturally calls them Navajos instead of blankets on account of them being so well-known and all."

"You say it's going to rain?"

"Sure will and down here, too. July, August, and into September you get it all. Comes in gully washers. You never camp in any kind of draw or arroyo or some storm you can't even see will likely come roaring down them dry beds and drown you before you know what happened."

Bucklin glanced at Jenny, who Burns had oddly chosen to ignore. "I'll need a hat for the woman then and two of your Navajos. Some jerked meat if you got it and…"

From somewhere out in the plaza, like a whispering alarm, the muffled jingling of spurs filtered through the front door causing Bucklin to turn cautiously toward the two seated men. Watching the doorway, he said evenly, "And some coffee."

Burns scribbled down the order, but continued to talk as he wrote. "How about some peaches? You'd never guess but these Zunis has been raising them in this desert for over a hundred years. Don't have any fresh, but I got some dried ones and they're good. I'll make you a good deal and they'll sure enough satisfy the sweet tooth."

A second Mexican wearing a pistol and large knife paused casually at the door, his large frame nearly blocking out the light. A moment later he strolled to the shelf of dry goods and began shuffling through the tin cans. He had started going through the blankets when two more Mexicans appeared, but these Bucklin recognized as soon as they stepped through the door. The tall one Jennifer had called Ramon, the other was Juan Garza. "That Injun in the corner," asked Bucklin hurriedly, "he a Zuni?"

Burns shrugged without taking his eyes of his list. "Navajo, I gather. Never talks much. He brings my blankets down from up north and I trade him the blue powder the Zunis mine out. Injuns from all over prize the stuff for the good paint it makes. Once when I was..."

As Burns glanced up at the two men that had just entered, his eyes flared with recognition and his mouth snapped tightly shut. With the color draining from his oval face he glared uneasily to the right then the left and finally at Bucklin. After tensely wiping his forehead with the back of his hand, he started for the rear door. Halfway through it he said nervously, "Excuse me, folks. I got to get your supplies from out back."

Sensing something was wrong, Jenny started to turn and ask Bucklin a question, but before her first word, she heard a voice that made her stomach turn.

"So, *Amigo*," taunted Juan Garza, "we meet again." Swaggering toward the seated Mexican who now raised his head, the bandit stopped at the table and picked up a bottle. "And you are so far from Albuquerque. You and your woman travel ver' fast. Like maybe somebody chasing you, I think."

Taking a drink of whiskey, he walked around the end of the bar, then stepped behind it and shoved his sombrero back on his shoulders exposing a bushy head of long, dusty hair. From the shelf he took two glasses and set them down in front of Bucklin. Filling each to the brim, he added, "I think maybe you got something you want to sell back to me and ver' cheap, I think maybe, too."

Ramon stopped just inside the door. Leaning a shoulder against its frame, he began rolling a cigarette. Behind Bucklin the shuffling sounds had ceased and the black eyes of the seated Mexican burned into him.

There was no decision, no choice to be made. There was only one path to follow and Sam Bucklin took it without hesitation. "This woman worth dying for, Garza? That the price you had in mind?'

Now standing no more than three feet across from Bucklin, Garza was suddenly off balance. Faced with four gunmen, he hadn't counted on an argument, much less a fight; but now he was unsure. Pointing a finger around the room he said, "Perhaps, *Señor*, you do not see there are four of us. You will be the one to die."

"Mister, I been shot up by better'n you," sneered Bucklin, "and I been speared and stabbed by Injuns and still left 'em scalped and ready for buzzards and maggots to clean up. I ain't died yet, but if today's the day, I won't be dying alone. Not by a large majority.

"I been stole from only once in my life and all but one of them I done read 'em from the Book. So now it's up to you, Garza. If you want to steal this woman you're sure as hellfire going to pay the price of trying to take her."

The dingy room fell into a deathly silence as a morgue-like stillness filled the air. Even the slightest rustle of a shirt sleeve or the scrape of a boot heel could trigger an explosion of point-blank gunfire, and in the close quarters, no one was ready to take a chance on getting shot.

"If you wan' this little woman bad enough to get killed for," said Garza cautiously, "why you tryin' to get her dead in here with you? Maybe she don' wan' to die already. I think she wan' more to be alive with us than dead with one loco gringo."

Seeing his chance, Bucklin paused long enough to see Garza sweat.

"All right, you ask her what she wants," he growled. "But, woman, if you choose to go for him after all I done for you, I want you clean out of my sights as fast as you can move…Do you understand me, woman?"

Jenny answered clearly, firmly, "Yes, Sam. I understand perfectly."

Garza relaxed slightly. then with both hands still on the bar leaned over close to Jenny and smiled threateningly. "So you wan' to be back with Juan Garza or maybe get shot down with the gringo? Maybe now Juan don' look so bad, eh? What does it matter so much to a woman which man has her? One man is like another."

Without warning Jenny's hand swung up from under the bar and the small Derringer exploded into the face of the grinning bandit, sending him spinning and screaming into the back wall. As Jenny threw herself to the floor, Bucklin's pair of Colts fired simultaneously at two different targets, but a split second behind their reports another deafening boom sent a searing-hot ball of lead into his side and out the front of his shirt.

Dropping the pistol from his left hand, Bucklin fell to one knee and spun around just as the large Mexican sent another shot over the top of his head. Catching his balance, Bucklin fired again, aiming instinctively at the center of the big man's brisket. Instantly the Mexican froze and with eyes wide open he stood motionless, gasping his last breath, then fully erect, fell face first onto the stone floor.

Rising slowly into a lingering cloud of silver-blue gun smoke, Bucklin came to his feet as blood began to drench his shirt. Ramon lay sprawled in the plaza where he had run a few steps before collapsing. The seated Mexican was still in his chair but as the last pulse of life left him, he rolled to one side until his head caught on the edge of the table and stopped him from dropping to the floor.

"He's gone," blurted Jenny frantically, "he's not dead"

Bucklin glanced behind the bar, then ducked under the planks and into the back room. Burns stood in the corner, pressing himself flat against the far wall. "Where's Garza?" demanded Bucklin, still holding a cocked pistol.

"I don't know," cried Burns, "he ran out the back. His hair was on fire."

Bucklin slipped to the back of the storeroom and peered out. No one was in sight, not even on the roof tops, yet he knew that in the maze of mud-walled apartments hundreds of Indians were likely watching him from the small windows and darkened doorways. Wherever Garza had gone it would be unwise, if not downright dangerous, to venture further into the Zunis' pueblo trying to find him.

Returning to the front room, Bucklin saw Jenny watching the door to the plaza and in her hands with both thumbs on the hammer was the dropped pistol. She could think and think quickly and without being told had picked up the revolver and covered his back. Or perhaps she was merely hoping for another chance at Garza. But either way, Sam Bucklin knew he had met an exceptional woman.

"He won't be back," he said. "His kind is always last to shoot and first to run."

"I shot too soon," lamented Jenny, as the Colt in her hand began to quiver.

"I was so close...he was so close to me." Lowering the pistol, she turned and looked remorsefully at Bucklin, but then caught sight of the blood-drenched shirt. "You're hit, Sam," she gasped. "You've been shot."

"More'n once. This time ain't too bad, though."

"But you're bleeding, bleeding badly."

As Jenny came toward him, Bucklin noticed the Navajo stirring for the first time since the shooting. "We get it bandaged good enough and that'll stop before too long," offered Bucklin, closely watching the Indian stand and go out the door to one of his pack burros. "I'll be all right."

Pulling a chair from the dead man's table, Jenny scooted it behind Bucklin. "Sit down and get your shirt off," she said worriedly and rushed into the storeroom. "I'll see what Mr. Burns has for bandages."

Unbuttoning his shirt, Bucklin half-listened to the commotion in the rear, but most of his attention was on the Navajo who worked at his burro and calmly puffed his pipe as if nothing had happened. A moment later he returned with a beaded leather pouch and set it on the bar.

"I am Jesus Arviso," offered the Navajo. Pointing to the pouch, he added, "For wound. It is used by Zuni, made from their plants. I use it many times."

Bucklin nodded, "Thanks. I'm Buck Samuels."

Jenny returned just ahead of Burns and was carrying a roll of cotton cloth and a pair of scissors. At the sight of Bucklin's bare back, she drew up, as did Burns.

From one side of his heavily muscled shoulders to the other, a white scar stretched from the tip of one shoulder blade to the bottom of the other. At the base of his neck on the right side a bullet had left its mark as had another that had exited just above his left kidney. And now, two inches below that round scar, his side was bathed in the bright red blood of still another wound.

As Jenny cut a large piece of cloth from the roll and folded it, Bucklin introduced the Indian. "Jenny Mason, meet Jesus Arviso. He's got some medicine to make a poultice inside that bag there."

Jenny hesitated, staring first at the Navajo, then at the pouch and finally back to the stoic Indian. "Thank you. You are very kind," she said, then began wiping the blood from the torn flesh on both sides.

Burns gawked incredulously at the three dead men. "You got three," he blustered, "three out of four, just like that?" Turning to Bucklin, he continued excitedly, "Damn it, man. Do you know who they were? You wiped out Juan Garza's band of cutthroats. They've been murdering through this territory for three years and nobody ever so much as laid a hand on them."

Bucklin winced as Jenny applied the poultice and began wrapping the wound. Trying to ignore the scalding pain in his side, he spoke evenly. "Garza ain't done, I reckon. He's a man that won't never stop thieving and murdering till he's dead. He's no different than an Apache or Comanche. And he can always find the likes of them there to do his dirt for him."

Still shaking his head in disbelief, Burns took the drinks Garza had poured and gulped them down his dry throat. The Navajo puffed on his pipe and watched patiently as Jenny tied off the bandage. As she finished and took the bloody shirt out the back door to wash it, the Indian put out his smoke.

"You want trade with Navajo?"

Bucklin's eyes narrowed, then he answered uncommittedly, "Navajo, Ute, Kiowa. All the tribes to the north that's got goods to trade."

"Sometimes there much danger for trade," replied Arviso, speaking slowly and choosing his words carefully. "Bandits, Mexican, white mans, Apache. Apache kill many. No trade, kill."

"You seemed to be doing all right," said Bucklin.

"Two men's better safe. Two and…that woman, more safe. Good woman. No fear."

Bucklin studied the Indian closely for a moment. Paying close attention to his eyes, he asked bluntly, "You don't trade with the Apache?"

Waving his brown hand in a short chopping motion, Arviso grunted, "Apache, no trade. Only steal, kill Navajo. Take sheep, womans, childs. No trade with Apache."

"What band?" asked Bucklin. "Who raids the most?"

"Jicarilla from east. Cabeza Blanca from all places. Many Navajo hungry, many. Some again raid white mens to north for food, guns."

"This here Cabeza Blanca, he a Jicarilla, too?"

"No. Ver' bad Apache."

"How far north are you headed?"

"To river San Juan. Many posts trade on river. Ute, Kiowa, Paiute, Mormons, come trade on river."

Jenny returned with the wet shirt draped over her arm and handed it to Bucklin. Catching a glimpse of several more scars on his muscular chest and abdomen, she quickly averted her eyes.

Painfully slipping into the cool shirt, Bucklin started fastening the buttons. "Jenny," he said with a softness in his voice, "this man wants us to ride together till we get to the San Juan country. He believes it'd be safer for us all. And I imagine he knows the shortest and best trails. That could save us some time, but I want to know how you feel about it. We can make it without him."

Jenny glared at the Indian, whose hair was more brown than black. From his ears hung two round, silver earrings and around his neck were several shell necklaces. He wore no breechcloth, but instead a belt of large silver conchos. He was like no Indian she had ever seen.

"You are a Navajo?" she asked half-speaking to herself.

"I am born Mexican," replied Arviso, surprising both Bucklin and Jenny as well as Burns. "Navajo take captive as child. Live as slave for Navajo. Now after Long Walk, am trade. Navajo call me Sotos."

"And you still live with the Navajo?" asked Jenny. "You haven't gone back to your family, to Mexico?"

Arviso shrugged with disinterest. "I was Mexican child. Now am man, Navajo man. No more Mexican."

Jenny flinched at the simplistic answer and unconsciously grabbed Bucklin's hand and held it tightly. "We must hurry, Sam," she said.

"We have to get Tommy away from them."

"All right then, Jesus. We'll ride together then, but we'll leave as soon as we get our supplies."

Arviso nodded and returned to his burros. "This Tommy you mentioned, ma'am, he your kin?" asked Burns.

Jenny's eyes had glazed with tears, but she managed to answer clearly.

"Yes. He is my child."

"I'm sorry to hear that, ma'am," offered Burns, shaking his head sincerely, "and I know it's none of my business, but there's no use you looking up north with Arviso. The Navajo had to give up all their captives when they were marched off to Fort Sumner. They haven't taken slaves since they were defeated several years back."

"My baby was taken one year and three months ago," struggled Jenny. "The Navajo weren't the ones that took him from me."

"Then why are you...?" Burns stopped short, then swore under his breath. "You're not going into Ute country?" he asked abruptly. "Not the Apaches?"

"We best be going as soon as we can," interrupted Bucklin. "If you'd fill that order, I'd be obliged."

Curious and unsatisfied, Burns glanced morbidly at the dead men.

"Mexican bandits are one thing," he said stepping behind the bar, "but Indians are a horse of an entirely different color, my friend. You'll be lucky just to get back alive, much less get that child."

After Burns went into the storage room, Jenny's tortured eyes grew distant and the repressed tears began trickling silently down her cheeks.

Bucklin put both hands on her shoulders and turned her toward him. "We'll get him back, Jenny, it won't be long now. He won't never be anything but your baby. Nobody else's but yours."

Jennifer Mason pulled herself closer to the blurry figure in front of her then hugged him gently. "Thank you, Sam Bucklin," she said weakly, "thank God for you."

Bucklin felt the warmth of her body through his cool shirt and the rise and fall of her chest as she pressed against him. It was a comforting feeling, a closeness kindled by tragedy and nurtured by a shared understanding of life's cruelty.

It had been five years since he held a woman, but that had been his wife and the sight of her mutilated body was burned into the fabric of his soul. She had been murdered by Indians while he was away. She had died because he was not there to protect her and now he was taking Jenny Mason into the heart of Indian country risking the same, if not worse, fate. He couldn't let it happen, not again. There had to be another way. "I won't let you down," whispered Bucklin, "not this time."

Jenny backed away slowly and wiped her tears. "I'm sorry, I don't want to be a burden. It's just that…"

Holding up a hand, Bucklin cut her off. "It's all right, Jenny. You could never be a burden to me. Not now. Not ever."

Looking up with a tearful glimmer of hope, Jenny blinked uncertainly. As her eyes cleared, she started to speak but, searching for the right words, she hesitated too long.

Returning with a bulging white cotton sack, two blankets, and a hat, Burns laid the load on the bar. "That'll be eight dollars."

Handing over a ten-dollar gold piece, Bucklin said, "Keep it all. I ain't got time to help bury them three. I'm taking their guns. You can have whatever else they got on 'em for expenses."

Jenny put on the hat, which was a size too large, and picked up the bag and blankets as Bucklin took the pistols. "If Garza comes back, you just tell him I took what all they had and you'll have no trouble. And if he wants any of it he'll know where to come looking."

"What do you mean?" asked Burns. "Where?"

"Just tell him. He'll know."

After tying on the new blankets and packing the dry goods into the saddlebags, Jenny and Bucklin mounted and waited beside the pack burros for Arviso who was nowhere in sight. A moment later he walked into the plaza, leading three saddled horses, two of them still wet with sweat.

"You kill mans," said Arviso simply, "now horses belong you. Other horse no here, gone. Man gone, too."

"You have a horse?" asked Bucklin.

"No more. Only burros."

Bucklin glanced appraisingly at the bandits' horses, a paint and two bays. "String the bays along with your burros, the paint is yours."

"*Gracias*," grunted Arviso then tied the geldings to the rear of the burros, making a train of six animals, four with goods for trade and two with the empty saddles of dead men.

"How far to Navajo country?" asked Bucklin.

"One sleep. Two sleeps to Fort Defiance."

"And to the river, the San Juan?"

"If no rain, four days' ride," answered Arviso as he straddled the paint and led the procession out of the plaza. "If rain, more days. Trade better at river."

After passing through a small peach orchard north of the pueblo, the Navajo led his pack train steadily to the northwest. Through most of the afternoon he followed well-marked trails, but occasionally took less visible ones used only by game animals. By nightfall, Bucklin couldn't make out any trail at all, but the Mexican-turned-Indian kept a steady pace winding his way through the rough and broken terrain as if it were broad daylight. By midnight they stopped at a camp that, although deserted, was evidently known to all who traveled north from Zuni.

The spring was well marked and judging by the empty fire rings and wagon tracks, the site was a common stopover for Indians, Mexicans, and whites.

"Where did the wagons come from?" asked Bucklin as he helped Jenny to the ground and held her until her aching legs once again steadied. "What are they hauling way out here?"

"Army wagons from Fort. Buy Zuni corn, wheat."

"Corn and wheat?" questioned Bucklin skeptically. "Those Zunis are farmers, Injun farmers?"

"Farm much. Good to raid, no fight good... But Navajo raid no more."

Too tired to eat, Bucklin unsaddled the horses while Jenny rolled out the bedrolls. As he and Arviso led their stock to water, Bucklin asked quietly. "These Navajo, they any trouble to a white man…or woman?"

"No trouble. Navajo follow white man road now. No trouble. Fight only other Injuns. Utes, Apaches, who come."

"What about the Mormons? I was told the Navajo are fighting with them."

"Some raid for guns, horses, food. No fight. Take only from Mormon. No more kill white man. Sometimes Ute, Apache still."

Bucklin rubbed the neck of one of the bays as it buried its nose into the spring and sucked up the water. "What do you know about this Cabeza Blanca?"

For a moment Arviso made no reply, but speaking from the darkness his voice revealed the tension on his face. "See him only one time. Only me. They many, but no see me."

"Then you know what he looks like?"

"See from not too far. Him big Apache. Bigger me, bigger you maybe."

"And his hair, is it white like they say?"

"No so white, gray. But no old man."

"Where did you see him?"

Arviso paused again. "Kill Rico close by Navajo Mountain. Take sheep, food, horses."

"Rico?" asked Bucklin. "What's that?"

"Rico is...mean rich. Ricos strongest of Navajo, trade much. Have many mans, guns, sheep. No take Long Walk to Bosque Redondo. Stay here. Army no find Ricos. Cabeza Blanca... he find."

Bucklin thought for a moment. Kit Carson had led the fight against the Navajo and his abilities were unquestionable, yet he had missed some of the most formidable Navajo. He had been unable to track them down, but the Apache was succeeding where Carson had failed. And that meant Cabeza Blanca was one of the most dangerous Indians in the territory.

"Anything in particular different about him, from other Apaches, I mean?"

"Him walk bad one leg. Big. White hair. Find many Ricos, kill many."

Folding his arms against the chill of the night, Bucklin debated whether or not to ask Arviso any more questions. Burns had said he didn't speak much, but the Navajo seemed in a talkative mood so he took a chance.

"You say he steals their sheep. He must have to drive them somewhere and that many animals would leave a whole lot of tracks, tracks that could be followed."

Even in the starlight, Bucklin saw Arviso look his way. "You follow Cabeza Blanca?"

Avoiding an answer, Bucklin countered with another question and hoped he hadn't aroused any suspicion. "Can't the Navajo track him down or even the army? He can't hide for long with all that stock to feed."

"No find Cabeza Blanca. He trade sheep quick to Mexican, Utes. Navajo no hunt Cabeza Blanca. Army no hunt Apache for Navajo. Give food, no more kill Apache. And food not enough to feed all."

"You mean nobody knows where he might be, where he might be hiding out. Nobody's seen where he keeps his squaws?"

Arviso gathered the lead ropes of his burros. "He have place like Ricos find place, only better. Many place hide in Navajo land. Hard look many places. Much danger to go. Soon you see."

Bucklin followed the burros to a picket line that had been strung between two large greasewood bushes and tied off his horses as Arviso secured the burros. A few paces beyond the picket rope, the saddles had been unloaded and Jenny lay in her bedroll already asleep. In the east the moon was beginning to rise and a gust of wind swept across the desert floor.

After gathering some branches for the morning fire, Bucklin ducked under the rope and walked quietly to the saddles, but suddenly drew up short as another gust of sultry breeze stirred the dark night. His bedroll and Navajo blanket had been neatly rolled out alongside Jenny's and the distance between them was scarcely a matter of inches.

"Cover your woman good," said Arviso a few steps behind him. "Rain come."

Stashing the wood under one of the saddles, Bucklin knelt down next to Jenny, eyeing the short distance between the blankets. It was dark and she was exhausted, but Jenny Mason would not allow such things to overcome her judgment. There could be no mistake, no doubt. On this night at least, she *wanted* him close to her.

Wondering about the blankets and how they had been arranged, Bucklin unbuckled his Colts and laid them next to where his head would be. Maybe it meant nothing, perhaps she knew it was going to rain or was it that she feared the Indian? Taking the Sharps from the saddle boot he stared at the sleeping figure next to him then carefully laid the rifle between them. Next to it he placed the shotguns. Whatever her reason it was based on trust...and possibly a delicate friendship. He could only hope.

After gently tucking Jenny's Navajo down over her feet and up over her shoulders, he rolled himself in his blanket and slid his Navajo over it. With his eyes on the stars and a breeze churning the cooling air, Bucklin tried to savor the moment, to realize how much she had changed, how far she had come...and how much he enjoyed her nearness.

Overhead the dark clouds of a brewing desert storm crept in to blot out the stars and in the distance an ominous flash of lightning lit up the northern horizon.

He struggled to keep his eyes open, but his thoughts drifted with the wind and Jenny's calm, even breathing quickly lulled him into a peaceful sleep, a sleep without dreams.

CHAPTER TEN

T he brunt of the downpour had fallen a few miles to the north and by morning the sky was cold and cloudless. Only the dripping shrubs and the rain-packed sand showed any signs of the storm that had thundered through half the night. And true to Burns' claim, the Navajo blankets made for a dry bed and good sleep.

After taking the branches from under the saddle, Jenny made a fire and put on coffee, then saddled the two bays while Bucklin helped Arviso load the pack train. When the work was done they returned to stand by the dwindling fire as they sipped steaming coffee and ate dried peaches and jerked beef.

"Today," said Arviso, breaking the damp silence, "we in land of Navajo. Navajo all way to river of San Juan. Reach Fort before sundown this day."

Bucklin glanced at Jenny then at Arviso. "You planning on stopping at Fort Defiance?"

"*Si*," grunted Arviso, "Good trade with Old Man William Leonard at fort. He have trade post there. See maybe Che Dodge. Him speak good English, only Navajo. Father white man since he small boy."

Throwing the dregs of his coffee into the ashes, Bucklin frowned to himself. "I'll have to think on it."

Arviso shrugged and took one last gulp from his tin cup. "Old Man William Leonard good trade," he repeated, then started for his burros.

Looking into Bucklin's troubled eyes, Jenny asked, "What is it, Sam? What's wrong?"

Bucklin shifted his weight from one leg to the other and began shoving sand over the smoldering ashes with his moccasined foot. "There's things I ain't told you, things that might cause trouble. Maybe not now, but later on."

"Can you tell me what it is?"

Watching Arviso until he mounted his paint horse, Bucklin answered softly. "I killed a white man back in Texas. Folks there know it weren't a murder, but there's others, others that are on their way to Fort Defiance, that say different. If they hear Sam Bucklin come through they'd send soldiers to fetch me back.

"On the other hand, if Harry talked, and I 'magine he did, the army from Fort Sumner has already sent a rider there telling them about a gun trader named Buck Samuels. And what's more, if the army finds out you was a captive, they'd make it a point to take you back to your blood kin."

"You could use another name," reasoned Jenny. "And I could go in...as your wife. They needn't know any more than what we tell them."

Shaking his head, Bucklin disagreed. "They'll have a, description of me. The name I use won't matter none too much."

"Then we won't go in," said Jenny simply. "We can wait for Jesus to start out again and then join back up with him."

Bucklin motioned toward the bays and as the two of them swung into their saddles, he scowled uneasily. "Jenny, it's going to get rough from here on out. Harder riding, more doing without food and water and sleep. And it'll be a sight more dangerous.

"I was thinking that now we'd met up with Jesus it might be best if you go to the fort. You could tell Jesus what you remember about the Injun's hideout and with his help I'm sure I could find it. You could go back to your kin-folks."

Jenny's cold blue eyes flared with shock then gradually narrowed into reflections of anguish and confusion. "I thought you understood, Sam. I can't go back. Not now, not ever! And I won't go anywhere without Tommy!"

Pausing briefly, her voice trailed off painfully. "Or you, Sam. I thought...I thought you understood."

Bucklin's saddle creaked as he turned. Facing Jenny, he studied her closely. "Fact is," he said, "I don't understand nothing lately...Five years ago, I lost my family, my baby, and my wife. I've had only blood in my eyes ever since. I thought about only one thing and did only one thing. A few weeks ago I was in Texas thinking I'd done all I could, but then come to find out there was maybe one more scalp to take. And it may be the one I dearly wanted most of all, the one from the Injun that killed my baby.

"Everyone I cared about was dead. And except for the hate that burned in me, I thought I was dead inside...then you came along.

"I scraped the bottom of the barrel looking for that last Injun, but never could find him and now it's you that can lead me to him. I can't rest till he's paid for his crime and I can't risk your life trying to kill him. But without taking you along there's a chance, maybe a good chance, I may not find him or your child." Bucklin sighed, then looked down at the ground.

"I do better alone...but being close to you brings a comfort I thought I'd never see again. No, Jenny, I don't understand. I don't understand nothing at all!"

The lines of frustration faded from Jenny's face. "We can work something out, Sam, something that will help us both. We have all day to come up with a solution."

Lowering her head, Jenny hesitated. As a fragile smile tugged at her lips, she glanced up. "And what you said, about how you feel when we are close...I feel much the same way. And that's...that's partly what I hoped you would understand."

Watching Arviso's burros cutting a dark trail into the smooth wet sand, Bucklin frowned thoughtfully. "Jenny, you been through a terrible ordeal. Your life's been busted up bad and some of the pieces ain't never gonna come back. Others of them won't quite fit back together like they used to, but you're a strong woman and you'll pull through.

"You're a fine woman, Jenny Mason, a fine lady. And any fool can see you come from a well-to-do family. When you get Tommy back and you're safe and sound...you'll start to see things different. And then I'll look different. It won't be long after, 'till you'll be ready to take up where you left off.

"You're feeling poorly now and have a powerful yearning to get back your child and that's only natural. I admire you for it and I respect you as much as I do any woman I ever knew. I'll be taking nothing from you nor asking for anything in return for favors, save the pride of having done you a service in your time of need."

The meager curve to Jenny's lips disappeared and her brow wrinkled with bewilderment. She urgently wanted to respond, to reassure him, but his words had a ring of truth and before she could gather her thoughts, Bucklin galloped out in front. As he motioned for her to follow, Jenny's smile slowly returned, only this time it had grown with confidence. "Sam Bucklin," she said to herself, "prince or pauper, no woman could hope to have a better man."

Three hours past noon Arviso halted his burros abruptly. As he leaned low from his saddle to study the trail below, Bucklin pulled his shotgun and galloped forward to join him.

A set of tracks broke the rain-crusted sand but now were completely dry. Shortly after the rain had stopped that morning, six shod horses had ridden toward them from the north, then suddenly charged off the trail to the northeast. From the west at least a dozen ponies had crossed their path at a full run. With their bare hooves pounding heavily into the red earth, their tracks quickly merged with those they pursued and angled in a wide arc toward the rocky bluffs that broke the horizon two miles ahead.

"No good," muttered Arviso, pointing to the upturned earth.

Bucklin nodded gravely. "Looks like a Yankee patrol got itself into trouble."

"Army come to Zuni always with wagon," grumbled the Navajo. "Why army come, no wagon?"

Glancing uneasily at Jenny as she rode up next to him, Bucklin answered, "Not 'nough of them to be out hunting Injuns. And with no wagon to truck it, they ain't likely after grain."

"No grain. No Injuns," agreed Arviso. "Maybe bandits. Juan Garza, maybe."

"Could be," said Bucklin warily, "or somebody else."

After explaining to Jenny what the tracks meant, he looked over the desert then saw the bluffs. "You think they're headed for those rocks up yonder?'

"*Si.* They go to rock with hole in it. Old pueblo there and water. Good place make fight."

"How far to the fort?'

"Too far to run for soldiers."

Bucklin wiped the back of his hand across his forehead. "How close will we be coming to that spot, to the rock with the hole?"

"Our trail go to water. Rock with hole in it only water before fort."

Jenny looked down at the tracks then at the rock formation in the distance. "Do you think the soldiers made it that far?"

"If they didn't," shrugged Bucklin, "there's no sense fretting over what come of them. Only chance they got is to get to cover and even then that chance ain't none too good with Apaches on your tail. They don't attack 'less they thought it all out and figured they was going to win. And there's no worse Injun to have to fight."

"Then what do we do?" asked Jenny.

"We go ahead slow and at the ready, but hope the skirmishing is over by the time we get there. Else we'll have a fight that's none of our business... unless it's Cabeza Blanca's band we meet."

Arviso's dark eyes flickered at the comment, but he made no other gesture of interest. After a thoughtful pause, he adjusted the Mexican pistol in his waistband, then nudged his paint cautiously up the trail.

Making frequent stops to listen and scour the terrain with binoculars, over an hour passed before the spring was in sight. Around it grew several large Cypress trees as well as a scattering of sage and greasewood. Beyond the trees a massive wall of red sandstone jutted vertically from the desert floor and in its center a gaping fifty foot hole opened into the blue sky behind it like a huge round window.

Directly below the opening at the base of the rock wall stood several crumbling breastworks of flat stone, the only remains of an ancient Indian dwelling. In front of it a dead horse lay on its side with a scalped soldier pinned under it and from the largest cypress a ghostly whisp of smoke swirled into view.

As they waited and listened from a safe distance, a low pitched wail echoed off the red bluff and drifted mournfully out into the empty desert.

"They're gone," said Bucklin, breaking the long silence. "We can go on in."

"But didn't you hear that?' whispered Jenny. "I heard something."

"I heard, Jenny, and so did Jesus. When we get close and I tell you to stop, you best stop right there and stay put. They left at least one of them alive up there and they only do that for one reason."

"What reason? Why would they leave him behind and not kill him?"

"Some Injun like kill slow," offered Arviso. "Apache much like."

Jenny grew increasingly agitated. "What do you mean?" she asked as her breathing grew more rapid. "What does he mean, Sam?"

"He means," began Bucklin callously, then realizing Jenny's growing concern hesitated. "Well, it's best not to know too much. You been through enough already. You don't need to see no more you'll have to forget, so just stay back when I say."

Jenny put her hand on Bucklin's arm. "But they took my husband alive. He was wounded, but he could have lived if...what did they do to him, Sam? What happened to him?"

"They killed him, Jenny," said Bucklin. "But please don't ask me no more than that. Just let's let the dead rest. We'll clear the slate when the time comes."

As they neared the spring, Bucklin dismounted and after helping Jenny down, handed her the shotgun and the horse's reins. "Keep a lookout," he warned, then slid the Sharps from its leather.

With Arviso at his side and the rifle loaded, Bucklin went first to the cypress where he'd seen the smoke. Rounding the far side, he found what he'd learned to expect. He had seen it before, but his gut still twisted with repugnant hatred.

Dangling by the tendons of his bloody ankles the body of a young soldier spun slowly over the ashes of a smoldering fire. Clenched into white fists, his hands had been tied behind his back. With eyes bulged in a terrified stare, his gray-blue lips hung open loosely and curved into a grisly smile. His ears had been cut out and where yellow hair once grew, a fire blackened skull protruded through a ring of charred flesh.

Swearing bitterly, Bucklin cut the rawhide off the ankles as he and Arviso eased the corpse to the ground.

"That's two accounted for," muttered Bucklin. Reading the tracks that pointed to the old pueblo, he started up the slight incline. "The rest of them will be up there."

Seventy paces further they passed the third body and dead horse. A few feet beyond was the first stone wall and sprawled behind it two more men lay in the blood-soaked sand. Both had been shot and scalped then stripped of their boots and clothing.

"At least these died easy," said Bucklin, then turned to check on Jenny.

Sitting in the shade of the horses with her arms locked worriedly around her knees, she flinched sharply as another moan hauntingly filled the air. She knew the cruelty of the Apache villages, but knew nothing of what occurred outside their confines. From Juan Garza she had learned of her husband's death, but until today she had not allowed her thoughts to wonder beyond that tragic fact.

"*Señor*," called Arviso from deeper inside the ruins. "Here soldier."

Hopping over the wall in front of him, Bucklin worked his way through the deserted rooms until he came to a courtyard. Stripped and laying face upward, the sixth man had been tied to stakes pounded into the rocky floor. His lips were cracked, his white skin baked red by the sun and dozens of yucca spines protruded from the soles of his feet and palms of his hands.

"He live," said Arviso. "No hurt bad."

Bucklin stood next to the tortured soldier for a brief moment, then knelt down beside him and took out his knife, but before he cut him free, Arviso stopped him.

"No cut now. Take out yucca, then cut. No have to hold down."

Grunting his approval, Bucklin sheathed the knife and started tearing the slivers of cactus from the soldier's hands as Arviso returned to his pack animals for water and bandages. Each time a spine was ripped from the tender flesh the half-conscious soldier jerked painfully, but rarely did he cry out. And in a matter of minutes the punctured skin was free of the bloody barbs.

After dressing the lone survivor in clothes gathered from the scattered dead, Arviso bandaged his hands and feet while Bucklin dribbled water past his dry crusty lips.

Taking a close look at the soldier for the first time, Bucklin started to swear, "Sergeant Wilkins."

At the sound of his name, the soldier's eyes weakly rolled open then closed.

"You know?" asked Arviso.

"Met him once," admitted Bucklin. "He's a sergeant from Fort Sumner."

Arviso bent over for a closer look. "Bosque Redondo soldier," he snorted in surprise. "See him on Long Walk."

"Well, he won't be doing no walking for a while," said Bucklin, then with Arviso's help hoisted the sergeant into the saddle of one of the extra horses and steadied him from both sides. "And if he can't sit his saddle we'll have to cinch him up behind me. We can't wait around for him to come to."

The water and jostling of the short ride down to where Jenny waited was enough to arouse Wilkins and as the horse came to a stop, his glazed eyes began to focus on what appeared to be two Indians holding him by the arms and legs. His eyes next wandered to Jenny and there, in dazed confusion, they held for several seconds before returning to those who held him up. This time he recognized the one on his left as friendly.

"Navajo? Dine?"

"*Si*," answered Arviso, then, seeing he could hold his balance, handed him the water.

Pawing the canteen with his bandaged hands, Wilkins gulped thirstily as the water spilled past the corners of his parched mouth and down through the dark whiskers on his neck. After heaving a sigh of relief, he rested the canteen on the pommel of the saddle and squinted at Jenny.

"Your wife?" he asked, then turned to Bucklin and squinted again.

For several seconds Wilkins did not move except to blink his eyes into better focus, but then his face twisted with hatred. "Damn. Damn my soul, if it ain't you, Samuels. You that got us all killed."

Bucklin's eyes were cold. "You got me mixed together with somebody else. I got nothing to do with this here."

Wary and unsure of his predicament, Wilkins made no reply, but Arviso confirmed Bucklin's story. "Him no kill," he said waving a finger in the air then pointing to the back-trail, "we far south this day morning."

"Can you ride?" asked Bucklin.

Wilkins sneered defiantly, "Where to?"

After sliding the Sharps back into place and helping Jenny mount up, Bucklin turned. "Fort Defiance."

"You? You're taking me back?" asked Wilkins incredulously.

"That's right," said Bucklin.

Wilkins paused, his eyes flickering with the thought of vengeance. "I can make it all right," he said enticingly as he nudged his mount to a walk, "and them at the fort would be mighty impressed. They'd look mighty favorable on what you done for the army today."

"Hold up," whispered Bucklin, riding alongside the Navajo. "I got words that need to be said and I don't want the sergeant to hear."

Arviso obligingly tightened his reins and allowed Wilkins to gain distance. Bucklin paused for a moment as the sergeant worked his way down the rocky trail. Taking a deep breath, he let it out slowly and shoved his hat back off his forehead. "He can make it on his own from here, but before you go on in I best lay some things out plain and simple.

"I ain't no trader, never have been one and my name ain't Buck Samuels. It's Sam Bucklin. I came to this territory to find Cabeza Blanca and to maybe kill him. All Apache warriors are my enemy."

Jesus Arviso glared stoically at the white man next to him, but said nothing. In his long silence, Jenny rode up to join them. Frowning worriedly, she asked, "What's wrong?"

Neither man answered for several seconds, then, with his penetrating black eyes riveted on Bucklin, the Indian spoke calmly. "Why enemy of all Apache have buffalo shield of Apache warrior?"

Reaching for the shield that hung from his saddle, Bucklin brushed the red dust from the faded painted symbols. "This was dropped by an Apache the day a band of them murdered my family and violated my sister. I use it like any Injun would, to turn bullets and arrows and sometimes a war club. It is useful to me...and a reminder of that day."

At the sight of the symbols, the Navajo's eyes flashed for an instant, but the change was almost imperceptible. With his expression softening slightly, he said, "Sam Bucklin speak truth. Kill Cabeza Blanca! For you, for Navajo, for all Dine."

Nodding in relief at Arviso's reaction, Bucklin replied, "Could be I'll do just that, but to do it I got to get close, like only a trader can do. I know how to do that, but there's something more to it now that I met Miss Jenny. This band took her boy child and I got to fetch him out too. She knows where the hideout is and how to get to it, but with what all's happened to the army patrol I'll have to light a shuck. I got to move fast 'cause they'll be after me.

"They'll tell you I trade guns to hostiles, but it ain't true. But it's best for now if they keep on believing that. It may help me out if Cabeza Blanca hears the army's after me for such. Anyway, now that things have changed it'll be too dangerous to take Jenny along with me."

"Sam," cried Jenny, her eyes full of shock, but Bucklin only raised his voice.

"But I don't want her at the fort or anywhere they can find her. I need a safe place for her to wait for me. She's been to their camp and can tell somebody that knows that country just where it is."

"You can't, Sam," protested Jenny. "I have to take you to Tommy, we have to hurry. We can't take chances on you getting lost. There's not enough time. You promised, Sam, you promised to take me with you."

Avoiding her eyes, Bucklin gazed into the remnants of a yellow-orange sunset. His saddle leather creaked as he shifted his weight and his brow wrinkled with a hint of confusion. "Jenny," he said, "it's been a long time since I cared about anybody but myself. And that's partly what's kept me alive. I can't be hunting Apaches and fretting over you at the same time. You'd be doing us both a favor by staying behind where I know you're out of harm's way... and besides that, what I got to do, what I been doing for all these years, ain't fit for you to see. I don't want you to have to carry it with you all the rest of our lives."

"Talk later," interrupted Arviso. "Soldiers come soon. We go to hogan. No find Jenny Mason in hogan of Navajo."

Slapping his heels into the belly of the paint, Arviso immediately turned the pack train off the trail and away from the fort. Climbing steadily to the east, with Sam and Jenny following behind, their tracks quickly vanished in a steep hillside of broken rocks. As night fell, they turned back to the north, but now rode easily along the flat top of a thousand-foot mesa.

An hour later the burros came to a halt just shy of what appeared in the darkness to be a sheer drop of several hundred feet. "Wait for moon," said Arviso, sliding to the ground. "Then walk."

Bucklin started to step down, but before he swung his leg over, he saw Jenny struggling hurriedly to get off her horse and he settled back against his cantel. When her feet touched the sand, her legs buckled only slightly but she clung to the stirrup and held herself up. After a moment she let her reins drop and walked into the night.

As she turned her back on him, Bucklin clenched his jaws and looked away, but it was no use. Before he could suppress it, a twinge of pain flickered in the darkness, a darkness where years ago a cold blanket of death had left only emptiness. Jenny Mason was a fine woman, a lady as courageous as she was beautiful. At this moment, however, feeling betrayed and helpless, she was simply a mother desperately searching for her child. And until they were brought together she would be drawn to anyone that helped her, even a homeless killer like himself. He had known it from the beginning, but still her kindness, her timid attraction to him, had kindled in him an irrepressible feeling that now had to be smothered at its first sign of life.

Having her along would only complicate matters if not get them both killed. And when he returned with her child she would eventually go back to her people, her own kind...or would she? Rubbing a hand over his face in frustration, Bucklin swore at his foolishness then gratefully caught a glimpse of the rising half-moon. "Damn my hide," he muttered bitterly, then stepped out of the saddle and checked his gear for a rough descent.

After retying a saddle string, he went to Jenny's horse and tightened the cinch. He was about to leave when he heard her footsteps approaching and on impulse decided to give the latigo a few unnecessary tugs. As she stopped behind him, he felt his stomach twist into knots. Facing her, he reached for the dangling reins. "I'm sorry, Jenny, for what you're feeling," he said. "I know how it pains you not knowing what's come of your child, fretting day and night and how it must gnaw at you, wondering if he's cold or hungry or hurt. I know what it's like, just the same as I know what it does to your insides when a lonesome wind starts to howl and somewhere out in the night you think you hear a baby, a baby all hurtful and scared, crying for its mama. Jenny, I understand how you feel. But what you want most to do ain't good for Tommy. You got to believe that. You got to stay back so I can give it my best shot."

Bucklin paused expectantly as Jenny took the reins from his hands, but she made no reply. "It's almost over, Jenny," he offered, but then, after a heavy silence, he added prophetically, "it's almost over for the both of us."

The winding path that led down off the mesa was deep, narrow, and often steep, but even in the faint moonlight Bucklin was amazed at how easy it was to follow. Even the rocks had been set aside or built into crude steps and where the rains would normally have washed it out the hillside was paved with blocks of flat sandstone. Like other Indian trails he had followed, this one had been used for generations, if not centuries, but after riding a few feet out onto the desert floor and taking a quick look back, he realized it was completely hidden from sight. Anyone not knowing of its exact location would never have guessed it existed; the thought suddenly disturbed him.

He had hunted Apaches from the woodlands of central Texas, into the parched plains, then across the rolling Llano Estacado, but this land was like nothing he had ever seen. From the flatness of open desert, blank walls of smooth sandstone jutted abruptly into the sky, towering overhead like enormous gods, while tabletop mesas broke the skyline with crumbling pillars of rock and twisted spires of stone. And in the confusion of shattered debris and sheer cliffs, even the clearest of trails could be hidden from sight, trails that would undoubtedly lead to hidden lookouts.

If this country was any indication of what lay ahead, the slightest daytime movement would be visible for miles in almost any direction. With virtually no vegetation for cover, he would have to ride only at night, or out in the open as a trader, pretending his presence was nothing he cared to hide. But if he rode openly, as Harry must have done, he would have no options. There would be no choice, but to go directly into the camp of Cabeza Blanca and hope to be accepted as Harry's replacement. If they didn't believe him, they would kill him. But if they did accept him, would they be willing to trade for Tommy? And if Cabeza Blanca was the scalp that had always eluded him, the one that haunted him most, what then? Bucklin swore under his breath as Arviso rode up to what appeared to be an eight-foot-high pile of dirt and sticks and dismounted. From the far side of the mound a faint light shown out into the night illuminating a long strip of the red sand and a few ghostlike branches of sage.

"Hogan," grunted Arviso. "My woman. You, your woman stay night here."

Sliding on her belly, Jenny eased herself down from the saddle to the ground. Letting her reins drop, she followed Arviso through a five-foot-high rectangular opening that led into the dwelling. From the top of the hogan, a faint whisp of smoke curled into the cool air and from inside voices spoke in a tongue resembling Apache and yet too different to be the same language. After tying his horses to some of the larger branches that lined the outside of the crude hut, Bucklin ducked inside, then stepped to the side, not wanting to silhouette himself in the doorway. In the center of the dirt floor a small fire burned and on the ceiling was a square smoke hole.

The edges of the hogan were lined with clean sheepskins and sitting on one of them was an attractive squaw clothed in a blanket-dress. Around her neck hung several shell necklaces and circling her waist was a belt of large silver discs. She wore leggings on her feet, and just beyond a tarnished silver wrist bracelet, a cigarette burned between her fingers. As Arviso spoke to her quietly, her black eyes moved slowly from Bucklin to Jenny, then back again, until they finally came to rest on Jenny.

After the Navajo squaw took a puff on her cigarette, she grunted and Arviso motioned for them to be seated. "My woman cook. You eat. I go to fort, talk to soldiers or they look for Jesus Arviso. Make trouble, maybe."

"Do they know where this place is?" asked Bucklin as he sat and folded his legs. "Where it is you live?"

Arviso smiled. "Army know nothing. Many Navajo, few soldier." Going to the small door, he bent over and paused. "You stay. Maybe I come back, maybe one more. Then we make ready you go."

Bucklin nodded uneasily and Arviso stepped out into the night. The woman tossed a small bundle of sticks onto the fire and in seconds the room brightened. The fine red dust on Jenny's cheeks was streaked with dried tears and seeing it, Sam Bucklin felt his stomach sour.

It was doubtful the squaw spoke any English and one glance at Jenny told him what he already knew, so for the next two hours they ate and sat in absolute silence. The fire crackled warmly and outside a horse occasionally blew and shifted its weight, but inside the hogan the air was heavy with bitter disappointment.

At last a wandering breeze drifted through the crude door, turning the stale air and offering a degree of relief, but a moment later one of the horses whinnied. Then in the distance another horse answered.

Instantly Bucklin scrambled through the door, barely making it to his feet before lunging into the blackness and jerking his 10-gauge from its scabbard. Running a few feet farther into the desert, he slid to the ground next to a small bush and rolled onto his stomach. With every sense alert, he cocked both ears of the shotgun then froze into a quiet indistinguishable shadow.

A few seconds later he heard a hoof kick a rock no more than fifty yards in front of him. "Hello to you in the hogan," called a voice from the same direction. "Jesus Arviso, a friend, has sent me. Sam Bucklin, I come in peace and I am alone. I am coming to the hogan with a message. I come slowly. Do not shoot."

Riding into view, a single horseman worked his way toward the doorway, stopping in front of it and allowing the firelight to make him an easy target. Slight of build and no more than five-foot-six, the man dismounted and, deliberately holding his hands away from his sides, stepped closer to the entry then stopped and waited. He wore a flat-brimmed hat and white man's clothes.

From inside the hogan the Navajo woman spoke and the answer was returned in Navajo. After a short pause, the words came again in English. "My name is Che Dodge. I have been invited to come in. The woman knows me well."

There was a long gun in the saddle boot, but the man wore no pistol or knife that Bucklin could see and by now Jenny would have her Derringer close at hand. She would be safe enough, so he let Che Dodge go on in, yet waited several minutes before making even the slightest movement.

The hogan was small with no windows and only one way in and out. It would make a perfect trap. He had always avoided anything even resembling one and the habit had saved his life more than once. Taking chances in Indian country was an invitation to death, but now there was more at stake than his own scalp...He had sworn an oath on the graves of those he loved to avenge their brutal murders, yet he had also given his word to Jenny that he would rescue her son. Keeping his promise was the last thing he could do for his family and it was the only thing he could do for Jenny. But trying to honor both commitments was pushing him to the edge.

Coming to his feet, Bucklin prowled deeper into the night, then warily circled the hogan, stopping every three or four steps to listen before going on. When he was satisfied no one was near, he eased the hammers of the shotgun down and went to the horse of Che Dodge. Taking the carbine from the saddle, he leaned it against the dark side of the hogan before ducking back inside.

Jenny leaned uneasily against the far wall with the Derringer laying clearly in her lap while the young man calling himself Che Dodge sat cross-legged next to Arviso's squaw, smoking a clay pipe. His hair, although cut short, was coarse black and his brown skin matched a pair of deep-set eyes.

As Bucklin stepped inside, he glanced up, then stared curiously.

"I'm Che Dodge," he said again, "and I'm alone."

Moving away from the doorway, Bucklin hitched his Colts into a better position, then sat down carefully. "What happened to Arviso?" he asked pointedly. "Where is he?"

"Still at Fort Defiance. Thought he might be followed so he sent me back instead." Dodge paused and puffed on his pipe. Gazing through the small cloud of smoke, his eyes narrowed appraisingly. "The army wants you mighty bad, say they'll hang you when they catch you." He took another leisurely puff then blew it out slowly. "A couple of peace commissioners come in yesterday with a U.S. marshal. They all want you in chains so they can cart you back to Texas to stand trial for murder. And Jesus tells me you just killed three of Juan Garza's men right in front of him, a matter Garza won't take kindly to at all."

Che Dodge paused and smiled. "Seems you're a man with a long past and a short future."

"A man lives long enough," growled Bucklin, "he makes some enemies. And I'm thinking you might just be one of them. Why'd he pick you to come looking for me?"

"He told me you was bound and determined to ride into the hornets' nest and needed somebody to come listen to your woman, then point the way. Only an Injun can do that and outside of Jesus, I'm the only Navajo in the whole tribe that speaks English."

"Che Dodge don't sound Navajo to me," said Bucklin skeptically.

"My father is Perry Williams and my mother is Navajo. Our place is four miles west of the fort at the mouth of a canyon. I'm the official interpreter for the fort and you're lucky I was there tonight."

"Why's that?"

"Sergeant Wilkins and his patrol stopped at the fort yesterday hunting you and telling how they been chasing all over after you. But nobody there cared too much. They got enough trouble just trying to feed everybody.

"Those peace commissioners weren't interested neither. Only that marshal asked them a few questions. But when Wilkins rode in tonight and told what all happened to his men and tied you in with it, they all pricked up their ears. Wasn't long before they pieced it together that Buck Samuels and Sam Bucklin was one in the same and wanted by all of them. By the time Jesus rode in, they were all worked up and started throwing questions at him from all sides.

"Old Jesus didn't bat an eye, just kept saying *no comprende, no comprende* until that Flitcher fella, that commissioner, pretty near had a frothy spell. They called me over to interpret in Navajo since none of them spoke Spanish either. And right there under their noses Jesus told me what he wanted done."

Bucklin studied the boyish-looking Navajo who suddenly seemed older than his years. "With all that was being said, how come you believe Arviso and side with him against the army and a pair of Washington people?"

"Two things," answered Dodge flatly. "That you were after Cabeza Blanca, an enemy of my people, and the mention of you being Sam Bucklin. My father travels often to the east and it's a name he's talked about in connection with the Apaches and Comanches."

Satisfied with Dodge's explanation, Bucklin sighed heavily as the tension left his shoulders. His eyes wandered to Jenny who had been listening intently. Pointing to her, he said, "This is not my woman. She's a lady. Her son's a captive in Cabeza Blanca's rancheria and I intend to get him back to her. She knows where the camp is and how to get to it, but I don't want her along having to show me the way." Bucklin paused, hoping Jenny would look his way, but after several seconds, he gave up, but chose his next words carefully. "And for the sake of her son, to give him his best chance of coming home…she will tell you everything she can about that country, the mountains, valleys, streams, washes, bushes, smells…the winds, sunrise and sunset, colors, shapes, animals, and birds. Everything. Then you can tell me where it is and how to get there by the fastest trails. Then I can get Tommy back as soon as can be."

After a prolonged silence, Jenny raised her head. Her eyes were clear and piercing as she looked at Bucklin, but the anger had faded into a quiet strength. "I will tell you what I can, but if you do not know the place, I will go there myself to point the way, even if I have to go with the military."

Che Dodge muttered something to Arviso's squaw and as she got up he said to Jenny, "That would likely get your youngin' killed. Lots of times captives are killed in a crossfire or are done in by the Injuns at the first sign of attack. Some Injuns would sooner kill their captives as give them back to the army. They see it as a sign of weakness."

The Navajo woman brought several small clay pots and set them down in front of Dodge and then cleared a wide area on the smooth-packed floor of the hogan. As Jenny began describing all the landmarks she could recall, Dodge began trickling colored sand from the palm of his hand onto the floor. Occasionally he would interrupt her with a question, but as she talked she remembered more detail than she thought possible and continually added bits and forgotten pieces as she went on.

Bucklin watched in amazement as the colored sand began to take form and where there had been nothing but dirt a red mountain would appear, then green sage and blue springs. There were dark shadows cast by the sun and streaks of brown where dry arroyos cut the desert and in several places where Jenny knew nothing, Dodge filled in more detail until after two hours' work, the sand painting was as good a map as Bucklin had ever seen.

Even Jenny sat back in bewilderment. "Do you know the place, this place, just as you've drawn it here?'

Dodge nodded, but with a puzzled look on his face. "It is a valley to the north. It is reached by following Chinle Creek. There is no other place like it, but we have looked there before for Cabeza Blanca and have not found him. And you say he is there. And from what you have told me, there can be no mistake."

Bucklin got up and squatted next to the painting. "So much of this country looks alike. How can you be so sure? Most of it looks like hell with the flames gone out."

Pointing to the rock formations near the center of the map, Dodge answered, "These rocks that she said looked like a left and right hand sticking up out of the ground and this one that looks like a chicken setting on eggs don't leave any doubt. This rock here we even have a name for, Yei Bi Chai.

This is the place all right. It is the valley of many legends, of gods and the home of the Navajo devil Chende. Some say it is a place of spirits. You'll see. You will know when you are there."

Suddenly with the same thought, both men glanced up at Jenny. It was Che Dodge who spoke first. "You have told us all but one thing. Where's the rancheria?"

Fighting an abhorrent flood of memories, Jenny Mason came to her knees and extended a trembling hand. Bending low over the map, she reluctantly pointed a finger then depressed it into a triangular pile of red sand opposite what represented three tall spires of rock.

"On that mesa?" questioned Dodge incredulously. "On top of the mesa?'

Jenny nodded weakly.

"I'll be damned," exclaimed Dodge in a half-whisper. "They must have found a way up, a trail even horses could use. No wonder we couldn't find them."

"How far's that from here," asked Bucklin as he read the lines in Jenny's tormented expression, "considering I'll be riding by day instead of night."

"A half-day's ride to the northwest," said Dodge, using his pipe as a pointer, "you'll run into Chinle wash. That you follow north for another full day until you see a long ridge, that looks like a big hair comb, off to the west. Along in there another wash takes out directly west. Cut through that comb ridge and this here mesa is ten miles or so straight ahead. I'd say a day and a half or two days if you go by day. If you live that long."

"I'm going straight in and making no sign of trying to hide," said Bucklin. "They'll know I come for a purpose and that'll make them curious enough to let me get close enough to parlee. Then I'll tell them I come to trade."

Dodge was skeptical. "And they'll believe you?"

"I have a name," said Bucklin calmly, "a name nobody knows, but them and me and one other'n. That'll convince them."

"Your life," shrugged Dodge. "Cabeza Blanca is the worst of the Apache and you know as well as anybody what that can mean. But Jesus said you would go, so he sent along something for you."

"What?"

"It's on the horse," said Dodge starting to get up, but was stopped by Bucklin's waving hand.

"I'll fetch it." said Bucklin. "What is it?"

"Jesus says it's the best weapon to throw against the Apache," answered Dodge with a faint smile. "It's hanging off to the side of my saddlehorn."

After carefully backing out of the hogan door, Bucklin returned in a matter of seconds with two brown jugs dangling from a rawhide thong. "Whiskey?'

"Sort of. It's tiswin. The Apaches brew it from corn and drink it whenever they can get their hands on some. It works fast, wears off slow, and a little of it goes a long ways."

Bucklin nodded approvingly. "I can use it," he said, then set the jugs down and squatted by the map studying it closely. "Did Arviso tell you the lady was to stay here?"

"Yeah, he did."

"It's her decision to keep put or go as she pleases and whatever she does is her own business. Nobody's to know she's here, nobody at all." Bucklin paused, then without taking his eyes from the map, added sternly, "And if any harm comes to her...for any reason...I'll kill whoever's to blame, white, brown, or red."

Dodge glanced at Jenny admiringly. "Jesus said as much. And more or less said he'd do the same thing. The Navajo respect a fighter, especially one that kills their enemy. Your woman...the lady...will be plenty safe."

"What about the squaws?" asked Bucklin, his eyes still scanning the details of the map. "You best tell them all to leave her be or the same thing goes for them."

"Navajo women aren't that way," replied Dodge with restrained indignation. "They don't torture captives and they're not beaten or butchered like they are in other tribes. They don't even saddle their husband's horses. They're treated well, not like slaves. Here it is the women that own the sheep of the family, not the men. We are Dine, the People."

Finally looking up, Bucklin gazed at the squaw for a moment. She was clean and her hair was neat. There was a look of confidence about her and one of satisfaction. The hogan was well organized and the edges were lined with clean beds of soft sheepskins and brightly colored blankets. There was no smell of human filth or decaying animals.

Coming to his feet, Bucklin said, "If all that's so, your folks won't have a hard time walking the white man's road. For those that don't choose to do that, there's only one thing to do with them."

Che Dodge sneered and tossed a stick into the dwindling fire. "The white man's road: Starvation and being treated like animals, herded back and forth across the country. They give out tags to men who used to hunt and fight so they can come in and get cheated out of food that's been promised and never comes. Some of the women have to dig for roots and the children go hungry.

"The Navajo have been beaten, but those like Victorio and Red Wasp, they will never take up your white man's road."

"You talk like you admire those two," said Bucklin, "and they're Apaches, your enemies."

"Sure they are, but they're at least Indian. Anyone able to keep fighting the white man is considered big medicine and a great warrior, somebody that's talked about around the campfires when the spirits are low.

"I was at a peace conference as an interpreter once and I heard Red Wasp speak and no other chief ever said it better. He stood up in the council and told how the paleface robbed them of their hunting grounds, destroyed their game, brought disease, stirred up his people, made whores of their wives, destroyed their traditions, and made orphans of their children. He said he fought for his former freedom, he fought for his wives and children, and he would keep on fighting for the love of all the gore. And he meant every word."

Considering what Dodge had said, Bucklin was quiet for several minutes.

When he finally spoke, his voice was unusually subdued.

"They say we lost more'n two hundred thousand men in the war and the north lost six hundred thousand more. All them died fighting over who owned this country and how it was going to be run and now it's all done from Washington. It was them that told us farmers there was land to settle out west, land that eight hundred thousand men got kilt fighting over the ownership of. I brung my family and we ruint nobody's game, or tradition or anything else, but they came and murdered my ma and pa, my brother, and my wife. They took my sister and used her as a whore until she lost her mind and then one of them hung my baby girl on a stick and let her cry, let her scream till she died."

Bucklin paused and picked up the jugs of tiswin. When he spoke again, his voice was laced with venom.

"And for that, if for nothing else, they're going to pay. The white man generally goes after the guilty, but the Injuns... they kill anybody. They kill just to kill, just for the so-called gore of it. They torture when they have the time in ways no white man ever dreamed of nor ever did in all the years of the North killing the South. Them like Red Wasp and Victorio and Cabeza Blanca live to kill. They don't plant the ground, they murder and steal their food from their neighbors and have been doing it for as far back as any of them can remember. The Apaches, Comanches, and Kiowa have been thieving and murdering down in Mexico for over two hundred years, but this here country ain't going to put up with that. They'll take the white man's ways or be killed and there's no two ways about it.

"I lost my way of life in the South, I seen my friends die and I been pushed off my land, but I ain't out torturing and murdering every Yankee man and woman and child I come across. I got no pity in me for a murderer. My family did nothing to nobody and now they're dead and, by damned, the red devils that done it won't live to cause that misery on nobody else. And where I leave off, there'll be a thousand just like me to finish the job. But right now, I got it to do and there ain't nothing going to stop me till I'm done or dead. You go tell that to your great warrior, Red Wasp, and all them like him. You tell him!"

With a smoldering rage, Bucklin stormed out of the confining hogan into the coolness of the open desert and went straight to his horses. The sand map had been thoroughly memorized and he knew where he would find Cabeza Blanca.

And now he could do it alone. There would be no encumbrances, no one to slow him down and no one to witness the savagery that lay ahead. He was free!

After looping the jugs onto the trailing horse, Bucklin checked the cinches of each saddle with a jerk, but instead of stepping into his stirrup, he hesitated as a gentle gust of wind brushed the heat from his face. He had not said goodbye to Jenny and the thought suddenly troubled him.

From the darkness he looked inside at Jenny. Her face was turned toward the door and softly illuminated by firelight. She was beautiful.

She had suffered beyond imagination, yet somehow had held onto her sanity and her dignity. She had counted on him, trusted him, but in her mind he had betrayed her and next to the loss of his family, nothing had affected Sam Bucklin so deeply.

With the heat once again flushing his skin, he said in a low, painful voice, "Goodbye, Jenny. Goodbye."

Bucklin turned the horse's head to the north and nudged him with his knees. Forcing his eyes ahead, he fought down the urge to turn and take one last look at Jenny.

Had he turned back he would have seen her face fill with concern at the sound of his departure, then notice her lips as they whispered a silent farewell.

CHAPTER ELEVEN

Two hours before dawn the moon dropped from sight and the stars darkened behind a threatening blanket of clouds. Night riding in Indian country had become a way of life for Sam Bucklin, but when it turned ink black even he had to stop. At the bottom of Chinle Wash he stepped down and, unable to sleep, started water boiling for coffee.

A small fire on a dark night was something he tried to avoid for in the dim light, surrounded by ghostlike shadows, he would stare at the meager flames. As they danced hypnotically, his thoughts invariably turned inward, only to plunge him into a deep, brooding grief that would last until the break of day. But strangely, on this bleak night, he wanted to remember it all, to forget none of the gruesome details of his family's massacre.

His father, brother, and his wife had fought hard, hard enough to make the Apaches even more vicious than usual. He had found their bodies with no arms or legs and all their throats had been cut. His brother's brains lay scattered over the ground and his mother had been scalped and left for dead. In his father there were fourteen arrows ,in his brother eleven, and in his wife three. His sister had been violated and ruined. And his baby daughter…how cold she was, small and helpless and agonizingly pitiful.

He had killed all of them he could find, but tomorrow, if Cabeza Blanca was the Apache his mother had described, he would be face to face with the leader of the band that murdered and mutilated his family, the red devil himself that had taken his little girl. And if that was to be, Bucklin prayed for the opportunity to kill him Apache-style, slowly, brutally and painfully. There could be no better justice than to torture him with the same brand of savagery that had been used on his only child.

Bucklin savored the coffee, drinking it languidly as he grew more melancholy and steadily more sorrowful. But for the first time in five years, instead of being consumed by grief, he found himself relishing an irrepressible sense of satisfaction. One way or the other it would finally come to an end. And if he were to die he had no intention of dying alone.

Going directly into the rancheria went against everything he knew about staying alive, but with what Harry had given him he had a good chance of riding in without trouble. And if Cabeza Blanca had learned anything while torturing Sergeant Wilkins and his men or if he had Indian spies at Fort Defiance, the fact that he was pursued by the military would only strengthen his story of being a gun trader. Hopefully it would at least give him time to work out a trade for Jenny's child and the chance to discover if he had finally found the murderer of his daughter.

He had killed Indians other than those he hunted when it was necessary, but before killing this one he had to know for sure. There could be no long anticipated revenge, no final rest, unless his guilt was unquestionable. After that was known, Bucklin would choose the time, the place, and the method to extract an eye for an eye and gloriously take his last scalp.

As he nursed the last swallow of a second cup of coffee, the skyline in the east was turning pale yellow above a huge black mesa. The clouds had all but passed over. The day would be clear and hot.

After tossing the dregs onto the fading coals, Bucklin walked his horses up to the edge of the wash and studied the terrain. The mesa to his right, a wall of stone some ten miles from end to end, still blocked the rising sun, but ahead of him he could see the creek bottom angling off to the northwest. A few minutes later, across twenty miles of broken desert to the west, he could make out what had to be the combed ridge of mountains Dodge had described. Somewhere along its base would be a pass that led into a valley of massive red stone monuments.

Once he was on the other side of the ridge any dust his animals kicked up would be visible to Cabeza Blanca who undoubtedly controlled the entire valley. Until then he would have to keep a sharp lookout for other bands of raiding Apaches and Utes. Even the Paiutes could be dangerous to a man alone, but considering the stories he had heard of Cabeza Blanca, most Indians would likely give a wide berth to the entire region.

Bucklin, however, was habitually cautious and instinctively wary. More like a cougar than a wolf, he crept along the edge of Chinle Wash, taking nothing for granted and leaving no shadow unsearched. When he reached the fork in the creek that led to the pass it was past noon, but he had covered barely ten miles.

After leaving the main branch of Chinle Creek, he rode west in the bottom of a shallow arroyo for another hour before stopping to water his horses at a stone tank that had filled with rain. As he ate some of the dried Zuni peaches, he crouched in the shade of a juniper and glassed the pass that lay five to six miles ahead across a sea of rippling heat waves. To reach it he would have to leave the protection of the arroyo, but with the terrain relatively flat and open, the distance would be covered quickly. However, if any enemy were to appear, his Sharps would easily keep them in check.

Catching wind of the peaches, the appaloosa and sorrel nickered hungrily from the bottom of the dry creek bed and

Bucklin took one last look through the binoculars. Walking back to the horses, he emptied the sack on the edge of the tank. While the horses ate he checked the caps on his pistols, filled his canteens, and calculated his next move.

Once he was on the other side of the pass he would ride directly for the rancheria, making no attempt at concealment. It would be clear to any observer he knew where the camp was and wanted them to know he was coming. To do anything else at that point would cause suspicion and invite disaster.

The Apache needed no reason to kill him and like the Comanche and Kiowa he had seen, all too often used torture and murder merely as a devilish form of entertainment. He could do nothing to arouse their suspicions. There could be no mistakes. And under no circumstances could he be taken as a captive.

Feeling the weight of the hidden Whitney revolver against his chest, Bucklin felt a chill run up his neck, then swung a leg over the sorrel. He had seen what was left of men and occasionally even some women that had been burned alive, skinned alive, and some staked over ant hills. One prospector, who had his stomach cut open and filled with scalding hot rocks, was still alive when he found him and begged for an hour to be shot before Bucklin obliged. Since that time he had always reserved his last shot for himself.

Cutting no sign as he crossed to the pass, Bucklin briefly scanned its entrance before riding uneasily into the narrow, winding passage. A few minutes later he caught sight of the valley beyond, but drew up short of the open desert. In the shadows cast by a jagged overhang, he reached for his binoculars and brought the glasses into focus.

The two formations Jenny had described as huge left and right hands reached into the skyline only a dozen miles ahead and behind them the long table-topped mountain of the rancheria stood darkly against the horizon.

Somewhere, hidden beneath three pinnacles of stone, he would find a trail, the trail that would finally end with Cabeza Blanca.

The valley, if it could be called that, opened into a vast plane of sand, sage, and juniper from which a score of mountainous red islands shoved their craggy walls a thousand feet into the sky. At the base of each, parched stream beds ran hazardously through piles of broken talus rocks then, like roots of a tree, cut their way out into the desert basin.

Lookouts from the rancheria would be posted and in the likelihood they possessed a stolen pair of binoculars, Bucklin tied the empty peach sack to the muzzle of his Sharps. His white flag would get him close enough to deliver Harry's message, but from there on there would be no turning back.

Swearing softly as he tightened the knot, Bucklin glanced at the open country. With the butt plate of his rifle resting on his thigh and the cloth overhead, he reluctantly left the concealment of the shadowy ridge and again started for the mesa. But this time, for the first time in his life, he rode deliberately into view of a treacherous band of Apaches.

A mile out from the ridge, he dropped into a deep wash and, coming out the other side, picked up a smaller arroyo that drained the flood waters from the base of the left and right-handed mesas. After following its edge for over an hour he pulled up where it branched northwest to the hands and southwest to the rancheria.

From where he sat there was nothing along the face of the rancheria's mesa that resembled the three needlelike points Jenny and Che Dodge had drawn out, but the southern edge of the mountain was still blocked from view by a smaller formation rising just in front of him.

With the sun getting low, the air had gradually grown hazy. Where there had been none before, shadows appeared on the towering walls of stone that now, in the changing light, had turned blood-red. Black streaks filled the cracks chiseled by centuries of relentless heat and with each passing minute the monuments of stone seemed to change.

For a moment, in the glaring sunlight, haze, and shadow, Bucklin felt an unexplainable reverence as the face of each monstrous formation took on a grotesque appearance. As if stirring with ancient life, they seemed to bend and stretch and then, with unseen eyes, to stare down at his unwelcome presence.

Feeling his skin crawl, Bucklin shook off the illusions and wiped his eyes. He had not slept in two days. He blinked hard and looked again. The moment had passed and he went on following the southwest fork of the arroyo yet, strangely, he was aware that somehow he felt like a trespasser, an intruder. A mortal in a valley of stone gods.

For another half-hour Bucklin rode into the dwindling daylight as the land surrounding him continued to warp and buckle in an unearthly sea of red. Recalling what Che Dodge had said, he thought it was little wonder that the Navajo believed this to be the home of their devil. Being dwarfed by angry stone giants was enough to make anyone superstitious, but when Sam Bucklin glanced down along the mesa to his left what he saw was far more threatening than anything imagined.

Rising out of the cliffs like the tines of an enormous pitchfork and less than a half-mile away, three pillars of rock caught the last rays of the setting sun. Their black shadows streaked the desert for thousands of feet to the east and, even though their tips glowed like beacons in the sky, the entire formation could only be seen from the place where he now held his horses. Had he approached the mesa from any other direction than the one Jenny had described, he would not have found the entrance to the secret trail.

Spurring his horse to a trot, Bucklin quickly covered the last mile and made it to the west side of the pillars just as the sun left them. Leaning back on the reins, he took a moment to listen. There was no sound but he knew someone was near, near enough to hear him or, if they chose, to shoot him.

"Soy el amigo de Baychen-day-sen," he announced in a loud clear voice. "I am the friend of Long Nose. *Mi, Apache trafico.* Trade with the Apache."

After calling out, Bucklin waited several minutes for a response, moving nothing but his eyes as they searched the twilight for anything he could use.

From a shallow ravine a few feet in front of him he saw where several horses had emerged then quickly disappeared into the broken boulders at the base of the pillars. As with the trail he had ridden with Arviso, this one's path could not be seen from below, yet he was sure it was here and it somehow led up the stone wall to the rancheria.

Sitting in the open, Bucklin waited with clenched jaws. This was likely the only trail to the top of the mesa and had circumstances been different, he would have crossed the valley at night and unseen. After locating the tracks he could have waited with his Sharps and ambushed any Apache that tried to leave their stronghold. It would have been the way he preferred but, admittedly, he would never have found the trail without Jenny's help. He reminded himself that it was her son he had sworn to rescue and there was only one way to do that safely. And there was only one way he knew of to get close enough to Cabeza Blanca to judge his guilt or innocence. After he had learned that and left with Tommy, things would be different. He could always return...day or night.

The dull clatter of unshod hooves broke into his thoughts as a lone warrior rode warily out from what had looked to be an impenetrable pile of broken rubble. With an army-issue carbine leveled at Bucklin, he motioned with his hand. *"Aqui,"* he grunted, then pointed sharply at something just out of sight in the direction he had come.

Swallowing hard, Bucklin nudged the gelding and led his horses past the suspicious, black-eyed Apache into the boulders where the trail's entrance lay hidden behind the twisted gray trunk of a dead juniper. With the lookout following closely on his heels, Bucklin paused by the dead wood to take the sack from his rifle barrel and slide it into its boot.

Thankful he had been allowed to keep his weapons, he breathed a quiet sigh of relief and with a guarded sense of optimism started up the steep climb. Allowing his horse to find its own way along the narrow path, Bucklin picked out what landmarks he could and etched them in his mind. In the darkness a horse could smell its way back down, but a man unfamiliar with the terrain would easily get lost in the night. He had no idea when he might have to leave or under what conditions and in Indian country it did not pay to miss even the slightest detail.

As often as the horses stumbled, it was clear the trail they followed was not nearly as old as the one Arviso had used and since the Navajos themselves knew nothing of it, a recent storm or landslide had probably opened it up. Apache warriors weren't known for their hard work and if any part of the trail had been improved the labor would have come from their squaws or captives.

Nearing the top of the mesa, a faint breeze stirred enough to cool the sweating horses and Bucklin stopped to give them a breather. A tinge of yellow lingered above the western horizon, but the evening stars were bright. They had risen no more than seven hundred feet, yet due to the rugged terrain, the climb had taken well over a half-hour. Going down, he could shave off at best ten minutes.

"Vamos," shouted the lookout and Bucklin reluctantly spurred his tired geldings over the last fifty feet. Before he reached the plateau where the fires would have been visible, the stench of the encampment told him where the lodges would be.

Only a few yards back from the precipitous edge of the mesa a dozen squat-looking teepees were lit with smoky cook fires. Inside some, Bucklin could see the grimy faces of squaws as they peered at him, but nowhere did he see any bucks.

Riding up from behind, the lookout ordered in Spanish, *"Siga me,"* and Bucklin followed him to the largest of the teepees. Pointing at the fire burning outside its closed flap he said, *"Espere."*

Understanding he was to wait, Bucklin dismounted and ground-hitched the horses to a clump of sage nearby, then with his arms crossed, stood facing the fire. The Sharps and shotgun were now behind him and out of reach, but he had the two Colts, the hideout gun, and his knife. For now, however, he prayed he would need nothing but a good poker face and a little bit of luck. As if on signal, the heavily armed braves came in from the darkness beyond the teepees and prowled closer to the fire. Their hair, bound by a band of twisted cloth or animal hide, was coarse and thick and each wore an oversized shirt of soiled calico. A long breech cloth hung down between their legs and knee-high moccasins covered their feet. Most wore cotton pants, some had army wool and, without exception, all their eyes were black and piercing.

Bucklin glanced around at the ragged band of renegades, noticing one of them to be Ute and another a Paiute. As yet there was no one fitting the description of Cabeza Blanca, but he forced a smile. *"Buenos noches, amigos,"* he said heartily. *"Se habla ingles?"*

Shining in the firelight, their copper faces were frozen in an unreadable stare. No one spoke as they gradually surrounded him, then another Apache, as large as Bucklin himself, appeared outside the circle.

His shoulders were broad and powerful and his chest was shaped like an oak barrel. The eyes, though shaded by heavy cheekbones, were set wide apart and his lips turned down in a menacing frown. He was no more than forty, but under his hair-band a crop of gray hair covered his head.

"Where Long Nose?" demanded the gray-headed Indian as he stepped into the circle. As he walked, he favored one leg.

"In jail at Fort Sumner with a busted leg," offered Bucklin, trying his best to sound at ease. "He give me his Apache name so Cabeza Blanca would know I'm a friend to Long Nose and to the Apache. Long Nose says Cabeza Blanca will trade with the friend of Baychen-day-sen."

"Who you?" growled Cabeza Blanca.

"I'm called Buck Samuels," replied Bucklin, and at that instant knew he had said the right thing.

The Apache leader looked back toward the two tied horses for a moment then asked bluntly, "Why soldiers hunt Buck Samuels?"

Bucklin smiled half in relief and half as a bluff. Cabeza Blanca was aware the army was after him and that would only work in his favor. "Because when they caught Long Nose, me and him were together. Only I got away and Harry didn't. They been after me ever since."

For a long minute the big Apache studied Bucklin critically then with a grunt, made his decision. "What you trade? What you have?"

Nodding cooly, Bucklin went to the trail horse and lifted the jugs. "I brung tiswin," he said holding it up. "We can palaver over a drink."

Abruptly taking the jugs out of Bucklin's hands, Cabeza Blanca tossed them to a brave next to him and muttered something in Apache. After an eruption of exuberant hoops and howls, the braves hurried off to another teepee as each scrambled for his turn at the whiskey. When they had gone, the gray-haired leader sat down cross-legged by his fire and following suit, Bucklin did the same.

"Long Nose trade guns," said the Apache gruffly, "you no bring many guns. Want trade guns."

"I can get plenty of guns," assured Bucklin, "and I can trade at the posts along the river to the north where you can't go. But first we trade small. Then when I come back, I'll have many guns and ammunition."

Cabeza Blanca thought for a moment as his eyes drifted slyly toward the two hitched horses. Missing nothing, Bucklin read his thoughts and commented shrewdly, "Harry won't be coming back. Whatever you were getting from him will have to come from me now. Without me there won't be no more trade."

"I see long rifle," replied Cabeza Blanca as if killing the white man had never entered his mind.

"That's a buffalo gun, shoots-far rifle. A gun I brung for trade."

There was a long silence broken only by the increasingly intoxicated screams at the far end of the camp, then the Indian glanced once more at the horses. "Know buff'lo gun. What want for long rifle?"

Pausing only long enough to take a deep breath, then quietly letting it out, Bucklin answered slowly. "Harry made hisself a good trade with the white woman he got from here. He said her child would fetch good money at a white man's town. I'll be giving that there long gun for the boy."

Cabeza Blanca tossed a handful of dry sage roots into the small fire, then, turning to his teepee, spoke in a choppy, low pitched voice. The flap which had been closed flipped open and a short fat squaw emerged with a child in her arms. Following her, a second later, was a Mexican.

The hair on the left side of his head was missing and where it had grown an oozing patch of burned skin reflected the flickering firelight. On his face a wide, humorless smile showed off a row of white teeth and as he stepped closer to the fire, Bucklin swore. "Juan Garza."

"So it is, *Amigo*," grinned Garza, "that we meet again. It is good to see you once more."

Bucklin glanced at Cabeza Blanca, who seemed uninterested in Garza, but took the child by the arm and forcefully sat him down by his side. "Bring rifle now. Maybe we trade."

With Garza's sinister eyes following him, Bucklin retrieved the Sharps and a blanket then spread the Navajo in front of Cabeza Blanca. As the Mexican sat next to the Apache he laid the rifle down between them.

Apparently having just woken up, Tommy merely yawned and stretched. Dressed in a long cotton shirt and his white skin covered with dirt, he would easily have passed for an Indian child. Only his small, blue eyes remained to testify as to who he was.

While Cabeza Blanca examined the rifle, Garza took out a pouch of tobacco and began rolling a cigarette. "So, it is the *niño* you come for?" he smiled tauntingly. "I think maybe you don't want him for money like you say. I think you do this for the woman, you trade for her little one."

As he paused to lick the paper, Garza's lips thinned into a hateful frown. "I think maybe...I take the child. I trade for him more."

Sensing a better deal, Cabeza Blanca put the rifle down. "What trade?"

Casually picking up a burning brand, Garza lit his smoke and glared across at Bucklin. "Three army rifles."

The Apache raised three fingers. "Three rifle?"

"Si, Amigo. Tres."

While Cabeza Blanca thought about the offer, Bucklin felt the heat rising in his face. "What use do you have for a child?"

"For the woman who did this to me," snapped Garza, pointing to his scorched head, "I take her child. Then you see me cut his throat. After that you take him to her. No one, no one does such a thing to Juan Garza."

Before the Indian could make up his mind, Bucklin quickly interrupted. "I brung more to trade," he said with an unusual calmness, then came to his feet and went to the far side of the horses.

From his lead horse, he took the double-barreled shot-gun and, after making sure both caps were in place, untied the buffalo shield and loosened the reins from the sage. He had little else he could bargain with and time was running out. There was only one thing left to do if he was to save Tommy's life.

Kneeling close to the blanket, Bucklin held the shotgun inoffensively with his right hand and laid the shield in front of Cabeza Blanca. "You bring such a thing to trade," laughed Garza scornfully. "This is all you bring here?"

With his eyes focused intently on the Apache, Bucklin began carefully wiping the red trail dust from the shield. Slowly revealing the markings that had been painted on it years before, he said, "It's not just any shield. This here one is big medicine. It was used by a great warrior who raided east of the *Llano Estacado.*"

Cabeza Blanca looked on stoically as more of the symbols were uncovered. "This particular Injun was shot by this here shotgun I'm holding and wasn't even hurt."

Suddenly, with a jerk, Cabeza Blanca shoved Bucklin's hand aside and hunching forward, violently brushed the last of the dust away with his shirt sleeve. When he straightened up his eyes had narrowed into shadowy slits and Sam Bucklin knowingly eased the outside hammer to full cock. There was no question, the Apache had recognized his own battle shield.

Oblivious to the drastic turn of events, Garza continued to scoff. "Only a fool would believe such a story, Gringo, and the Apaches, they are no fools."

Ignoring him, Bucklin went on as the muzzle of the shotgun gradually swung around. "It was a woman that shot that Apache. That was five winters back and that woman was my mother. And the Injun that dropped this shield murdered my baby and it's took me five years to finally run him down."

Garza blinked in confusion as his smile went flat, but Cabeza Blanca sat still, his face frozen in an unemotional stare. "You heard the name Buck Samuels," said Bucklin with a lethal edge to his voice, "so maybe you heard of Sam Bucklin, too. It was the Bucklins you kilt back in Texas and now it's time to pay the last farthing."

Finally grasping what was happening and the shift in the shotgun barrel, Garza paled with shock, then his eyes caught the movement of Bucklin's thumb reaching for the second hammer. In a wave of panic and utter desperation, his hand flashed down for his pistol, but a hurried blast from the 10- gauge took off the top of the Mexican's head.

Before Bucklin could recover from the recoil, the Apache threw Tommy headlong across the fire and into his shoulder, knocking him off balance.

Falling backward, Bucklin fired again as the Indian dove for the rear of the teepee and landed out of sight.

Scrambling to his feet, Bucklin threw the shotgun into the night, then scooped up the screaming boy and shield with one arm and grabbed the Sharps with his free hand. Racing to his horses, he threw the Sharps into the scabbard on the trail horse and tossed the shield over his back and jerked the reins free. With Tommy squalling under his arm and Cabeza Blanca yelling for his half-drunk Apaches, Bucklin slung himself into the saddle and plunged over the mesa's rim and down the pitch black trail.

A rifle exploded behind him and the rear horse went down, tearing the reins from his hand just as a second shot nearly knocked him from his saddle. The startled gelding lunged forward then clattered down the path as Bucklin caught his balance and more shots rang out only to ricochet off the rocks over his head.

In a matter of seconds he was safely beyond reach of their bullets, but the savage screams of Cabeza Blanca seemed for a moment to be following him. Feeling his back as the sorrel stumbled recklessly down the mesa, Bucklin found no blood. The slug that almost knocked him off his horse had been turned by the thick buffalo hide, but when the appaloosa fell, he lost the Long Tom shotgun and the Sharps, his only rifle, and the country ahead was wide open.

At the bottom of the mesa he drew up to listen. Tommy was whimpering softly and the sorrel, nervously catching its wind, danced about gingerly. From above he heard the sound of horses, yet they were much farther behind than he expected. Were they too drunk to follow or had he been lucky enough for his fallen horse to have blocked the narrow passage? Whatever the reason for the delay, he was grateful and wasting no more time, he started for the combed ridge at a gallop. If he could reach the pass without being run down he would at least have a chance. If they caught him before that it would be a short fight.

Although stars provided the only light, when the moon rose it would be half-full and more than bright enough to follow his tracks. For now, however, in the darkness, even an Apache could not read sign at a full gallop. They had seen him ride in from the east, yet he had mentioned the trading posts along the San Juan River. If they believed he was heading north he would gain some time, but if they guessed he was trying for the pass the lack of moonlight would make no difference at all. His horse had had no rest and little feed and the rocky ridge was nearly twelve miles away.

Clamping the reins between his teeth as he rode, Bucklin held onto the child with one arm and pulled off his buckskin jacket. Folding it the best he could, he laid the soft deerskin over the pommel and front of the saddle's seat, then swung Tommy around. The gelding had a smooth gait, but without the supple cushion to protect his bare legs the constant rocking against hard leather would have drawn blood before they reached the first arroyo.

The demanding ride would have been hard on any horse, but as tired as the sorrel already was he would bottom out by the time they reached the ridge, if not before.

Even if he did make it, with the Apaches on fresh mounts, there was no way to stay ahead of them for long and once through the pass it was eighty long, empty miles to Fort Defiance. He would have to have another horse.

Passing the outer edge of the small mesa, Bucklin veered sharply to the northeast. Somewhere in that direction he knew he would cut the drainage of the large arroyo he followed the day before and the short cut would put him one mile closer to the protection of the narrow pass. If he could get through to the far side and the Apaches pursued on horseback he would ambush them from the rocks as they came in single file.

At close range he could kill one and, if he was lucky, two or three.

As the others turned and ran for cover his only hope was to rope a dead Indian's horse before it bolted by him or back into the pass. If he failed with his lariat, there would be no more chances. The Apaches would come over the ridge on foot and eventually surround him. If they didn't kill him outright, Sam Bucklin would do it himself.

A half-hour after taking the shortcut he found the wash he was looking for and turned east along its bank. With the sorrel beginning to tire, its gait was growing rough, but when Bucklin glanced down at the child, he was astonished. With his tiny head bobbing with the rhythmic pounding of the hooves Tommy was barely awake. He had not cried since being thrown by Cabeza Blanca and now, in the midst of losing his mother a few days earlier and being spirited away by a total stranger, he was falling asleep in the saddle!

The Apaches taught their children from birth not to cry and would kill captured children that cried too much. Fortunately for little Tommy he learned quickly…and he had Jenny Mason for a mother. Had she managed to teach him early on not to be afraid? Or was it something else, something that came from within? Why was it some women captives that had been returned to their families found it possible to gather the shattered pieces and go on with their lives while most, like his sister, had been ruined permanently? Not even their worst nightmares could have prepared any of them for what they endured, yet some did not wither even though they faced the same unspeakable abuses. They suffered the same horror, felt the same shame and humiliation, yet somehow a few survived.

Sam Bucklin had heard of such women and marveled at their courage, but until he discovered Jenny Mason, he had never met one. Now that be had, he wanted nothing worse than to reunite her with her child. And at times he had found himself wanting it even more than the hated scalp of Cabeza Blanca.

Over the next twenty minutes the sorrel covered three more miles, but then started to falter and as the moon began to rise, Bucklin eased him to a standstill. Tying the reins to a juniper with Tommy asleep in his arms, he retraced his back trail until he could hear without the horse's heavy breathing filling the air.

For several seconds he listened for any hint of pursuit, but there was nothing. As he stood waiting, Tommy stirred and shifted his weight, causing Bucklin to cradle him with both arms. The moonlight bathed the round face with a soft silver-blue glow and what had been a dirty-faced little orphan was transformed into an innocent sleeping angel.

Gazing at the wondrous change, Bucklin held Tommy a little closer, then his eyes filled with a longing sadness. "I miss you, Elizabeth," he whispered. "Daddy misses his baby girl."

Clutching the child to his chest, he went back to the juniper and, after stuffing the buckskin jacket inside his saddlebags, took hold of the reins. Instead of mounting the fatigued horse, he started off in a dog-trot with the gelding trailing behind. Without the two-hundred-pound load, the horse could recover some of its strength and, even with Tommy in his arms, Bucklin could easily make the next two miles on foot. After that it should only be another two or at most three miles to the entrance of the pass. Once there he would be safe until dawn.

When he started the trot, Tommy woke up suddenly, but after a few minutes merely laid his head back against Bucklin's chest and tried to hang on. When the moon had risen the thickness of two fingers above the distant ridge, the dog-trot ceased, the miles were behind them and little Tommy's grip was still tight. Like his mother, he was one Sam Bucklin would always be proud of, one that would have plenty of sand at any age.

Again covering the saddle with the jacket, Bucklin paused to listen, then mounted up. With Tommy secured in front and the combed ridge illuminated by moonlight, he once more spurred the weary gelding into a gallop. A black notch in the gray wall of rock was barely visible, and on a hunch, he rode directly toward it. In a matter of minutes there was no question it was the entrance to the pass and a short time later he trotted into the passageway. After one more mile of virtually blind riding, he emerged out the eastern end of the narrow crevice and back onto desert sand.

A quarter-mile to the south he found a patch of dried grass and sage within a half-circle of junipers. Exhausted by the long ordeal, Tommy was deep in sleep and did not waken when Bucklin carefully wrapped him in his blanket and laid him down under a stunted tree.

After unsaddling the worn-out sorrel, Bucklin led him to a good stand of feed and hobbled him. He would not wander far and what grass was there only covered a half-acre. The horse was spent, yet with a night's rest and something in its belly, it might be of some use by morning.

From his saddlebags he took a long strip of rawhide and tied one end tightly onto his cinch ring and the other, in a close-fitting bowline, around Tommy's ankle. He had no time to fool with a two-year-old child and here he would be safe. And whatever the outcome, in the morning he would be easy to find.

Hanging his powder horn and pouch over his shoulder, Bucklin knelt to pick up the shield and horse-hair rope, then looked one last time at the sleeping boy.

He had the same fine features as his mother and apparently would share her courage and strength. With Jenny to raise him, he would grow into a good man, the kind a growing country was going to need, but if tomorrow turned sour and the Apaches were to take him, what then? And what would come of Jenny if Tommy were never returned? Would it be too much even for her? Would she eventually end up like his sister?

Blocking the thoughts from his mind, Bucklin pulled the blanket down over Tommy's feet. Standing slowly, he looked north along the edge of the ridge. The Apaches would likely wait until morning to come through the pass, especially if they still thought he had the shotgun. But with them you could never be sure. They might even try to ride around the ridge and come at him from the south or north. But if he remembered the sand map correctly, that would be an extra twenty to thirty miles for their horses to go. If they did that he would at least stand a fair chance of outrunning them with the sorrel.

CHAPTER TWELVE

B ordering the last fifty yards of the pass, its rock walls were no more than ten feet high and barely wide enough for two horses to ride abreast. Lying motionless in a shallow depression, Sam Bucklin watched the trail beneath him and waited patiently for his chance to strike.

The night, like any other, was full of sound, the rustling of gentle breezes, the trickling of sand, the occasional rattle of dislodged pebbles. There were claws that burrowed, wings that fluttered, and feet that scurried through the night and each time the fragile silence was broken, Bucklin knew enough to suspect something larger. No Indian could move more silently than the Apache. But they too could be heard if a person knew how to listen.

Just past midnight there was some movement down the ridge to the north of him that continued until it faded away into the desert, but from the passage there was nothing until just before dawn. Then, from deep within the pass, a horse kicked a stone.

Crawling to the edge of the crevice, Bucklin peered into the blackness and removed his hat. Holding it flat behind his ear to magnify any trace of sound, he held his breath. A moment later he detected the hollow wooden echo of hooves walking slowly over solid rock. They were coming and would be in sight by first light.

Easing back into the depression, he took out both pistols and, after double-checking the caps, laid them in front of him next to the lariat. The Apaches were wary and would be watching for an ambush, but he would not move until the last second. Until then he would be virtually invisible to anyone unless they were standing beside him. When they were within fifty feet, he would begin firing with both pistols, aiming to kill the first Indian, then the horse and rider next in line. If he was lucky, very lucky, he could block the pass behind the leading horse and rope it as it came running beneath him. It was a long-shot at best. But there would be no better time and no better place; it was here, it was now, or it was never.

The eastern horizon faded gradually into a dusky yellow while the blazing morning star reigned briefly in its realm of twilight. A wandering coyote barked plaintively one last time and from out of nowhere a hot gust of wind swept up the ridge, then was gone. For a long while Bucklin heard nothing save the muffled beating of his heart, but as the sky lightened and the stars dwindled away the dull thuds of a war horse's hooves drifted down the narrow corridor.

With the lariat over his shoulder and both fists locked around his Colts, Bucklin listened for the approaching horse and inch by inch worked himself closer to the top of the wall. Lying flat on his belly, he eased the hammers of the pistols back, timing the clicks of the cylinders with the steps of the first horse. Feeling his body stiffen with anticipation, he took a deep breath and held it.

When the lead horse took one step more he sprung into a half-crouch with both barrels already aimed at the Apache's body. But where the Indian's chest should have been there was nothing. The blanket over the horse's back was empty. Alarmed and confused by what he saw, Bucklin froze for a split second then frantically threw himself down and rolled just as a bullet buzzed over head and exploded against the solid rock ridge. As he grabbed for the rope and flung himself over the ledge of the pass, he heard the delayed boom of a Sharps.50-caliber.

Landing hard on his back, he was stunned for a moment, then, staggering to his feet, he leaned back on the rock wall to catch his breath. One of his ribs felt broken, but had he not realized in time what had happened, the heavy lead slug of the buffalo gun would have cut him in two.

An Apache now had his rifle and instead of riding through the pass had sent his horse through as a decoy and come over the ridge during the night. Hidden three or four hundred yards out in the desert he had watched up and down the pass for something to move and when it did he was ready and waiting.

The Apache had caught him in his own trap and now would be closing in for a better shot. There was only one path of escape and if he acted quickly, one slim chance to get out of the pass alive. The horse he so desperately needed would have to be used as a shield against the buffalo gun.

Bucklin glanced a few paces away at the startled animal that stood watching him then, speaking softly and building a loop in the lariat, he cautiously walked toward it. Having been trained for war, the horse had not spooked badly and after pondering the dark passageway to the rear, it turned its head and waited calmly for the lasso to fall around its neck. Jerking off the blanket that covered the saddle, Bucklin took the reins and looped the coiled lariat over his shoulder. Hooking his right foot into the left stirrup and hanging on to the horn with both hands, he kicked hard with his heel. As the horse broke into a run he folded himself against its side and immediately after hitting the desert veered sharply to the northeast and away from Tommy.

Just behind the pounding hooves, a lead slug smashed into the rocks as the big bore roared again. Caught off guard by the unexpected move, the Apache's shot had missed entirely and now the pony was running at full speed.

Bucklin knew his rifle and it would take a few seconds to reload another cartridge, yet even at two hundred yards a well-placed bullet would tear through the horse's side and kill him. He would have to drop off as soon as he hit any kind of cover and at all costs get out of the rifle's deadly sights.

The second shot came before he was ready, but the speeding horse was hit in the flank, knocking it sideways and nearly off its feet. Weaving badly, it stumbled into a shallow arroyo, then went down as Bucklin threw himself clear and dove for a two-foot-high embankment.

Scrambling for cover, Bucklin rolled himself against the bank, then looked back where the horse had fallen. In that direction the embankment disappeared entirely and ahead of him it was barely six inches high. Just above him on the top of the bank was a scrubby juniper bush. Other than that, the only other cover was fifty feet down the arroyo where it once again cut deeper into the desert floor.

With the other Apaches on the way there was little time, and he was trapped. Or was he? Bucklin had never known an Apache to risk his life needlessly and neither would this one. Certain that his quarry could not escape he would wait patiently for the others, then they would surround him for an easy kill.

The Apache would keep his eyes on where the white man lay and if necessary would wait the entire day without moving a muscle.

Taking the lariat from his shoulder, Bucklin slowly reached up to the juniper and tied a knot around one of the branches. Keeping out of sight, he crawled forward a few feet to where the bank dropped low then gave the rope a tug. The branch shook slightly, but enough for an Apache to notice.

Flat on his belly, Bucklin inched his way out in the open knowing that the short bank would not conceal him completely. Digging with his toes and fingers, he moved at a snail's pace as the sun slowly rose and beat down on his back.

Every few inches he gave a jerk on the lariat then let it slip through his fingers before moving on. If the Apache watched the bush he could make it to cover and work his way further into the desert, but if the Indian caught sight of him trying to escape he would get a bullet in the back at any given moment.

For almost an hour he shoved himself down the dry creek-bed as sand caked his sweating face and neck. He had gone thirty feet and given his last tug on the lariat before letting the end go. Without the distraction of the moving branch to protect him, he plowed onward, but even slower than before.

When Bucklin finally reached the deeper part of the arroyo, two hours had passed and he had heard nothing. Where were the other Apaches? If they had been waiting to come through the pass they would have been there long ago. They must have gone some other way. Around the ridge? Through another pass? But one Indian had come alone, come in the night, and outmaneuvered him.

Bucklin sat up against the steep bank, brushed the sand from his face, and thought of the tiswin and what Arviso had said. It made drunk Indians in a hurry and only one of them had not been drinking. Cabeza Blanca.

Flattened beneath the bank and heading into the rising sun, Bucklin hurriedly crawled over the sand with his knees and elbows, putting distance between himself and the dead horse. The shot that knocked it down had been fired much closer to the ridge than the first shot which put the Indian near the pass and almost in line with it.

The arroyo drained steadily to the east and after almost an hour of crawling, Bucklin was a mile from where he had fallen. Rising in a crouching run, he bounded up from the streambed and across the desert in a wide arc.

Staying low and making use of what cover there was, he dashed from one hiding place to another, stopping just long enough to check his position, then pushing on. Judging from where the three shots had been fired and their angle, he took his best guess where the Apache lay in waiting and after circling quickly to the rear, he started warily for the spot he had picked.

Mentally drawing a line out from the entrance of the pass and another along the angle of the third shot, Bucklin knew within an acre of where the Apache would be. When he could see the arroyo where his horse had gone down, he aligned himself with the last bullet's trajectory and drew one of his Colts. Bending low and painstakingly settling each foot before lifting the other, he crept forward on cat's feet.

Advancing in absolute silence, he studied every shadow, every tuft of sage and branch of juniper. He did not look for an Apache, for they were not to be seen. Instead, his eyes searched for a moccasin, a lock of black hair, or a fold of calico, any fragment of the landscape that did not belong. It was all he would see, but it was all he would need.

The closer he got to the Apache, the more carefully he moved. With every sense alert, he now stopped after each step and with his head slowly turning, scanned every inch of the terrain in front of him. If he took one step too many and entered the Indian's line of sight he knew it would be his last.

His right side was growing warm from the sun when its heat stirred the morning air. As it drifted faintly by him everything but his eyes abruptly came to a dead stop. He could smell the Apache. He was almost on top of him, yet he had seen nothing.

The only immediate cover was a knee-high juniper but to go any farther was out of the question. It would have to do. It grew only an arm's length away, but when he shifted his weight toward it, a jackrabbit darted out from under it and, ducking its long ears, burst through a row of sagebrush then buck-jumped a pile of rocks on its way to the arroyo.

Instantly dropping to one knee, Bucklin caught a flicker of movement forty paces ahead in a tangle of sage. When he saw the flash of metal, he fired and rolled to his right amidst the answering roar of a buffalo gun. Coming back up on both knees, he fired twice more then rushed the Apache before he could reload.

Halfway to the swirling cloud of blue smoke, he glimpsed the square head of Cabeza Blanca, but before he could shoot, a red-hot pistol ball slammed into his hip and spun him to the ground. As he hit, he fired again, then rolled over twice behind the trunk of a large juniper.

There was no return fire, only the hiss and churning of sand as the Apache slithered away unseen, but heading for the pile of rocks. A few feet away, Bucklin saw the heavy barrel of his Sharps protruding from the crumpled sage. The Indian had left the cumbersome rifle behind. It would be pistols at close range now...if he did not bleed to death first.

Both sides of the rock pile were visible from where Bucklin lay and nearly free of sage, but his position was no better. Neither could move without being seen as long as it was daylight. He could not be certain if he had hit the Apache and it made little difference. They did not die easily and, like the rattlesnake, could kill with their last twitch of life.

Pressing his palm over the oozing hole on his hip, he holstered his smoking pistol and took out the other. After replacing one of the caps, he put it within easy reach and grabbed his powder flask. As he brought it up, his hand froze in midair. In the distance was the muffled rumbling of a dozen or more fast-moving horses.

They were coming at him from the south and must have ridden around the ridge while Cabeza Blanca had traveled over it. There was no time to reload. If he wanted to kill Cabeza Blanca before he died, if he was to finish what he had sworn on his family's graves to do, he had to make it to those rocks. With his bloody hand he pulled the small Whitney revolver from under his jacket and palmed the loaded Colt with his other. He had come too far, he was too close. He could not fail now. The thundering hooves began to echo off the ridge as Bucklin struggled to get his legs under him, then, limping badly, he bolted from behind the trunk. He took only three quick steps, then dove as another pistol shot rang out.

Rolling again to his right and into the sun, he lunged forward, fired at the smoke and felt a bullet burn the skin off his back. He fired recklessly, then scrambled to his feet, blasting away with both pistols.

With a wild scream, Cabeza Blanca sprang from behind the rocks, his left arm dangling, his calico shirt caked with bloody sand and his pistol belching fire and smoke.

Instinctively, Bucklin leveled both pistols and knocked the Apache off his feet, firing two shots through his heart. The powerful Indian crashed into the sand. A leg kicked and Bucklin put another round into his chest.

The dust from the racing horses was rising a quarter-mile away as Bucklin desperately searched the body for Sharps cartridges, but finding nothing, he sat back and took a deep breath. The Colt was empty, but the pocket pistol had two caps left. He would only need one and he calmly shoved the pistol behind his belt and slid out his scalping knife. At least he would take the last scalp.

"This is for you, Baby Elizabeth," he said clearly, then knelt beside the large head of his child's murderer. With the tip of the blade, he flicked off the Apache's hair band then, sinking back on his heels, glared at the corpse in shock.

Unbelievingly he peeled back the thick eyelids as horses and riders came storming at him in a tight group. Jerking out the Whitney, he thumbed back the hammer and forced his eyes from the bloody corpse. But again what he saw was unbelievable. The men charging with rifles drawn were in formation. And they wore blue. Lathered and blowing hard, the horses fanned out around him as some of the soldiers dropped from their saddles and came running. One of them was tall, lanky and out of uniform. "You all right, Sam?" It was Bigfoot Wallace who got to him first. On his chest was a U.S. marshal's badge.

Bucklin stared incredulously at the Ranger, then in a cloud of bewilderment he said, "This here is the one Bigfoot. The one that done it all, he kilt them."

Taking the cocked pistol from his hand, the Ranger smiled, "Well, you done made a good Injun out of him, Sam. He won't..."

"But look at him close," interrupted Bucklin. "Look at him."

Wallace glanced at the young soldier next to him, then back at Bucklin. "I see 'im, boy. You got him good. Now let's see about gettin' you patched up. Yore leakin' all over the sand."

Bucklin angrily shook his head and pointed with his knife at the white band of skin around the Indian's forehead. "See that? You see?" he insisted. "And his eyes. They're hazel. Cabeza Blanca was a white man! The one who kilt my baby was white!"

Shoving his tattered hat back on his head, Wallace leaned forward and swore. "Damned if you're right, boy. Damnit to hell! And after all this time."

Two more riders came in escorted by a pair of soldiers, but Bucklin paid no attention until he heard Jenny's voice cry out. "Sam! Sam, you're alive!"

Holding Tommy in her arms, she rushed over to Bucklin, then gasped at the blood. Turning suddenly, she said, "Hurry, Jesus! He's hurt bad!"

Bucklin looked up from the white Indian and into Jenny's pale blue eyes, eyes that filled with fear. "You found Tommy," he said as the words wavered with a growing pain. "He's a fine boy."

Setting the child down, Jenny went to Bucklin's side and began removing his bloody buckskin jacket as Arviso trotted over with a Navajo blanket and a medicine bag.

"Most of the bleedin's from his hip," said Wallace after looking at the gash along his back. "We got to lay you back, boy, and take a look at that bullet hole."

Bucklin nodded light-headedly as Wallace and Arviso helped him onto the blanket, then eased him back. A lieutenant came into view and stood over him briefly, then disappeared.

"We meet again, Señor," said Arviso. Opening his bag he took out a piece of linen and folded it into a square. Handing it to Jenny, he added, "And somehow, you are alive still."

Bucklin blinked his bloodshot eyes and studied the Indian. "You saw Cabeza Blanca up close once. Did you know he was a white man?"

Arviso took out his knife and shrugged. "He is Apache."

"Take another look then," argued Bucklin. "Tell me what you see there."

Jesus Arviso glanced casually at the dead man. "You wear the skin of a deer, but you are not a deer. A man is what he is in his heart. His skin is white, but his blood, it is Apache. The man you kill this day is Cabeza Blanca. He is Apache."

Slipping the knife under Bucklin's pants, Arviso slit them open from the waist to expose the bullet hole in his bare hip. Without being told Jenny immediately pressed the cloth over the wound and held if firmly as the Navajo made a poultice to stop the bleeding.

Sam Bucklin awkwardly looked away from Jenny's concerned eyes. Bigfoot Wallace grinned knowingly, then said, "You ain't asked what I'm doin' way out here, Samuel. Ain't you one bit curious?"

Bucklin turned his head and stared once more at the dead renegade. After a long pause, he rolled his eyes toward Wallace. "I was wondering on it just before you cut my britches right here in front of everybody."

Wallace broke out laughing. "Well, ma'am, he's a tad bashful, but once you get to know 'im he's not so bad. Boy, you're lucky we brought Miss Jenny along or you'd've been buzzard meat already. She brung us right here in a hurry. And along the way we run into a band of Apaches. She knowed who they was, that they run with this Cabeza fella so we lit into 'em. Otherwise they'd of been here and kilt you by now."

"You fought with Apaches?"

"Yep. We was camped along the ridge and they came along just at first light. Miss Jenny, she saw 'em ridin' in. Might have caught us off our guard if'n she hadn't warned us. But we was loaded for bear by the time they cut our trail and then we set 'em off with their tails tucked. Got two, maybe three of them red devils."

Bucklin thought for a moment while Arviso laid the poultice over the wound and Jenny left to get a canteen. "Well, that explains why I ain't dead, but what about the rest of it? You out here with a marshal's badge and bringing the army after me. And I left Jenny in a safe place, at Arviso's. How'd you find her?"

Wallace fished a small plug of tobacco out of his shirt pocket and, after offering a chew to Arviso and then to a private standing guard, bit off a piece. "As fer what I'm doin' here," began Wallace as he chewed heavily, "I was hired by them Injun commissioners back in Texas to run you down. When you lit out they was fit to be tied.

"They wanted you, especially that there Flitcher feller, they wanted you bad and I figured they meant business. So I told 'em how you weren't no friend or kin of mine and how only a Injun fighter like me could ever hope to fetch you back. They got me the badge so I come to tell you to light a shuck. I come all the way out here with them two and I ain't never heard so much ignernt pallaverin's about Injuns in all my born days."

Jenny returned with the canteen in one arm and Tommy in the other.

After Bucklin took a welcome drink, she sat next to him with Tommy crawling into her lap. Glancing at her for an instant, Bucklin dropped his eyes.

"How's Tommy? He had a rough night."

"He's fine," replied Jenny warmly, then, placing her hand on his arm, she continued. "I can never thank you enough for what you did. He means everything to me, everything. But I know you understand that."

"Yes. Yes, I do, Jenny. But you owe me nothing. A man don't need no kind of payment for doing what's right."

"Well, now," broke in Wallace, then spit a brown stream of tobacco off to his side, "to get on with the story, I was there at the fort with Coyler and Flitcher when the sergeant come in all cut up and told his account of what you done for him. Then Jesus here, he come in, too. But I didn't pay him much mind at the time. Only later on, that no-good Che Dodge come to the fort askin' questions and we all got curious."

"What kind of questions?" asked Bucklin with an edge to his voice.

Wallace spit again and wiped his chin whiskers dry. "Seems he figured for certain you wasn't coming back and thought there might be some reward money if he knew the whereabouts of a white woman captive. He never said nothin' in particular, but it weren't no time till the army figured out who he was talkin' about, that is to say the captive was Buck Samuels's woman. And pretty soon he was spillin' his guts and the army was mountin' up to go get her.

"Seein' as how I was duly sworn to bring you back to Texas and the commissioners was claimin' they had more say in the fracas than the military, they allowed as I could ride along."

Glancing up at the private, Wallace paused to smile. "Now this army's no different than those back home and they don't care no more for this Injun Ring than we do, so me and the lieutenant had us a little talk on the way to Arviso's hogan. And right away we come to an understandin'."

"Understanding?" asked Jenny. "What kind of understanding?"

"Well, it weren't no perfect plan at first, Miss Jenny, but when you was so all-fired certain you was gonna ride with us, it got even better. No matter what, Sam was to be turned over to me, but seein' the kind of woman you was and...and that there was more to your fearfulness than just your youngin', I was plumb proud of myself the way it come together."

"What are you driving at, Bigfoot?" asked Bucklin.

Wallace shook his head. "Fer a Yankee, this lieutenant ain't so bad and he ain't dumb neither. Once I told him how I knowed you and who you was, it didn't take no time to make a believer out of him. Buck Samuels, Sam Bucklin. He caught on quick enough and he had heard of you, boy. And he weren't about to turn you over to no Injun lovers to be put in jail for killin' Apaches."

"What about that mule-skinner I shot?" asked Bucklin. "Them carpetbaggers was claiming I murdered him and you know a Confederate ain't got no chance at a fair trial."

"Well, sir," smiled Wallace, "what happens to you after you're turned over to me is my business. And we all ain't goin' back to the fort. That was our deal, me and the lieutenant's."

With a puzzled glance at Bigfoot Wallace, Jenny asked sharply, "What are you going to do with him?"

Wallace scratched the side of his bony jaw. "Sorry I didn't tell you sooner, Miss Jenny, but Sam and me go way back. That killin' was self-defense, besides. I know 'cause I was there. He ain't goin' to no Yankee jail. I was figurin' more on California, Oregon, maybe. Good ranch country out that way. Good place to raise a family, too. A good place to start over for the both of you."

Sam Bucklin frowned. Turning his head away from everyone, he stared silently into the open desert. After a moment Arviso nudged Wallace and motioned to the private. "The bleeding stop soon. I think the lieutenant, we go speak to him, all of us."

After looking at the pair in front of him, Wallace grinned agreeably and unfolded his long legs. "Yep," he said, ambling to his feet, "we're gonna be needin' a few army horses and enough grub to last us till we can get these two back to your hogan."

Jenny watched the three men go, then looked down at Sam Bucklin. Tommy rolled his fingers in his mother's hair as he leaned his sleepy head on her breast. She smiled uncertainly at the face turned away from her and waited patiently.

"I'm sorry they have the wrong idea about us, Jenny." Bucklin said finally. "I didn't mean to bring you any shame. I can straighten it out directly. And I'm sure Bigfoot will help you get back East. He's a good man. He'll get you there safe."

"And what will you do now, Sam Bucklin? Where will you go?"

Bucklin shrugged. "As soon as I can ride I'll find a place and hole up until I'm mended. After that...who knows. Maybe I'll go on West like Bigfoot said. I never gave it much thought... what I'd do after. Thought I'd go back to Texas I reckon, but now that's out."

"Sam." Jenny's voice was soft, yet strangely demanding, and Bucklin rolled his head toward her and looked into her eyes, eyes he had tried to avoid. "I am going to stay with you until you are well. I'll hear of nothing else, Sam."

Bucklin clenched his jaws. "You can't do that, Jenny. Your kinfolks are waiting to get word on you. It's best you get back to them as soon as you can."

"No," said Jenny firmly, "I will send word that I am well. That I was rescued and I am safe with Tommy. There is no need for worry."

"They'll be wanting to see you, Jenny, and Tommy, too. They'll be wanting to care for you, to do what they can to help."

Jenny sighed and took Bucklin's hand. "Sam, they are to know nothing. Only that my husband was killed and Tommy and I were saved by a wonderful man from Texas. Anything else would only spread the grief and shame. It would hurt them more than I could bear. I know them, Sam, and it is better this way."

Sam Bucklin felt his hand tighten around Jenny's, felt its smallness, yet its strength.

"If I can do anything, after I'm on my feet, anything for you at all, I'd be obliged if you'd let me help out until you got settled."

Jenny Mason smiled, "That could take a long time, Sam. A very long time."

Allowing himself to look deeply into the ice blue eyes above him, Sam Bucklin saw a brightness in them, a warmth he had not seen for five long years.

"There's nothing I'd like to do better, Jenny. And when the mending's all done and this is put behind us, maybe we could...well, I'd surely want to know how you and Tommy was doing from time to time. I might could visit once in a while."

"When we're both ready, Sam," said Jenny as she squeezed his hand gently, "there will be no reason for you to come visit. It will be time for you to stay."